Reflections of Loko Miwa

CARAF Books
Caribbean and African Literature
Translated from French

Editor
CARROL F. COATES

Advisory Editors

Clarisse Zimra

J. Michael Dash

John Conteh-Morgan

Elisabeth Mudimbe-Boyi

Reflections of Loko Miwa

Lilas Desquiron

Translated by
Robin Orr Bodkin

Introduction by
Marie-Agnès Sourieau

. . .

UNIVERSITY PRESS
OF VIRGINIA
*Charlottesville
& London*

.

Publication of this translation was assisted by
a grant from the French Ministry of Culture
Originally published in French
as *Les chemins de Loco-Miroir*,
© Éditions Stock, 1990

First published March 1998
Second paperback printing October 1998

∞ The paper used in this publication meets the minimum
requirements of the American National Standard for
Information Sciences—Permanence of Paper for
Printed Library Materials, ANSI Z39.48-1984.

Library of Congress Cataloging-in-Publication Data
Desquiron, Lilas.
[Chemins de Loco-Miroir. English]
Reflections of Loko Miwa = Les chemins de Loco-Miroir /
Lilas Desquiron ; translated by Robin Orr Bodkin ;
introduction by Marie-Agnès Sourieau.
p.   cm. — (CARAF books)
Includes bibliographical references.
ISBN 0-8139-1752-2 (cloth : alk. paper). —
ISBN 0-8139-1753-0 (paper : alk. paper)
I. Bodkin, Robin Orr, 1946– .   II. Title.   III. Series.
PQ3949.2.D445C4813   1998
843—dc21   97-25472 CIP

CONTENTS

. . .

Introduction by
Marie-Agnès Sourieau
vii

. . .

Bibliography
xxix

. . .

Reflections of Loko Miwa
I

. . .

Glossary
185

. . .

A Brief Guide to Kreyòl
Pronunciation
193

. . .

Select Bibliography of Sources
for Kreyòl Terms
195

. . .

INTRODUCTION

. . .

Lilas Desquiron has lived in Belgium and France for the past thirty years, joining the ranks, although not quite for the same reasons, of the large literary diaspora of Haitian intellectuals who fled the Duvaliers' political tyranny and its resulting social and economic chaos. Indeed, since the 1960s, Haitian writing has been most prolific outside the island, in places where material and spiritual conditions have been more conducive to artistic creation. *Reflections of Loko Miwa*, which is aimed at a readership located outside its narrative space, reflects this internationalization of Haitian literature.

Like many of her long-exiled compatriots, Desquiron deals in her novel with her country's complex historical and social structure. She attempts to reestablish her severed connections with the past and assess the consequences of that severance on reality. Thus, the testimony of her novel adds to the recent analysis of a number of critics who have observed how Haitian novelists, especially women, frequently address their nation's political and social dilemmas in their fiction. In her 1979 study of women novelists of French-speaking countries, Guadeloupean writer Maryse Condé argued that Haitian women authors did not deplore their personal fate in their work, "for their major preoccupation was that of Haiti on the whole, Haiti with its social complexities and political dramas. . . . It is almost impossible to separate their personal life from that of the country."[1] In a recent interview, Yanick Lahens, born and based on the island, said of her country's women writers that they "plunge more directly into what makes up the day-to-day fabric of our relationship. They bring to light this historical and cultural dimension that is usually kept hidden."[2]

Reflections is structured by such complex forces. Through a narrative approach reminiscent in part of the folktale, the author portrays the reality of Haiti's social and political fabric while bringing to light the historical and cultural dimensions of a nation whose spirit has been stifled by a dreadful oppression. The text is divided into thirty-one unnumbered chapters that can be seen as comprising three equal parts, each ending with a catastrophic event resulting in the disruption of the social order.[3] The narrative is shared by several individual and collective voices framed by the voice of Cocotte, the main storyteller. This multivoiced approach allows the author to defy the notion of a single reality and incites the reader to play a dynamic role in the process of signification. Thus the reader becomes an insider within the community and must confront its intricate nature and its tense and secretive atmosphere. This narrative structure also enables the representation of all social groups in their diversity and contradictions: the mulatto bourgeoisie, the black bourgeoisie, the urban black middle and lower classes, the urban proletariat, and the peasantry. Their distinct discourses are heard simultaneously and consequently are preserved as alternate visions of official "history." In *Reflections*, Desquiron inscribes the reality of her country, especially alluding to the abuses of the Duvalier era through the remembering of Haiti's torn history and corrupted social fabric.

. . .

Originally from Jérémie, a coffee-exporting harbor situated in the Gulf of Gonâve on the west coast of the island, Lilas Desquiron's family belongs to the small, literate upper class, the privileged mulatto elite, also referred to as the "caste," made up of landowners, merchants, and occasional politicians and writers. Her great-grandfather, A. T. de Saint-Aignan Desquiron, composed *L'Haïtiade*, an epic poem in eight cantos. Among her mother's ancestors were Laurent Bazelais, chief of staff of Dessalines at the time of the Haitian revolution, and Jean-Pierre Boyer-Bazelais, a leader of the liberal party in the 1860s, killed in the siege of Miragoâne in 1884.

Her father, Jean Desquiron, to whom her novel is dedicated, managed an import-export business. More recently he has published *Haïti à la une*, an anthology of Haitian journalistic articles in six volumes, covering 1724 to 1934.

During my September 1994 interview with Lilas Desquiron at her Paris home, she explained the circumstances of her upbringing that triggered the writing of her novel. She left her native town at the age of two, when her parents and other members of their families settled in the capital, Port-au-Prince. There, with some of their affluent Jeremiean friends, they strove to re-create the atmosphere and dynamics of their previous comfortable lifestyle. Through photographs and numerous stories told by Desquiron's paternal grandmother, and later by her father, the town of Jérémie acquired a mythical dimension that haunted her childhood. Her progressive parents gave her an unusually broad education. She attended a Catholic school where she was, she reports, exposed to the social diversity of the capital. Her secondary education complete, she was sent to Belgium, where she studied ethnology at the University of Brussels. She eventually wrote a master's thesis on the African origins of Vodou, published by Librairie Deschamps in Port-au-Prince in 1990. A film critic and a scriptwriter for French television, she now lives in Paris.

During our interview, Desquiron reflected upon the context of racism that pervaded the atmosphere of her upbringing in spite of the open-mindness of her close family circle. Light-skinned and therefore praised for her desirable complexion, she ironically felt more attuned to her African ethnic heritage than to her obvious biological link to the white race. But because of the color discrimination that obsessively dominated her environment, she felt compelled to suppress the manifestations of her black sensibility. Thus, at an early age she understood the meaning of epidermic prejudice and its tragic consequences to her country. Since Haiti's independence in 1804, this aberration has remained taboo within Haitian society, creating unsolvable tensions between the privileged mulatto minority and the destitute black majority.[4]

Desquiron's remarks coincide with those of ethnologists, historians, and other scholars of Haiti who have been studying the relationships between phenotypes and political privileges, economic power, social intercourse, and sensuous relations. "Wisdom recommends that one recognize that indeed a black man can be set apart from a white. The main thing is to know whether their differentiation constitutes the signs for superiority or stigmata for inferiority," wrote Jacques Roumain in 1939.[5] From the beginning of the Republic of Haiti, the development of the nation has rested on this oppositional distinction between blacks and whites, or more precisely between light-skinned mulattoes and blacks, Pétion and Dessalines, Rigaud and Toussaint Louverture, North and South, Nationals and Liberals. In a recent essay scrutinizing the complexities of Haitian national sensibility, Léon-François Hoffmann writes that it has been shaped by the "ambiguity of a history that is both a reservoir of national pride and a source of national shame, [and it] is paralleled by the ambiguity of racialism." He continues, "while this internalization of anti-black racialism is far from unknown in the rest of the Caribbean, it is especially shocking and paradoxical in the country which has always defined itself as the Black Republic."[6] If ideologically Haitians maintain that they are of African descent, the powerful European-educated elite has effectively internalized white attitudes. Early in Desquiron's novel, the black peasant Cocotte sarcastically comments on that very fact. The rich mulattoes of Jérémie, she says, hide in their big pretentious houses which "turn their backs to this magnificent view of the sea below," symbol of their origin and of their dubiously acquired wealth (5). Moreover, they strive to protect their pale skin "from the fierce Caribbean sun with an almost maniacal care, as if they could hide the original sin of their negritude beneath a pale epidermis" (6).

These mechanics of power and submission correspond to skin color and came about after the colony of Saint-Domingue became the Republic of Haiti. The making of the Haitian nation demanded a new writing of history that became entangled in the question of "color." When Dessalines drafted his constitution in 1805, he annihilated the tripartite division of whites, people of color, and blacks, creating one category for Haitian identity that absorbed all other distinctions: "the generic word *black*" (article 14). However, the dilution of the color issue through this new legislation imposed an artificial epidermic reconciliation of the former free, who were mostly mulattoes, and the newly free, who were mostly black. The forging of the national Haitian identity depended on the blackening of the population by definition. The Haitian mulatto elites, who had been lightened as well as debased by the French, disavowed Dessalines's classification. By adopting European intellectual and aesthetic norms, mostly French, the mulattoes progressively began to distance themselves from their African origins, favoring light-skinned pigmentation and encouraging marriages that would "improve the race," that is to say, whiten it.[7] The pervasive and complex white-color prejudice since the country's independence is the harsh underlying reality represented in Desquiron's novel. This reality is forcefully articulated by Alexandre, the black politically-engaged protagonist through an internal monologue addressed to his lover, the mulattress Violaine: "You know better than I the revulsion Jeremian mulattoes have for that Negro they all carry within themselves and have desperately relegated to the most obscure part of their memory. You're aware of their very real fear, which is of of course absurd, of falling back into original sin, of regressing toward that primitive source" (59–60).

That color discrimination was never discussed openly and objectively might have exacerbated the reality of class and race conflicts and the profound resentment felt by the black middle-class striving for legitimacy. Their frustrations, ranging over the span of this white/black conflict, found an outlet in the lure of racial and cultural authenticity, eventually reaching to an ideological obsession that would bring black fascism to power in 1957. As Michael Dash points out, "the arguments for the political ascendancy of a black elite were closely allied to the growing interest in ethnology and the customs of the peasantry. An authentic black nation needed an authentic culture and religion."[8] This is why during the U.S. occupation, from 1915 to 1934, several ethnographers, among them J. C. Dorsinville and Jean Price-Mars, had a great influence in reconstructing an "authentic" Haitian identity. In his celebrated work, *So Spoke the Uncle*, Price-Mars stresses the importance of Africa's contribution to the peasant culture of Haiti and defends Vodou as a legitimate and vital component of a national folklore, "that is: the lore of the people, the knowledge of the people". The book, defined by its author as "an ethnographic stroll," created the basis for the "Indigenist" movement, a racial mystique implying the existence of an authentic black essence.[9] Racial theories thus provided Haiti's history with an ideologically comprehensible system and unity as well as a vision of order and security; they also fulfilled the emotional needs of a nation in constant crisis.[10] This Africanist ideology, which found its concrete political outlet in the so-called *noiriste* movement, would give François Duvalier the opportunity to implement his segregational politics of racial purity and manipulate the masses for his own purposes. Indeed, Papa Doc based his dictatorship on black supremacy with the support of certain Vodou priests in order to counteract, and eventually eliminate, the powerful influence of the mulatto elite. He was able to put his plan into operation, partially because the mulatto elite were altogether contemptuous and fearful of the powers of Vodou. Duvalier "proclaimed the existence and superiority of an 'authentic' African personality within the black Haitian, and, like all racisms, it was also mystical in its evocation of a collective ethnic identity rooted in blood and suffering," writes James Ferguson.[11] Because the *noiriste* discourse denied the bourgeois mulattoes any Haitian "authenticity," it had an essential appeal to the vast majority of underprivileged Haitians, and it revealed the radical split within the country's society. In this context, Lilas Desquiron noted that her parents and relatives became threatened by the excesses of Duvalier's racial mystification. By becoming political activists, they attempted to oppose his regime's constructed nationalism. Thus the young Desquiron experienced at an early age the prejudices related to her pale pigmentation and the insecurity brought by extreme social tensions. Her present reassumption of her African ancestry—her Negro part, as she stated—coincides with the assertion and celebration by most Haitian intellectuals, even those whose physical features are essentially European, of their belonging to the African race, hence of their fundamental Haitianness. Desquiron insightfully recognizes that she is practicing a model of strategic essentialism. By placing herself in this tradition of patriotic pride and thus bonding with her African ancestors, she recovers in her novel the ethnographic elements asserted by the indigenist movement.

Thus the character of Violaine, who possesses many physical and social similarities with the author of *Reflections*, should be considered in the context of Haitian letters and history as well as that of the political situation of the island. Since the beginning of colonization, on most of the Caribbean islands there has been a fantasized figure who has stirred the imagination of many people. Régis Antoine has noted the presence, for three centuries, of the seductive, island-born mulattress in French letters. She is the female of mixed blood "created by the pleasure of slave masters and promoted to the level of symbol of the islands . . . that would guarantee her a literary reputation."[12] Functioning as a symbol of the Caribbean collective image, Violaine is also emblematic of Haiti's obsession with the beautiful light-skinned mulatto female described at length by historians of Saint Domingue, such as Moreau de Saint-Méry and later captured by poets and novelists such as Marie Chauvet, Jacques Stephen Alexis, and René Depestre. As Joan Dayan writes, "the mixed-blood or mulatto mistress somehow became the concrete signifier for lust that could be portrayed as 'love.' Moreau de Saint-Méry envisioned her as 'one of those prietesses of Venus,'" her entire being given up to pleasure.[13] Violaine fits remarkably well this stereotype of the sensual mulattress, a combination of fiery passion and excessive beauty, "unbelievably desirable, yet . . . dangerous," and so orgasmic that she represents a permanent scandal and threat (59). Her destiny is to be beautiful and passive, erotic and consummated by male desire. The author of *Reflections* attempts to subvert this powerful myth of the colonial and postcolonial discourse that has perpetuated this vision. Indeed, Violaine refuses all subordination and discipline. As her betrothed Philippe Edouard aptly reflects, she has "escaped the laborious rearing that fashioned and molded us, the children spawned in this country of pain"(102). Desquiron graphically reveals the consequences of Violaine's insurgence by allowing her to be cruelly chastised by her own people, that is to say, evacuated from her mystifying role. And as a consequence, she disappears from the story as well as from official history: she becomes transparent, Desquiron's mark of the nonexistent fantasy.

Like many of her compatriot writers, Desquiron uses the symbol of the mulattress to deal with the problem of Haitian identity especially for women of African ancestry. Represented by Cocotte, the black woman is negated by her opposite, the mulattress Violaine. In spite of the fact that Cocotte tells most of the story, acts as a key preserver of history, and is an active participant in the narrative, the reader knows very little about her. It is worth noting that she does not have a life of her own, and undoubtedly not a love life. She is devoted to her *marasa* sister. Her principal role is to reflect or report Violaine's body, mind, and her eventual destiny.

Moreover, to grasp fully the meaning of *Reflections*, it is crucial to understand the 1950s and 1960s mentality of the old French colonial city of Jérémie, and of the President-for-Life's special hatred for its mulattoes. Elizabeth Abbott writes that, when François Duvalier came to power, Jérémie was "Haiti's most color-obsessed city, with a structure akin to apartheid and every aspect of life defined by color/class lines. Residential segregation was absolute."[14] The city was a microcosm of Haiti's social structure. Abbott reports the tale that Duvalier said to a favored black officer, Jérémie's commandant Abel Jérôme, that "there are three kinds of mulattoes, the nationalists, the anti-nationalists, and the mulattoes of Jérémie. . . . Those, Jérôme, are the most rabid mulattoes of all."[15] Jérémie's wealthy, arrogant, and independent-minded light-skinned Europeanized elite was the stark reminder of Papa Doc's past humiliations. It represented everything he despised, feared, and longed to annihilate. An attempt by a guerrilla movement to overthrow his regime would soon give him the opportunity. In August 1964, Jeune Haïti (Young Haiti), a resistance group based in the United States and led by twelve university-educated Jeremiean mulattoes and one black, a motorboat mechanic politicized in New York, landed at the village of Dame Marie on the tip of the peninsula, miles away from their original destination of Jérémie. From the beginning of their invasion, and very rapidly, the scattered and poorly armed rebels (called *les Treize*) were brutally crushed by

Duvalier's militia. This terrible repression—including torture, rape, and summary executions—directed specifically against the Jeremiean families of those members of *les Treize* came to be known as the Vespers of Jérémie. Duvalier was able to avenge himself by terrorizing, persecuting, and finally decimating several of these families of Jérémie through the ferocious diligence of his personal militia, better known as *tonton makout*. According to Desquiron, the savage raid by Duvalier's henchmen could only be pulled off successfully because of "the silent complicity of the entire town" (interview, 16 Sept. 1994). This tragic episode, the most important among several invasion attempts from abroad from 1958 onward, exemplary of the paroxysm of hatred between blacks and mulattoes, serves as the underlying historical reality of the novel. Indeed, through the fictional character Alexandre—who leads an invasion and an aborted general uprising—Desquiron intended to commemorate the fate of the writer Jacques Stephen Alexis (interview, 16 Sept. 1994). He is believed to have been murdered by the *makout* during a 1961 insurgency against the Duvalier regime. In fact, several times in the text a nameless figure is mentioned who suggests the personality and the fate of Alexis: "he was a famous writer, very tall, very black, but also with that distinguished air of a leader" (113). Alexandre's story reflects the painful history of the country.

Another key element for reading *Reflections* is an understanding of Vodou as an incontrovertible construct of Haitian identity. The narrative is fundamentally inscribed within the heritage of Guinea, that is, within the framework of the Vodou gods that would eventually create, as Joan Dayan says, "the rituals of memory" to be seen as "deposits of history."[16] Since the telling of the ceremony of Bois-Caïman, a key event in the revolution (14 August 1791) by which Haitians continue to construct their identity, Vodou has entered both written official history and the ritualized imaginary of the people through a complex system of myths. The word *Vodou* is African. It is used by the Fon tribe of Dahomey to mean *spirit*, *god*, or *image*, but its survival in Haiti is intrinsically linked to the successful revolution of 1791 and the improbable ceremony retold by every historian of Saint-Domingue. But, if Vodou's ritual practices reenact the spirit of liberation, it is important to keep in mind, as

Joan Dayan points out, that "the lwa most often invoked by today's vodou practitioners . . . were responses to the institution of slavery, to its peculiar brand of sensuous domination."[17] In other words, the invocation of the spirits constituted in the past a reaction to the white master's power. The followers of Vodou often reenact in their worship the links of servitude. Thus the life of the spirits thrives: serving the gods means to tell the history of the people beyond official history. This in turn, serves to tell their spiritual heritage while establishing an incontrovertible Haitian identity.

It is not easy to talk about the *lwa* of Vodou since there are thousands of them and any *lwa* can have multiple emanations depending on locale, a particular ritual, an individual's needs, or other factors. Originating from numerous tribes of Africa, the spirits came to the New World with the slaves and underwent multiple transformations that would make it difficult to identify their place of origin and original function. Moreover, because any Vodou initiate can, once dead, be turned into a spirit by a priest, some *lwa* are specifically Haitian. Most *lwa* live "under the waters," in an indeterminate place called Ginen (Guinea), and dwell with the ancestors. Since no one really knows what goes on in their world or how the gods relate to each other and to the dead, "talk about them usually ends up being about the ways in which men and women serve or resist their 'mysteries,' or how the gods themselves respond to the vicissitudes of life in the corporeal world."[18] The *oungan* or *manbò* serves as intermediary between the believers and the supernatural powers and must periodically visit the *lwa* in search of renewed powers. "There is little difference between the supernatural society of the *loa* and the Haitian peasantry which imagined it. The spirits distinguish themselves from men solely by the extent of their 'knowledge,' or, which is the same thing, their powers. They are all country people who share the tastes, habits and passions of their servants," writes Métraux.[19] Thus the faithful expect the *lwa* to respond to their needs and to offer assistance in practical matters of life.

Vodou worshippers are divided into cult groups, and they gather around an *ounfò* or temple. The *oungan* or *manbò* who directs the ceremonies is usually assisted by *ounsi*, or servants of the spirits, who make up the corps de ballet and the choir of the temple. The only difference between the appearance of the *ounfô* and that of a house of ordinary folk is the outside *peristil*, a sort of open shelter offering protection from inclement weather. Colorful posts support the roof, and ritual dances pivot around the *poto mitan* (central pillar), which is venerated during the ceremonies as evidence of its particular holiness. It is "the way of the spirits" by which the *lwa* enter the *peristil* when summoned. The *bagi* (inner sanctuary) is a room located at the far end of the *ounfô*. It contains brick altars in the form of arched platforms filled with ritualistic objects, such as jugs containing *lwa*, all manner of pots and bowls containing the souls of the initiated, thunderstones or *lwa* stones, playing cards, rattles, and divine emblems.[20]

In spite of a number of antisuperstition campaigns led by the Roman Catholic Church from the 1930s onward and backed by the government, Vodou as a religion has been able not only to survive but also to react defensively to the many forms of oppressions in the lives of Haitians. There are five Vodou ceremonies in *Reflections*, revealing the importance of these rituals in people's lives and their consequences within the country's social and political fabric. The title of the novel, *Reflections of Loko Miwa*, refers to the *lwa* Loko, who is the spirit closely associated with trees and their curative leaves. Loko is a guardian of sanctuaries and a healer who protects the *doktè fèy* (healer). He is also the spirit of mirrors who gives eyes and knowledge, that is, simultaneously vision and acumen, and reflection. In other words, Loko allows the mirroring of the self, both body and mind.

In *Reflections*, Loko is also the *lwa* who protects the *marasa* who mirror each other. This braiding together of myth, ritual, and reality is often reflected in Haitian literature. Gemination is, indeed, a recurrent theme in Haiti's letters from Emeric Bergeaud's *Stella* (1859) to Marie Chauvet's *Folie* (1968). Twin figures are implicitly present in Jacques Stephen Alexis's *Les arbres musiciens* (1957; The musician trees) and *Le romancero aux étoiles* (1960; Romancero of the stars) and fully part of the plot in Jacques Roumain's *Gouverneurs de la rosée* (1944; trans. *Masters of the Dew*, 1947). According to Alfred Métraux, twins may be quite threatening because they are invested with potential evil powers, but they are always honored.

They embody a paradoxical alliance of opposite irrational forces: unity and duality.[21] Maximilien Laroche also remarks in his study of gemination in Haitian letters that "twins and *lwa marasa* as personification of law and power represent the conjunction of two spaces, one concentric, the other eccentric." This reveals, Laroche says, that Haitian culture is basically formed by "a double space" governed by the concrete possibility of the union of opposites.[22] According to this definition, the *marasa* in the novel would represent the hope of communion and understanding, the promise of true love and harmony. Mystical sisters are also related by blood from "the time of Guinea," that is, from their common African heritage, thus signaling the possible reconciliation of a divided society. As importantly, Laroche notes that the first fictional representations of gemination appear in traditional folktales in the Kreyòl language. The tales about Bouki and Malis (see, for example, Alexis's story, "Le dit be Bouqui et de Malice," in *Le romancero aux étoiles*) reveal the primacy of issues of race, color, and class prejudice in Haitian's society and their possible resolution.[23] In *Reflections*, the twinning communion of the two heroines from the two completely opposite worlds—the rich city girl from the fiercely prejudiced mulatto caste and the poor black girl from a rural, mountain community—allows the author to expose the deep-rooted contradictions of Haitian social structure. In Jérémie, a town "corrupted by prejudices, . . . suspended like curdled milk because of its absurd hierarchies," the *marasa* are powerless to transform their society (37). If their bonding appears on the surface to establish some sort of unity, it also exacerbates the conflicts of their community to the point at which they will be outcast and silenced.

In the first part of the narrative, the voice of the then-eighty-year-old Alma Viva Jean Joseph, known as Cocotte, born in a poor and very dark-skinned family of plantation workers, alternates with Violaine's, born into a rich mulatto family. The two girls, born the same day, share the burden of telling the crucial event of their lives; they are mystical *marasa* with power akin to those of the *lwa*. The Delavigne family must accept the decree since Violaine's paternal grandfather, against the unwritten law of his social class, married a black peasant from Cocotte's village. Cocotte is therefore brought to live and work in the Delavigne household from the age of eight, indicating the reality of Vodou's feared influence to connect social classes that would not otherwise have intimate relationships. In spite of Violaine's fair complexion and hair—she is characterized as a *chabin*—she has also inherited the African genes of her grandmother. Violaine has been betrothed since birth to Philippe Edouard, a Jérémie mulatto, "the perfect product of this complex alchemy of crossbreeding" (102). However, she irremediably falls in love with Alexandre upon his return from Port-au-Prince, where he was fighting against the regime of François Duvalier. The irruption of Alexandre into Violaine's life is the first catastrophic event and the direct indication of the unfolding drama.

In the first pages of the novel, Cocotte informs the reader of the fragmentation of her society, and more specifically of the distancing, colonialist attitude of the rich mulatto merchants from the rest of the population. The language they use furthers the fracture of Haitian society and its mechanism of repression. They speak French with their own kind but Kreyòl with their servants.[24] Franz Lofficial writes that "French is the language of fine speech and solemn occasions. It functions as an external obvious sign permitting the identification of the speaker's social status."[25] Cocotte also reveals in this first chapter that the representation of Haitian society is far more complex than the apparent rigid division between blacks and whites, poor and rich. She intimates that it is actually the unpredictable, mysterious ties that weave social relationships. The invisible powers of the *lwa* play a determining role in all people's destiny despite the mulattoes striving to repress their black African heritage. Indeed, it is generally acknowledged that, while claiming to despise Vodou as a set of deplorable superstitions, many members of the Haitian elite fear its supposed malefic powers and secretly consult *oungan* on occasion. Officially, however, they show their unquestionable allegiance to Roman Catholicism, and almost never to Vodou, all the more because their participation in the Roman Catholic Church is a synonym of social position. "There are always seven veils to be stripped away before the truth hidden behind life's comedy can be seen," Cocotte remarks (7).

What is Cocotte's role behind life's comedy? This is Desquiron's underlying question. Is she not, along with her condition of *marasa*, a reenactment of the young black slave woman who, before Independence, often had an intimate bondage with a white Creole or a free mulatto woman? According to Pierre de Vassières, who writes about Saint Domingue in the years between 1629 and 1789, there existed a complicitous intimacy between those women who thought themselves superior and those who served them. De Vassières writes: "Nearly every young white Créole owns a young mulâtresse or quarteronne (quadroon), and sometimes even a young négresse, whom they make their 'cocotte.' The cocotte is the confidante of all the thoughts of the mistress (and this reliance is sometimes reciprocal), the confidante of her loves."[26] In Desquiron's novel, Cocotte not only plays the role of confidante, but she is a necessary part of Violaine's identity, she is the mirror in which Violaine can contemplate her own body's duality and express the impulses of her African heritage.[27] Paradoxically, Violaine exerts a certain amount of control over Cocotte if only because of her superior social status. She remains the mistress who is often served by her *marasa* sister. The Delavigne family's compliance with the decree by the *lwa* to make Violaine and Cocotte "sisters" signals a kind of ruse to reaffirm the superiority and power of their caste. This, in turn, recalls the central undercurrent of Desquiron's text and reminds the reader that the central role of Vodou rites is to reenact the deep-rooted memories of mastery and servitude.

In the second part of *Reflections*, Violaine embarks on her tragic destiny under the guidance of the *manbò* Man Chavannes, when Violaine is to be punished for transgressing absolute taboos: she is pregnant with a black man's child. "There's no place for a child in your life. In their infinite wisdom the *lwa* are going to take it back," says Man Chavannes (88). "Mounted" by Papa Loko, Man Chavannes must perform the abortion. Thus, the priestess of Vodou undergoes a *crise mystique*, whereby the spirits descend and take possession of one of her "two souls."[28] She becomes both the vessel and the instrument of the *lwa*'s personality and decisions.

It is clear that the spirits of Vodou are not only part of Haitian sensibility, they also play a crucial role as guardian of the country's social order. In this respect, Aunt Tika's comments are particularly revealing when she refers to the role of the *bòkò* Eliacin, the sorcerer she has summoned to carry out the decision regarding Violaine's fate: "His duty is to carry them out, ours is to command" (106). If the several Vodou ceremonies in the text do, indeed, create a symbolic universe for the recovery of Haiti's African identity, they also suggest that, when necessary, the elite (the Delavigne family) manipulate the cult they would rather shun, and in Desquiron's novel, engage in sorcery for their own benefit. Through Vodou, the Delavignes exert control over the status of their family and, by extension, over their social class as a whole.

In the third and final section of the novel, the saddened gravedigger tells the story of Violaine's burial and exhumation. Against all established rules, she is given some salt to eat, the forbidden food for *ʒonbi* since one grain suffices to dispel lethargy and renew their will power. If Violaine is able to escape her zombified state, she recovers only a semblance of life; she remains a walking dead person. The end of Violaine's story is told by three different groups of voices. There are those of the children, those heard at the Vodou ceremony when the *manbò* Clermézine invokes Agwe, and finally the background voices of the market during the reunion of the *marasa* in Port-au-Prince. The last catastrophic event occurs when a famished child shoots down the *pigeon-lwa* who was to guide Alexandre to freedom. The reader senses, then, that Alexandre will die in prison. As for dezombified Violaine, deprived of her full consciousness, and effectively muted, she is now the constant companion of Cocotte under the protection of Papa Loko.

The living dead haunt the imaginary space of Haitians. No fate is more feared than to be made into a soulless body. According to Métraux, *ʒonbi* are recognized "by their absent-minded manner, their extinguished, almost glassy eyes, and above all by the nasal twang in their voices—a peculiarity which they share with the Gede, spirits of death."[29] Not only does the *ʒonbi* tell the experience of slavery, that terrible mutilation of being, but he represents the legacy of colonization and hybridization that is a contemporary reality. This hero-god from a horrific colonial past has survived in order to infuse ordinary people and devotees with a sense of independence and hope. "Variously reconstituted and adaptable to varying events, [Jean Zonbi] crystallizes the crossing not only of spirit and man in Vodou practices but the intertwining of black and yellow, African and Creole in the struggle for independence."[30] Thus, like Jean Zonbi, the zombified cross-bred Violaine exemplifies the history of dispossession and anonymity of her people born out of the experience of slavery. But equally important, she bears testimony of the Haitians' never-ending struggle for freedom.

The tales of zombification of beautiful white- or light-skinned upper-class women permeate Haitian literature from Alexis's "Chronique d'un faux amour" (Chronicle of a false love) to Depestre's Hadriana in *Hadriana dans tous mes rêves* (Hadriana in all my dreams). The common thread in those works as well as in movies staging this magic process is the zombification on her wedding night of a beautiful white girl coveted by a lower-class, dark-skinned *bòkò* who administers the poison in order to subject her to his commands, especially his ominous sexual longings. Therefore, the Gede, the *lwa* of death in the Vodou pantheon, are also powerful spirits of eroticism. As Lizabeth Paravisini-Gebert writes, the various versions of zombification, such as those told by Alfred Métraux, Zora Neale Hurston, or Katherine Dunham, "posit sexual desire—the erotic—as a fundamental component of the zombified woman's tale, hinting at, although never directly addressing, the urge to transcend or subvert race and class barriers as one of the repositories of the sorcerer's lust."[31] The implausible consummation of dichotomy of white female–black male is at the core of Haitian erotic imaginary. The female's heinous zombification is the result of her social and sexual inaccessibility since her lustful victimizer is from a lower class and darker color, thus physically revolting by definition.

Reflections draws upon this basic tale: Violaine is a beautiful, light-complected, good-hearted young woman born into a prominent family but engaged in a sexual union with a black man of humble background. She dies "mysteriously" in the prime of her youth, and is buried in a "gossamer gown of white tulle, which is spangled with silver sequins and surrounded by what appears to be a translucent cloud" (137). This dress, reminiscent of a virginal wedding gown, is the favorite burial outfit of female *zonbi*, who usually "die" on their wedding night or wedding anniversary. However, Desquiron's story offers some significant variations and consequently, subversions on the same theme. Violaine's zombification results from her own passionate love and self-initiated assuaged desire for the poor, black, handsome Alexandre. She transgresses the social lines that decree that she can experience sensual fulfillment only with a man of her own background and pigmentation. She uses her eroticized body to straddle an otherwise insurmountable barrier of race and class. As a consequence, she loses her privileged status and her white body. She falls victim to her own caste that loathes the other and punishes its transgressors by rape and by divesting them of their being, both body and mind. Philippe Edouard victimizes her, taking on the role of the *bòkò* with soiling sexual desire, whereas black Alexandre is transformed into a heroic figure, the possible savior of his country. Philippe Edouard is an active participant in Violaine's zombification, and it is only by reducing her agency that he is able to take possession of her now-empty body. Dissociated from her will, Violaine is returned to the condition of her slave ancestors, those victims who were silenced by the plantation system. She has been unable to breach the race and class obstacles of her society. On the trails of Loko Miwa, Violaine reflects on her condition: "I barely know where I come from. My memory is full of black holes and fleeting, confused, even preposterous visions" (150).

From the outset, Violaine's name announces her fate. It contains two significant French words: *viol*, which means "rape," and *(h)aine*, "hatred." Violaine's name symbolizes the harrowing history of her country. "Our past, molded out of fear, consists of uprooting and rape that has transformed us into a variegated throng, a people torn apart at our very core," Violaine laments (41). She echoes René Depestre's comments: "this obsession with the zombi is . . . the most interesting fact of cultural life in Haiti. And further, it corresponds to a reality which is the state of the Haitian people. . . . Haiti is a zombified country, a country that has lost its soul. Political and colonial history has plunged Haiti into an unrelenting state of total alienation."[32] Violaine's zombified fate is exemplary of the dissociation between the Haitian people's body and their will that centuries of brutality have perpetuated. Cocotte, the privileged witness of the mulattoes' way of life and of Jérémie's society, understands that she must liberate herself from Haiti's various oppressions. But the "trails" to this freedom are harsh, painful, and eventually lead her nowhere. Through Violaine's ordeal, Cocotte's own world collapses and her destiny parallels her *marasa* sister's. Cocotte is not whole anymore. She, too, is returned to her past of "fear," "uprooting," and "rape" when she must submit to the sorcerer's sexual desires in an effort to free Alexandre. Still a virgin, she expresses her harrowing experience in these terms: "He crushes you with his weight. You can hear him moan through his heavy breathing. A burning dagger opens you, penetrates you, tears you in two, as he continues to gasp for air. The taste of vomit fills your mouth" (175).

It is important to note, near the end of the novel, the intertextual intrusion of Isidore Ducasse, also known as Tonton Dodo, in Violaine's quest. The name "Isodore Ducasse" evokes the French poet of uncertain origins on the margins of America, and French poetry, the Comte de Lautréamont, whose masterpiece *Les chants de Maldoror* (trans. *Maldoror*, 1965) is a meditation on the forces of evil. In Desquiron's novel, Isidore Ducasse's affectionate nickname is "Tonton Dodo," or "Uncle Sleep." One of the recurrent themes in *Les chants* is Maldoror's obsessive fear of sleep and his relentless struggle against its threat. Trapped in some sort of magnetic numbness, Maldoror is battling against the central tragedy of life. His urge to be lucid and awareness of his lack of consciousness constitute the struggle of his work. In *Reflections*, Isidore Ducasse has an ironic role. He attempts to cure Violaine from her "sleep" and loss of speech by leading her on the *lwa*'s trails. He is a sorcerer and, like the poet, a wordsmith, a magician of the word. Papa Agwe "mounts" Isidore and enables him to speak for Violaine, thus allowing her to break her silence. Violaine is begotten by the ocean and reborn in its midst, painfully rising like her ancestors from the bottoms of the slave ships. The intrusion of the literary figure of Lautréamont in the narrative allows Desquiron to address a twofold question that remains unanswered in the French poet's work.

What is the role of the writer within society and what function can literary creation have within culture?

Violaine and Cocotte's tragic stories are about Haiti's socio-political and sexual taboos and their destructiveness. Lilas Desquiron is part of the small group of Haitian women writers who are subverting the former patriarchal discourses to confront the harsh reality of their country and show how it affects their personal lives. As Yanick Lahens has said, "it is the (Haitian) women who sought to pave the way for a new form of literary expression, free of black consciousness and Negritude, free of social realism and of Marvelous Realism."[33] In that sense, Desquiron's novel shares many aspects with the works of Haitian women writers such as Marie Chauvet, the most original fiction writer of the 1960s and 1970s, Nadine Magloire, and Jan J. Dominique. Like Desquiron, these authors center on the situation of women who rebel against the confines of their world and break the silence imposed upon them. And as did Marie Chauvet in *Amour* (1968) and Nadine Magloire in *Le sexe mystique* (1975), Desquiron breaks the silence on female sexuality. In the social and literary context of Haiti, Violaine's displayed eroticism implies a subversive critical stance toward Haitian patriarchal culture. She initiates the sexual act with Alexandre—who graphically describes making love to her—and she masturbates with a tree when she returns to consciousness from her zombified lethargy. The author of *Reflections* proves that Haitian women are as capable as men (Depestre, for example) of writing erotic fiction.

Desquiron is opposed, however, to a simplistic feminist reading of *Reflections* because she feels that "the North American feminist struggle is irrelevant to Haitian women" (interview, 16 Sept. 1994). However, it is impossible not to compare Violaine to other Haitian female characters who are struggling for self-identity and empowerment within the context of their country's violent political scene. Like most "feminists," Violaine is trying to breach the obstacles of her bourgeois world and to revolt against the submissive roles prescribed for women. She also has the courage to defy the racial and class prejudices of her society, and to assume fully her African heritage. She challenges and ultimately subverts the assumption of her country's reality but becomes its victim because of her courage and assertiveness. Her zombification is the symbol of the collective amnesia and silence imposed by Haiti's long history of violently repressive dictatorships. For a time the novel sustains Violaine and Cocotte, the *lwa marasa*, as representing the hope of social reconciliation, but this is not the final outcome. The narrative offers a reminder of Haitian history, a regressive vision of a very complex reality.

Marie-Agnès Sourieau

NOTES

1. Condé, *La parole des femmes*, 82. My translation.

2. Zimra, "Haitian Literature," 86.

3. See Carrol F. Coates's analysis of the narrative structure in "Lilas Desquiron," 101–2.

4. See Hoffmann, "Haitian Sensibility," 368–69.

5. Roumain, "Griefs de l'homme noir," 204. My translation.

6. Hoffmann, 369.

7. See Dayan, *Haiti, History and the Gods*, 25–27, 234–35. See also Fanon, *Black Skin, White Masks*, for a psychoanalytical discussion of the curse of color afflicting black women and their dream of "lactification" as destructive imitation of the externals of the dominant "white" society.

8. Dash, *Literature and Ideology*, 112.

9. Price-Mars, *So Spoke the Uncle*, 11.

10. Dash, *Literature and Ideology*, 100, 112.

11. Ferguson, *Papa Doc, Baby Doc*, 34.

12. Antoine, "The Caribbean in Metropolitan French Writing," 352.

13. Dayan, *Haiti, History, and the Gods*, 56.

14. Abbott, *Haiti*, 62–63. Abbott writes: "Intermarriage between black and mulatto was acceptable only if the black was a successful male and the mulatto a woman, for no mulatto man dared disgrace his family's name by darkening its blood with a black wife. Even casual social intermingling was limited, and mulattoes partied at the exclusive Excelsior Club, while aspiring blacks had to be content with the Essor Club. Politics especially was skin-colored, with Jérémie's mulatto elite ruling the city ever since Haitian independence."

15. Abbott, *Haiti*, 120.

16. Dayan, *Haiti, History, and the Gods*, 35.

17. Dayan, *Haiti, History, and the Gods*, 36.

18. Dayan, "Vodoun and the Voice of the Gods," 37.

19. Métraux, *Voodoo*, 94.

20. Métraux, *Haiti, Black Peasants, and Voodoo*, 65–70.

21. Métraux, *Voodoo*, 146–53.

22. Laroche, *Le Patriarche*, 136–37. My translation.

23. Laroche, *Le Patriarche*, 137.

24. "Haiti is an ambiguous nation, and the ambivalence of its language is the foremost proof of this," writes Ghislain Gouraige in *La Diaspora*, 134. My translation.

25. Lofficial, *Créole-français*, 38. My translation. Privilege of the elite, French is a barrier to upward social mobility. Only a small minority of school-age children learn to speak it as if it were their mother tongue.

26. Quoted in Dayan, *Haiti, History, and the Gods*, 57.

27. In Depestre's *Hadriana dans tous mes rêves*, the white Hadriana, zombified in her coffin, sees her black double in bridal veil dancing for her.

28. Depestre says in regard to the Haitian metaphysical question of the two "souls": "each human being is composed of a 'gros bon ange' and a 'petit bon ange' (big and small good angel). The body is 'le cadavre corps' opposed to 'l'esprit' (spirit), but no simple dichotomy is allowed here, since to understand the distinction between the gros bon ange and the petit bon ange, we would have to think about something like mind and soul, but the division is not hard and fast." Dayan, "France Reads Haiti," 141.

29. Métraux, *Voodoo*, 283. As the tradition goes, during the 1804 massacre of the whites on Dessalines's order, a mulatto from Port-au-Prince, known as Jean Zombi became infamous for his horrifying brutality. Mentioned by several historians of Haiti as a key figure during the liberation of the country from the French, his real existence remains a mystery, but his fame endured as the most demonic and therefore the most influential spirit of the Vodou pantheon.

30. Dayan, *Haiti, History, and the Gods*, 36.

31. Paravisini-Gebert, "Women Possessed," 52.

32. Dayan, "France Reads Haiti," 147.

33. Rowell, "Interview with Yannick Lahens," 442.

BIBLIOGRAPHY

. . .

Works by Lilas Desquiron

FICTION

Desquiron, Lilas. *Les chemins de Loco-Miroir.* Paris: Éditions Stock, 1990. Reprint, Paris: Press Pocket, 1991.

Desquiron, Lilas. "From *Les chemins de Loco-Miroir.*" Translated by Jean Desquiron. *Callaloo* 15, no. 2 (1992): 484–89.

ESSAYS

Desquiron, Lilas. *Racines du Vodou* (The roots of vodou). Port-au-Prince: Henri Deschamps, 1990. Awarded the 1990 Deschamps prize.

Studies and Reviews of Lilas Desquiron and Her Works

Bailby, Edouard. "Un roman qui met à nu l'âme du pays: Roméo et Juliette en Haïti" (A novel laying bare the country's soul: Romeo and Juliet in Haiti). *Jeune Afrique* 30 (Jan.–5 Feb. 1991): 76–77. Review.

Chemla, Yves. "L'autre dans le miroir. Essai sur la représentation de la société dans le roman haïtien" (Mirroring the other: essay on the representation of society in Haitian fiction). Université de Paris-XII, 1993. Doctoral dissertation.

Coates, Carrol F. "Lilas Desquiron et les vêpres de Jérémie: *Les Chemins de Loco-Miroir*" (Lilas Desquiron and the vespers of Jérémie: *Reflections of Loko Miwa*). In *Elles écrivent des Antilles.* Edited by Suzanne Rinne and Joëlle Vitiello, 95–103. Paris: L'Harmattan, 1997.

Desquiron, Jean. *Haïti à la une. Une anthologie de la presse haïtien de 1724 à 1934.* Port-au-Prince: L'Imprimeur II, 1993–97. 6 vols.

Hell, Jeff. "Feu pour feu. Une Volte-face surprenante" (Return fire: an amazing volte-face). *Le Nouvelliste* 5–6 Jan. 1991, 1–2. Review.

―――. *Le Nouvelliste*, 19–20 Jan. 1991, 2–3. Review.

Shelton, Marie-Denise. "Haitian Women's Fiction." *Callaloo* 15, no. 3 (1992): 770–77. Passing mention.

Zimra, Clarisse. "Haitian Literature after Duvalier: An interview with Yanick Lahens." *Callaloo* 16, no. 1 (1993): 77–93. Passing mention.

General Bibliography

Abbott, Elizabeth. *Haiti: The Duvaliers and Their Legacy.* New York: McGraw Hill, 1988.

Alexis, Jacques Stephen. "Chronique d'un faux amour" (Chronicle of a false love). In *Romancero aux étoiles* (Romancero of the stars). Paris: Gallimard, 1960.

Antoine, Régis. *La littérature franco-antillaise (Haïti, Guadeloupe, Martinique).* Paris: Karthala, 1992.

―――. "The Caribbean in Metropolitan French Writing." In *History of Literature in the Caribbean.* Edited by A. James Arnold, translated by J. M. Dash. Amsterdam: J. Benjamin, 1994.

Bellegarde-Smith, Patrick. *Haiti: The Breached Citadel.* Boulder CO: Westview, 1990.

Bonniol, Jean-Luc. *La couleur comme maléfice. Une illustration créole de la généalogie des Blancs et des Noirs* (Color as curse: a Creole illustration of the genealogy of blacks and whites). Paris: Albin Michel, 1992.

Condé, Maryse. *La parole des femmes* (Women's words). Paris: L'Harmattan, 1979.

Dash, J. Michael. *Haiti and the United States. National Stereotypes and the Literary Imagination.* New York: St. Martin's, 1988.

―――. *Literature and Ideology in Haiti, 1915–1961.* London: Macmillan, 1981.

Dayan, Joan. "France Reads Haiti: An Interview with René Depestre." *Yale French Studies* 83 (1993): 136–53.

―――. *Haiti, History, and the Gods.* Berkeley: Univ. of California Press, 1995.

―――. "Vodoun and the Voice of the Gods." *Raritan* 10 (winter 1991).

Depestre, René. *Hadriana dans tous mes rêves* (Hadriana in all my dreams). Paris: Gallimard, 1988.

Deren, Maya. *The Divine Horsemen: The Voodoo Gods of Haïti.* New York: Delta, 1972.

Desmangles, Leslie G. *The Faces of God: Vodou and Roman Catholicism in Haiti.* Chapel Hill: Univ. of North Carolina Press, 1992.

Fanon, Franz. *Black Skin, White Masks.* Translated by Charles Lam Markmann. New York: Grove Press, 1967.

Ferguson, James. *Papa Doc, Baby Doc: Haïti and the Duvaliers.* Oxford: Blackwell, 1989.

Fick, Carolyn E. *The Making of Haiti. The Saint Domingue Revolution from Below.* Knoxville: Univ. of Tennessee Press, 1990.

Gouraige, Ghislain. *La Diaspora d'Haïti et l'Afrique.* Québec: Naaman, 1974.

Hoffmann, Léon-François. "Haitian Sensibility." In *History of Literature in the Caribbean.* Edited by A. James Arnold, 365–78. Amsterdam: J. Benjamins, 1994.

Hurbon, Laënnec. *Comprendre Haïti. Essai sur l'Etat, la nation, la culture* (Understanding Haiti: essay on the state, nation, and culture). Paris: Karthala, 1987.

———. *Voodoo: Search for the Spirit.* Translated by Lory Frankel. New York: Abrams, 1995.

Hurston, Zora N. *Tell My Horse.* Philadelphia: Lippincott, 1938.

James, C. L. R. *The Black Jacobins.* New York: Vintage, 1963.

Laroche, Maximilien. *Le Patriarche, le Marron et la Dosa* (The patriarch, the maroon, and the dosa). Sainte-Foy, Québec: Groupe de Recherche sur les Littératures de la Caraïbe, coll. Essai 4, 1988.

Lofficial, Franz. *Créole-français: une fausse querelle* (Creole-French: a bogus quarrel). Montréal: Collectif Paroles, 1979.

Métraux, Alfred. *Haiti, Black Peasants, and Voodoo.* Translated by Peter Lengyel. New York: Universe, 1960. Originally published as *Haiti, la terre, les hommes et les dieux,* Neuchâtel: La Béconnière, 1957.

———. *Voodoo in Haiti.* Translated by Hugo Charteris. Intro. Sidney W. Mintz. New York: Schochen,1972. Originally published as *Le Vaudou haïtien,* Paris: Gallimard, 1958.

Nicholls, David. *From Dessalines to Duvalier.* New York: Cambridge Univ. Press, 1979.

Ott, Thomas O. *The Haitian Revolution 1789–1894.* Knoxville: Univ. of Tennessee Press, 1973.

Paravisini-Gebert, Lizabeth. "Women Possessed: the Eroticism and Exoticism of the Representation of Woman as Zombie." In *Sacred Possessions*. New Brunswick: Rutgers Univ. Press, 1997.

Price-Mars, Jean. *So Spoke the Uncle*. Translated by Magdaline W. Shannonn. Washington, D.C.: Three Continents Press, 1983. Originally published as *Ainsi parla l'oncle*, Compiègne: Imprimerie de Compiègne, 1928; new edition, edited by Robert Cornevin, Ottawa: Leméac, 1973.

Roumain, Jacques. "Griefs de l'homme noir" (The black man's grievance). In *La montagne ensorcelée* (The enchanted mountain). Paris: Éditeurs Français Réunis, 1972.

Rowell, Charles H. "Interview with Yannick Lahens." *Callaloo* 15, no. 2 (1992).

Trouillot, Michel-Rolph. *Nation, State, and Society in Haiti, 1804–1984*. Washington, D.C.: Woodrow Wilson International Center for Scholars, 1985.

Reflections of Loko Miwa

To Jean D.,
my friend,
my brother,
my father.

Cocotte

Life is long, indeed too long. It just never seems to end. The Guinean spirits slipped into my cradle a tangle of yarn I've never quite managed to unravel. Violaine, my sister, left some time ago to join our ancestors on the other side of the great water. As for me, my hair has turned as white as the Caribbean glistening in the sunlight. As for me, a shriveled old mango left out in the sun too long, I can barely walk. On the other hand, my eyes are still pretty good. Wonder why that is. I can still impress my neighbors not only by how far into the distance I see but by my accuracy as well. Even in the dead of night I can see clearly—a veritable frizzy-headed old owl, I'm telling you. My tireless eyes are an accursed gift from the *lwa*. Each day of my interminable life, their mischievousness has condemned me to contemplate the town of Jérémie stretched out like a sick beast at the foot of my little mountain. The town is always within sight, right there before me, evil, infected, swollen from envy and bile. And yet, from afar, one might think of it as a jewel with the corolla of its bay spread in front of the verdant, foamy tops of its rounded hills. Along the golden curve of its beach, the *kay chanmòt*, the two-storied houses of the rich merchants, with their wood-laced facades, turn their backs to this magnificent view of the sea below. Yes, it is true! They have literally turned their backsides to this vast expanse of blue, to the tenderness and fury of that living water.

I have had to live four times twenty years in order to understand the blindness of these men and women so filled with arrogance that they've considered this heavenly bay nothing more than a receptacle for the water draining from their sewers. We should have been able to foresee it. We should have been able to discern they were incurably closed off to any kind of emotion just by looking at their pretentious, gingerbread houses with their facades turned away from all the natural beauty and directed instead toward the streets in order to plunder and amass their sacrosanct money all the more. No doubt about it, they were blind to all that gradation of blue behind them, to its languid curve like that of a *kreyòl* backside, in short, blind to all the wonders teeming within this dream inlet. On the other hand, you had to see them firsthand in their famous literary circles, reciting poems like Lamartine's "Le Lac" or Musset's "Namouna" without ever missing a beat or a single rhyme. Yes, for things like that, they were indeed specialists. Filling themselves up with *tafya* while babbling like monkeys about the moon and the wind. Yes, they were all very good at that! But as for me, I'll tell anyone and everyone who wants to listen—and may lightning strike me if it isn't the truth—these people have never been shaken to the bone by anything other than hatred and jealousy. And that can even be seen inscribed in the very geography of the town itself. The mulatto merchants of Jérémie are all descendants of pirates. They are all vendors of *pakoti* and exporters of coffee, cocoa, or campeachy wood, and they are all as proud as can be of their pale skin. They protect it from the fierce Caribbean sun with an almost maniacal care, as if they could hide the original sin of their negritude beneath a pale epidermis.

We could go on forever about the extraordinary range and variety of their prejudices. Moreover, we should never forget that, as the most intimate secretion of this southern peninsula, they were the impure product of its loins, the children of its foolish ways. These feverish-eyed mulatto men and women were in fact the only authentic *Kreyòl* before the Eternal Spirit. Complicated and vigorous bastards, they had bubbled up out of the prolific and frenetic couplings of freed slaves and whites from nowhere or from everywhere, that is, from every possible experience. Indestructible and lethargic, they were at the same time excitable, heavy drinkers of punch, who kept their minds clouded over with its rum and their words bombastic. Hmmph, just some more "high-strung mulattos from Jérémie!" (Yes, in fact, that's the way people from Port-au-Prince refer to them to show their disdain, thumb their nose at them or simply give them a hard time.)

They built the town in their own image: gaudy, laid out in jigsaw fashion, and forever unfinished. It was their private kingdom, their home playing field, if you will; and they ruled the game like monarchs, according to their own wishes. Until the day it all came crashing down, but that's another story altogether.

In the old days, the people who lived up in the hills, the peasants who came down to sell or buy something on Gran Ri had to get off their horses, hold them by the bridle and approach in a respectful manner. Yes indeed! I'm telling you how it was because my elderly grandma repeated this story to me from the time I was just a child. Our black-skinned patriarchs with that tranquil look who, while kings in their own gardens, had to walk humbly in the middle of Gran Ri as they led their horses behind them. But you know, nothing is so simple in the land of Ayiti Toma because that same peasant, who used to be seen hat in hand holding his horse by the bridle and selling his coffee on the stoop of the store, was linked to his mulatto client by mysterious *pwen*, which in certain circumstances made him the master. And that too is another story altogether. There are always seven veils to be stripped away before the truth hidden behind life's comedy can be seen.

The rest of the town radiates chaotically from the old kiosk. From the Plas Zam to the cirque, Jérémie climbs all the way up to the now-dusty terraces of long ago with its alleyways, its children's cries, and its itinerant tradeswomen. And then Korido Trezò tumbles down with its loose, brick stairs from Ri Gouvènman to Gran Ri. Today, a strange silence hangs over it all and shrouds my sleepy little city, my Sleeping Beauty. It's as if the actors had deserted the stage, abandoning behind them a lavish decor that time had insidiously begun to attack.

And the Grandans, that silvery river rippling like a beautiful eel, still sensuously slips its ringlets out onto a plain so fertile that fruit ends by rotting on the vine there. It continues to cradle its *pipirit*, small bamboo rafts that almost sink when loaded down under the weight of various fruits and tubers. Even today, this hard labor still goes on. All of the so-called important people in the city have disappeared, but the peasants remain, enduring as best they can. A long time ago when I was just a child, I used to load those rafts, too. Back then it was always a celebration, but all that is so far away now. And yet memories are starting to come back in reverse order, unfolding before my eyes, so much so that at first the voice of a little girl no bigger than a palmetto bird will speak. Smooth as a slippery stone from a stream, she had large, inquisitive yet peaceful eyes while her woolly plaits fell on skin as velvety as a sapodilla. A petite little girl, she is spending her last night in her native village, nestled in the hollow of a mountain far from the city.

· · ·

I'll never forget it. It was the night I turned eight. Angélique had come at sundown. She only made this kind of effort on special occasions. Having smoothed my hair with oil, she then spent hours braiding it in complicated twists and turns. I still remember my face in the mirror, glimpsing it as I passed. It resembled the faces of all girls leaving for the city, with the borrowed air that the fear of the unknown and especially a first hairdo for going out seem to impart. My head was wrapped in a scarf in order not to spoil my beautiful hairdo, and I curled up on my mat for the last time in the main room of our house. The night was filled with the tolling of the anoles and the musical breathing of tree toads. I was sad to leave my elderly grandmother as well as my friends. I knew I would miss swimming with them in the river along with our interminable hopscotch games and the rounds when our high-pitched voices massacred the words to such childhood ditties as "Les Oignons" or something like "La Petite Boiteuse." But the adults in my family had explained how I wouldn't have to fetch water from the well anymore. In the city it just sprang right up inside the houses. The thought of spending my days without having to lug a heavy water gourd up and down mountainous footpaths pleased me more than anything. And yet, I was afraid. The whole story of my departure for the city was too much to carry about, too heavy for a little girl. Our lives here on earth are full of mystery and sudden shifts in direction. Bearing this in mind, you will come to understand perhaps how my destiny became strangely interwoven with that of my sister Violaine.

The story of how we both came into the world was told to me on more than one occasion. I was born in the canal on the edge of the coffee plantations, in that canal where all the women went to give birth. My mother was sixteen at the time. She had a little, bulging brow along with all the courage of our race packed into her body. She pushed me out into the world without raising a single cry to the sun which, on that day and at that precise moment, was just coming up over the apricot-colored hills. Grann Nannie, who was lending a hand, hugged me close to her heart and, after having coated me with all the obligatory decoctions against werewolves, the evil eye, malevolent breezes, fever, enteritis, and navel infections, held me out to the four directions of the wind, saying, "With your permission, Great Master, here is Alma Viva Jean Joseph, who has come amongst us with her full complement of joys and sorrows. I commend her to your care, Oh Spirits of the water, my *lwa*, Oh my *mistè* and all my Saints! And with this I say *ayibobo!*"

It is, I think, the only time my full name was ever spoken aloud in the village. Almost immediately thereafter everyone began calling me affectionately "Cocotte" because of my resemblance to a bird with ruffled feathers but also because it was useful to have a nickname to ward off wrongdoers out for blood.

At the same time in a big house in Jérémie, Violaine came into the world only to be immediately wrapped in a lace cocoon. Whereas the wiry back of my mother had been braced up against a partition tapestried with banana leaves from the canal, Violaine's mother, who was the color of brown sugar, twisted painfully among her batiste bedclothes. Her child's fervid screams resounded as incongruously in that padded ambiance as might a clarion call. But, despite the silk and Valenciennes lace, it was with genuine love and care that old Vénus anointed the child, coating her with the same decoctions used on me, those always prepared from sacred leaves, those preparations that made us all part of the "Begotten," part of those people thought to be capable of surviving the worst kinds of misery. And then to the East, to the West, to the North and

South, Marie Athanase Cléonice Violaine was presented to the *mistè* of our ancestors, those from Africa, those who, although denied whenever surfacing in our daily conversations, are always present from birth to death at all the crucial moments in our lives. Will anyone ever dare speak of this gag forever tied over our mouths, of these scales virtually bolted to our eyelids, or this weight always right there, pressing down upon our backs? Words only dry up on our barren tongues. Who will break this oppressive silence that has stifled our spirit ever since those savage nights languishing in the hold of a slave ship?

It had always been written that Violaine's mother and mine would bring into the world *marasa* girls, *dosou-dosa* twins. And afterward, it was up to us to pursue patiently the arduous task of maintaining the breath of life between our two worlds: the countryside, that refuge of the *lwa*, and the city where money and education were to be found. Ay, what a burden! What an undertaking for us, poor little hummingbirds that we were, to celebrate and promote this impossible union! And yet without it, without this fragile thread maintained by our ancestors across generations as well as nations, none of us in this damnable world would even be able to breathe.

Little Violaine was no sooner asleep in her cradle than her mother like a restless animal began to stir, anxiously waiting (I've always pictured Madame Delavigne, as beautiful as a sugar-coated almond on her embroidered pillow, with that black braid of hers shining next to her cheek). On that particular day she would not have to wait long. Almost immediately after I was born, Papa Da had hurriedly set out for Jérémie with the small dishes and pitchers for Violaine. It was very important that the rituals take place without a hitch. Nothing is more feared than angering the spirit of the *marasa*. Everything was, therefore, carried out according to the rules. All of our relatives from up in the mountains took care of the preparations in the *ounfò*. Violaine and I were sanctified by the *lwa rasin* and the talisman that linked us both together was handed over to them for safekeeping.

The night after we were born the first ritual of the *marasa* took place. The *oungan*, the old broken down priest, the venerable *papa lwa*, prepared libations along with inspirational words to give strength to the Spirits. Then, he stuffed our umbilical cords into our small, individual pitchers. Next, a lock of our baby hair was taken along with tiny clippings from our fingernails and earnestly deposited in the *bagi*. Later, a piece of linen soaked in the blood from our first menstruation and a tuft of our pubic hair would also be plunged into the mysterious heart of these pitchers sheltered in that same *bagi*. The adults carried all this out without ever saying a word. As for Violaine and me, we absorbed every last detail like the very air we were breathing.

Twenty-one days after my birth, Madame Delavigne, who, as had been planned, was to be my godmother, came to my village and held me over the baptismal font in that small mountain church where Saint Michael had been designated the patron saint. To this day, I'm still afraid to go inside of it because of the dreadful monster he is piercing with the tip of his spear. This monster, with its long, curling tail, its huge red tongue, and its body all covered with pustules, is hideous and frightening. Truly, it is a peculiar idea, I find, to portray it right there like that in a church in which children are to be baptized, where young people pledge their faith before the eyes of the Lord, and where the last rites are given to the dead— but so much for that! That particular day, the day of my baptism, Saint Michael's chapel was abloom with verbenas and bougainvillea.

The new Christian I had just become passed from a Breton priest's hands to the more paternal ones of the *oungan*, who took his turn at performing the necessary rituals for protecting me against evil spells, *wanga*, or any ill-intentioned people because, after all, Evil does exist. And it was to him, the *oungan*, the village elder, that Madame Delavigne had promised to come seek me out on my eighth birthday so I could be raised with my *marasa*, Violaine.

Violaine

My first childhood recollection is literally not much more than a naive painting. There's always a dense jungle that appears to be too green, with splotches of excessively strident colors. Among all the others, it's always this one, strong and precise, that rises from the depths of my memory, perfumed with mint and anise, with the very perfume of the mountains surrounding Jérémie.

I'm just a little package now being tossed about in the back of the Jeep. We're barely able to climb up the rocky road that runs along the side of the mountain. The dawn's watercolor hues have already faded and a cottony mist lingers on, trailing its wisps here and there. My stomach is a little upset after being jostled around by the road but also by the memory of that enormous piece of cake I wolfed down last night with my friends when they came to celebrate my fifth birthday. Even at this early age I'm feeling old and a bit important, but above all nauseated. For the very first time, I'm accompanying my mother to the coffee plantation. Alone with her, I'll finally get to know our village: the very same village that lords over our lives and from which the all-powerful coffee comes, along with fresh vegetables, our Sunday *kasav*, and "problems." It's in this same village that basic, essentially mysterious happenings are always taking place and where "our people" live, as they often say back at our house and not without a certain arrogance in their voice.

And suddenly, after a turn in the road, there's a violent shock. The village just leaps out at us! It's right there before us and yet at the same time there's a kind of tranquillity coming from its small huts, all of which are the color of candied sugar and perched like a flock of hummingbirds around the *kay mistè*. That's where I come from. I have always known it, but today this certainty rushes through me with the power of a dream. Indeed, this is where life began for me. I even know where to find the ancient *mapou*, feeling the urge to curl up passionately within the invigorating tentacles of its roots and let myself be taken over by the vitality of its soul. It's that maternal womb, that female tree that has engendered us all.

The smell of roast coffee, wisps of blue smoke rising out of fire-places near the tiny huts, long lines of children with their necks stiffened under the weight of a water calabash balanced on their head, the dull thud of wooden pestles, the bleating of small mountain goats, or the rhythmic walk of men with hoes on their shoulders—all this seems familiar to me and at the same time overwhelmingly new. Half asleep, I was placed on a mat in the shadowy light filtering from the *peristil* in the temple of the *lwa*, precisely where day-to-day life unfolds. In fact, a young woman is ironing there now. I can see her powerful back, rippling as the iron passes back and forth across her steaming laundry. Some children are shelling red kidney beans for the evening meal while a few chickens peck here and there. Because of their proximity to the sacred place, these humble gestures seem imbued with a certain nobility. There, on my mat, with my heart pounding against my ribs, I'm wide-eyed as I take it all in. I can even smell the odor of the nearby *bagi* with its soaked herbs, magic powders, and that sickly sweet stench of dried blood from the sacrifices.

But now right in front of me stands a little girl about my age. Completely black and very small, she's watching me without batting an eyelid. I don't dare speak or even utter a single sound. She's right there. I'll just have to be content with looking at her for the moment. An image surging up in my mind begins to shimmer within the haze of my thoughts: two almonds lying side by side in that intimate, twin compartment of their common husk. Harmony found again at last. And along with it goes the sensation of a thirst finally quenched, of wholeness, of loneliness abolished.

That day, I thought a great deal about the two reconciled parts of our entwined existence. Though incomplete, it suddenly seemed promising, like the sort of reflection we catch in the darkened waters of a pond. It was a violent and fleeting sensation whose intensity I could never capture again. Perhaps, the only privileged means of reflecting the truth of our double existence, of our two lives joined together through the will of the *lwa* was through the transparent candor of childhood. She and I were to be *marasa* from beginning to end.

Later on, in a kind of mutual dependence that became a part of our lives, we lived next to each other without ever discussing it. But from that day on, when we saw each other for the very first time, we were caught up in the turmoil of a magnetic storm. Words falter when attempting to express this secret because, like a magnet's attraction to metal or the shudder of a mother tree receiving a graft, it can never be sufficiently explained.

Cocotte

The day after my eighth birthday, I finally got to know the town of Jérémie a little better. Summoned by Madame Delavigne, Papa Da took me in tow along with all my clothes, which had been washed, starched, and ironed. It was almost everything in the world I owned tied up in one neat bundle, from a chambray dress to a flowered print for Sundays to my white one with its matching scarf for the Feast of the *Marasa*, and two pairs of muslin shorts. I wore my only pair of shoes (my mountain sandals were left behind in the cabin).

We set out into the frosted dawn that covered the foothills. And I have to say I shall never forget the Caribbean Sea's entry into my life. Yes, it was that same deep blue that jumps out as it unfolds before you like some magnificent flower. I can still hear Papa Da whispering at that moment: "Just look at it. Look at that!" I'd been dozing while riding along clinging to his back, lulled to sleep by the monotonous gait of the horse as it ambled along. And, having never seen anything other than the foothills around our cabin, my incredulous young eyes drank in every bit of that spectacular view for the first time. To this day I still haven't grown tired of it. Each morning when I come out of my hut, I rediscover the Bay of Jérémie through the eyes of the little girl I was back then.

Papa Da's horse reached the Plas Zam. It was market day, and the place was just swarming with people: women from neighboring villages were loudly hawking their vegetables, arguing with one another, then bursting into raucous laughter. The children tried to break into all this brouhaha with their high-pitched voices, shouting "pralines," "who wants cinnamon for five *kòb*," anybody for "star anise," or "get your leaf remedies here." Sometimes a girl carrying on her head a heavy basket laden with *kenèp* would sing-song at the top of her lungs: "Here are the soft ones, soft *kenèp*!"

The gossipy old women who had come to do their shopping punctuated their haggling with powerful slaps to their hips accompanied by a Homeric *kipe*! I remember, just as if it were yesterday, a girl not even as big as me, who, with the agility of a ballerina, would sell coffee to the men standing next to their horses. A platter with a pot of hot coffee and porcelain cups balanced on her head, she fluttered about without ever spilling a drop. Yes, she was a very graceful child; I can still see her now. No doubt one of the numerous *restavèk* of the ladies in Jérémie's high society.

Finally, we arrived in front of the Delavignes' house. It was rather large and sat at an angle to the market place. On the second floor, a wrought-iron railing ran from one end of the facade to the other. Later, in seclusion on this balcony, where I was sheltered by the hardy shoots of the rose bush crawling up the length of the columns and encircling the twisted bars of the railing only to form small, forgiving alcoves of freshness, I spent hours on end dreaming in the company of its rusted metallic birds as well as its grape clusters that had been eaten away by verdigris. Down below was the store with its multicolored bottles, its *kleren* and kerosene barrels, and its sacks of grain. And on a shelf nearby were the coffee scales. The Delavignes lived upstairs. Papa Da, a little impressed by all this, held my small hand firmly in his huge, calloused fist as we climbed the mahogany staircase leading to the living quarters. Once in front of the Delavignes' door, Papa Da let go of my hand for a second as he removed his straw hat and wiped the perspiration from his face with a checkered bandanna. But almost immediately thereafter I nestled my trembling hand back in his. Everything here seemed strange to me: the big house, especially the staircase (where could I have seen anything similar, since the small huts in our village have but a single floor?), as well as the smells drifting through the Venetian blinds with their big-city aroma that disoriented my mountain-child sense of smell. And then, a tall, buxom woman wearing an immaculate apron opened the door for us. Her voice made you think irresistibly of that smooth quality of a fine cane syrup. It was Nounou's voice, a voice that knew how to soothe any kind of distress. In a very pleasant way she had us sit down, then disappeared into the mysterious depths of the large house.

Moments later, it was Madame Delavigne's turn to make her appearance in the dimly lit room where we had been seated. In her mauve-flowered housecoat, her black hair cascading around her shoulders, she seemed quite thin. Without even looking at me, she went directly to Papa Da. They spoke quietly, and their conversation ended almost as soon as it had begun. Indeed, everything had already been said at the time of my birth. At that point Papa Da came over to me, raised me up into his arms and said simply with an immense tenderness in his eyes (now suddenly teared over), "Behave yourself. I'll return soon. Your godmother will take good care of you."

"Please don't leave, don't leave me all alone, I beg you, Papa Da!" My voice was no more than a little bleating in his ears as I continued to cling to his powerful neck.

He put me back down and then, stiff as a board, marched out of the room. I felt as if I had just plunged into a whirling black hole. Nothing of my familiar world remained, nothing at all, except my little bundle that I clutched close to me with all my might. Madame Delavigne looked at me long and hard, then ended by caressing my chin dreamily (was she looking for some other face as she scrutinized mine so thoroughly?).

"Ti Cocotte, you'll see, you'll be happy here. We're going to take care of you, but we're going to have to fluff up your feathers a little, my little girl. You're thin as a rail!" And after an affectionate tap on my cheek she was off.

I could hear her ring of keys rattling against her hip as she traveled throughout the rest of the house. She left me to myself in my own little corner. The smell of iris that was to haunt my childhood from that point on filled the living room. It mixed in with the powdery smell of wallpaper splashed with lavender garlands as well as a faint trace of mildew from the carpets. This room was not often used. On that particular morning it was inordinately striated by golden rays passing through the Venetian blinds. Subsequently, but ever so slowly, my fears slipped away as the whole house began seeping into me through my nose, eyes, and pores. I started to breath again, to move about. Though still lukewarm, my blood began to flow once more beneath my skin. I settled in, intensely but rather serenely, to wait. And I waited. Then suddenly, I sensed what seemed to be the rebellious presence of a cat. At first it seemed that there was nothing more than an unruly mane reflecting every sparkle of sunlight that came into the room. Then I could make out something untamed, golden-skinned but possessing a muzzle constellated with red spots like freckles. It's Violaine. It's really her. She's right there in front of me staring at me with her tiger-yellow eyes, just as she had a long time ago at the *peristil*. And in turn with my silvery eyes I try probing into her very soul. She's all crouched over, her eyes bulging to the point they seem to engulf her cheeks. You could even go so far as to say she looks like a wildcat. With my dress smartly spread around me and my hands calmly positioned on my thighs, I watch her without batting an eyelash as she continues to sit there with her chin on her fists. She's fire, I'm water. It's as if I am struck by lightning as I finally realize that the ancients, the people from olden times, really "knew." They were the ones who nourished our souls with the same *marasa* dishes long ago, the ones going all the way back to the Ginen of our ancestors, the very ones who made us incomplete, linked, one to another, fragile and all alone, yet when reunited, strong and powerful. Of course, we knew all that but would not have known how to say it because we were afraid and then, at that particular moment, an emotion just too intense to express had us in its grips.

Violaine

I have to go back to school today. In my schoolbag are my slate and chalk, along with a gray-covered speller. I'm desperate. It's absolute torture. With strong strokes of her comb and brush, Nounou is trying to untangle a thick shock of my *chabin* hair. Why do this? Why try to disguise me as a model little girl? If anything, I'm a daughter of this earth where walking about barefooted with your hair down and flowing freely should be an inviolable privilege. But just try to tell that to Nounou, who's untangling and brushing my hair more vigorously now than ever.

"No, I don't have silky hair like a magazine beauty. Mine is kinky. It's kinky and it's going to stay that way!"

"We'll just see about that, *pitit moun!* Watch what happens with this: a little Trichopherous and beef marrow. Everyone knows that even nature has to give in to that mixture. And then from this day on, you'll have to put your life as a wild thing behind you. It's high time you began to look like a real little girl. So, if you braid your hair tightly every day you'll see, my *chabin*. I'm telling you, that hair of yours will soon be as soft as cane syrup!"

The uniform required by the nuns, a long-sleeved white blouse with a pleated navy blue skirt, white bobby socks, and buckle-down shoes (which is completely incongruous, given the sun and the meandering alleyways of my pirate city), is an attempt to transform me into a perfect little girl for my Jeremiean mother. But alas, all this is in vain because I'm the one who has to wear it.

My childhood was a perpetual struggle by the adults against my "vigorous" and "rebellious" nature, as they termed it. No one could have suspected back then that this struggle would have such a tragic outcome. My mother did everything in her power to break me of my "bad instincts." I was both her joy and her nightmare, but, as she used to say, God had given her only one child. So, she had always tried to do what was proper. She had married my father, the lightest mulatto ever, protected her skin and hair from the sun by religiously anointing her body and face with a combination of lime juice and starch to maintain their pale color, and cared for her hair with avocado pulp and beef marrow. What's more, she had almost lost her Jeremiean accent after spending two years at the Convent des Oiseaux in Paris and would use *Kreyòl* only with her servants (ay! ay! and on those occasions it reclaimed all its racy features as it flowed from her mouth with a virtuosity that was a pleasure to hear). In addition, she belonged to a family that for several generations had relentlessly endeavored to repress all traces of its African heritage. As her daughter, why was I so different? My hair could easily be taken care of and my skin, after all, was rather light. But for some reason, everything about me made her unhappy. I looked at people too brazenly, she said. My walk was too provocative as I swayed from side to side, and then there was that mania I had of squatting down with my legs spread wide open and drawing up my dress between my thighs as if I were selling fried foods or something. How scandalous! Yet, there was nothing provocative about my attitude. I was just myself, filled with all the vitality of my ancestors, those "others" as they were called. In similar fashion, she disapproved of my taste for native foods, especially spicy ones generously doused with hot sauce. She also found unacceptable the way I danced, laughed openly, or fit in comfortably with the "common folk"—all of which was simply part of me, without any affectation whatsoever. She knew it all too well, my dear mother, and that is what made her suffer. She bore her cross without uttering a word. In that regard she was clearly, authentically Haitian: the people from my country are interminable talkers whose exuberance is widely known, but the irony is we never actually talk about what counts. Our conversations never even begin to skim over a subject genuinely close to our hearts. We conjugate all the nuances of "hmmm" in order to muzzle our speech, to prohibit it from getting too close to our taboos, frustrations, or real sufferings, those we endure without being able to do anything about them. We make a lot of noise in order to avoid facing head-on what would otherwise be too painful. That's just the way we are. Our heavy eyelids only partially hide our eyes. People often say that because of this we have "a proud, haughty look" but, in reality, we are only taking refuge behind our heavy eyelids.

At the beginning of the school year, I remember I was envious of Cocotte. Instead of going to a big school surrounded by tall, metal fences, she attended Mademoiselle Nini's school in the morning with the other *restavèk*. As a result, I was crushed by all this; and the sadness of being separated from my companion became part of a violent revolt. Cocotte excelled in her studies and enjoyed them, as well. She would have the right to continued schooling at a reduced rate, but I attended the only girls' school that provided access to the University of Port-au-Prince. Unfortunately, I was only mildly interested in anything that forced me to stay closed inside. But what was even more painful was having to give up the freedom that Jeremiean girls enjoyed up to the age of receiving their diploma. Until the age of ten, we were allowed to roam around like little runaways with all the other children in the city. The teacher came for two hours in the morning to give us spelling and arithmetic, then we were cut free for what was thought to be "real life." Of course, what I learned in the street was much more valuable to me than anything that came from school, books, or my family. In all likelihood, our parents must have known this. They had to know that everything we would need in order to survive in the strange world in which we were going to evolve could not be found in books. Thus, our most tender years were entrusted to those true sages, to the best mentors possible, the humble men and women of Jérémie, whose generous hearts entered into our own forever. In spite of my sorrow and anger, I did not fear for Cocotte. Indeed, I was even quite serene thinking of her making her way in the world. She knew better than anyone the clever ways and secrets of that madman's game we would inevitably have to play. She would know how to take care of herself and ultimately win.

Cocotte

I'm ten years old. Violaine and I are going to school for the first time. We know how to read, write, and do a little arithmetic; but today, we have to rejoin the flock. And after that, there will be no more confusion. Violaine is going to go to the school for young ladies and I'll be in the company of the *restavèk*, the girls from the countryside being raised in bourgeois homes. I'll learn how to embroider, make desserts and pastries, put together a menu, write a list of provisions flawlessly, in short, everything that a servant for the wealthy should know how to do. I'm somewhat humiliated. Everyone knows children sense these things. But in contrast to Violaine, I've never had any trouble conforming to rules. It's my fate and what can I do other than give it my best? Violaine, despite all her tantrums, would never be able to change a thing. This is our first separation and it hurts, but I find consolation as best I can. I have new sandals, a red and white checkered dress, along with red rosettes in my hair. As for Violaine, in her uniform and patent leather shoes she resembles a thoroughbred that has just been saddled for the first time. I hardly recognize her since her hairdo makes her look so proper, and a little sad. She's suffering through the whole thing. But, lucky girl, she'll certainly like learning from books. She'll be able to put all her time and energy into her studies.

Violaine had a marvelous gift for telling stories. Her most devoted listener was Philippe Edouard, the eldest son of the Rougemonts, our closest neighbors. Often, at night, we would stay at the far end of the big garden. Philippe Edouard would scale the wall separating his parents' property from our own and then the fun would begin. Violaine would recount in her own way those same stories with which Nounou had reared us. *"Krik? Krak!"* And with those words, suddenly, a legend out of the depths of time, from the banks of Mother Africa, was carrying us away on its great wings.

So, once there was a magical fish called Tezen that made a beautiful girl fall madly in love with him. Every night she would sing at the water's edge calling him forth. You could hear her soft, plaintive voice resonating against the rocks: "Tezen, my dearest Tezen, my love fish, come up, come up to the surface!"

Then the marvelous fish would rise to the surface amidst a surge of phosphorescent bubbles, and the celebration would begin. He would take his beauty down deep into the water bewitching her for another night. Each day, the young girl, who was already passionately in love, fell more and more under the sway of his powers.

We were all fascinated by the story of this mysterious fish, and then Violaine would always begin to sway, becoming an alluring eel herself, imitating Tezen taking his fiancée down into the weeds at the bottom of the spring, those same treacherous water plants that one day, after being charmed by a jealous sorcerer, would become entangled in the girl's hair, imprisoning her there forever.

Philippe Edouard never took his eyes off Violaine. But then again, had he ever stopped spying on her, following her everywhere, pining after her with that intense gaze of his? From the moment they were born, his parents and the Delavignes had agreed the two would marry later. And Philippe Edouard took all this very seriously because Violaine belonged to him. She was his fiancée. Somewhat bothered by his oppressive adoration, Violaine kept pushing him away, sometimes violently, sometimes with a strange kind of affection. After all, she actually did love him. But did she really see him? She almost never seemed to look at him directly, always appearing to be somewhere else, lost in a daydream. Although she was always the one whose passionate attention could be directed at the most insignificant insect or who could enthusiastically lose herself at play, she slipped into a type of lethargy when Philippe Edouard appeared, because of his singular inability to capture her attention. Since I used to watch him closely, however, I found that his boundless love for Violaine made him different from

all the other young men. Every time I think of him, I see him hanging out in a tree or lurking behind Venetian blinds or some other
cover in order to spy on his little wild savage. That famous day
when all the girls were supposed to wear white dresses, he was
there devouring her with his eyes, perched atop the garden wall.

Madame Delavigne had Jérémie's finest seamstress make a
dream dress for Violaine, who was not yet twelve years old. It was
the most beautiful dress ever made for a young woman in this town,
an extravaganza of organza flounces sprinkled with English bouquets, streams of pearls, and raised satin stitches done in the old
style. Indeed, all the finery fit for a princess! Even the bride whose
procession Violaine was supposed to accompany didn't have a dress
as richly embroidered. But this accursed dress made me tremble
with fear. I was unable to keep myself from smelling its evil fragrances. Inexorably, it made me think of the ceremonial shroud
they wrap around wealthy people when they die. It horrified me.

The day of the wedding, Violaine's aunts and Madame Delavigne's close friends were like a swarm of bees buzzing around her
from early morning on. They made a big fuss over her hairdo. How
were they going to give an "appropriate" appearance to this cop-
per-colored, frizzy mass? After seemingly endless palaver and several tries, they decided to smooth it out once and for all with a hot
iron, then imprison it in a hair net adorned with small silk flowers.
Strangely, Violaine let herself be moved about like a puppet, without squirming, as her eyes stared vaguely off into the distance.
Once everything was finished, from the last touches on the hairdo
to the tiny diamond earrings and gold-studded necklace around her
neck as well as a strip of satin encircling the dress, everyone
stopped to admire her. "Just look how beautiful she is! She's as
beautiful as the Virgin Saint of Altagras! Or even an angel in a
stained glass window!" It was true. Stunned by her appearance, I
just gawked at Violaine. They had made her over in such a way that
she now resembled a picture right out of a missal. But I knew things
would not unfold so simply, so I waited in my corner, terrified, for
the unavoidable cataclysm. Standing straight as a candle, Violaine
was looking at herself in her mother's oval mirror. Her face hard-

ened with a savage look as her eyes began to glimmer like two yellow flames in the shadowy light.

Suddenly, she bounded out of the room like a wild beast. The swarm of people buzzing around her hardly had time to realize she had disappeared, dissolved into space with her embroidered dress and diamond earrings.

"Surely, she'll come back," said Madame Delavigne concerned about this unexpected turn of events. "I only hope she doesn't crumple her dress too much."

But I knew exactly where Violaine had gone. Ever so quietly, I eased outside and headed for the back of the garden. There, spread close to the enclosing wall was that dark green mass of a century-old bougainvillea that our dreams used to transform into a jungle. It was an imposing edifice of vegetation. At least a meter thick, it ultimately sheltered all our childhood secrets. Over time, we had managed to make a pathway through its thorns leading to a woody sanctuary as large as a ballroom, which, on that day, was riddled with intermittent spangles of sunlight. I knew Violaine would take refuge there, like a hunted animal. Sure enough, that's where I found her. I remained motionless at the edge of this leafy cradle so I could watch her every move. Calmly, she had begun to exorcise the blond angel with which her mother had tried to imbue her. Only I could feel the searing wound this masquerade was causing. It was obvious she couldn't allow this "other" who was suffocating her to remain intact even for an hour.

But gradually, as her eyes remained closed, her true face reappeared. The little saint from the stain glass window vanished into thin air, and life once again began to palpitate around her flaring nostrils and sensuous mouth. Then, she began, slowly at first, to stir, taking back the body they were trying to steal and divert from its primitive calling of freedom, sexuality, life, dance, Africa, and, finally, scandal. She began to reclaim her wandering, indistinct body they were trying to embalm as if in a lace shroud. Then came dancing, a masterful, though quite serious, *kasè*. She threw her head back, letting it hang loose on her shoulders as if detached. Then her back followed suit with a short and powerful creeping movement that sent her pelvis into a perfect back and forth gyration as lascivious as the Serpent God to whom this *yanvalou* step was dedicated. And on and on she danced to chase away death. She danced as a water Simbi, a little African serpent disguised as an infanta. And still she danced on, fervently defiling all the golden tabernacles of the New World, ripping away all the bonds with which they shackled us, unraveling all the hair shirts with which they tortured us. Violaine continued to whirl around and around, shaking her hips with a redemptive violence. And in so doing, it was Banda, the most carnal of all the Spirits, whom she honored with her liquid loins.

For a long while she remained alone, immersed in the mysterious land of her dance without uttering a word or even a sigh. And when she had thoroughly cleansed her spirit, when she had reassumed her inherent skill of being able to juggle her two identities, *both* of them (fiercely protecting the one most often attacked), when she had at last reestablished the soul that was uniquely hers in its proper place—that all-powerful soul they wanted to muzzle— Violaine, that complete and consenting hybrid, reopened her eyes, straightened out her rumpled clothes, and left her hideaway.

When she finally reappeared in that living room draped in mauve garlands, her mother's desperate look told her she had successfully performed her task. However, there was nothing to say, everything was in place. The dress fit for a queen didn't have a single unwanted crease in it, but Violaine had become Violaine once again.

Violaine

The Feast of the Marasa has always been the best day of the year for me. In the first place, to see my very Catholic mother submit to rules established by the Guinean *lwa* is an intense pleasure. In a solemn and determined way she goes about it without saying a word, not wanting to upset the Spirit of the Marasa because the goal is to cajole the Twins. Their anger or frustration can be the cause of great misfortune.

At two o'clock in the afternoon, Cocotte and I are supposed to take off all our clothes and climb into a large enameled bathtub warmed by the midday sun and filled with the aromatic leaves Nounou has rubbed between her hands before sunrise. Her mixture of orange tree and spicebush leaves gives the water a pleasing aroma. We are required to sit motionless and wait. Soon women from the *ounfò* will come to massage us all over with leaves from the tub and smoke-dried sour oranges.

Once allowed to stand in the tub, which, by the way, is located in the back of the garden, we take up the ritual refrain the women have been murmuring as they rub us. Then new strengths begin to traverse our tiny limbs and, already, I can feel deep in my loins the rhythm of those dances performed during the ceremony of the Marasa.

"In the mist of the night" (as the old ladies from Jérémie say to designate that moment of grace just after sunset when the birds bed down), they wrap us in bright, white sheets that crackle from the starch and hurriedly whisk us off to the *ounfò*. There, all the children of our clan, Cocotte's village, and even those of my father's clients have been brought together, resulting in a joyous din of sound. Oh, no! You won't find my friends from the wealthy side of town there! In that group everyone pays homage to the *lwa* like my mother, without telling anyone about it. Everyone looks very beautiful with eyes shining brightly from the pleasure of the feast. The twins, of course, have the place of honor. Dressed in our white outfits, we're seated on a mat in the middle of the *peristil* with the other pairs of *marasa*. They stuff us with all kinds of delicacies, while we throw what seems a thousand tantrums in order to affirm our authority. With gentleness and some amusement, the adults go about the task of waiting on us hand and foot. We're children, but also little gods.

Then comes the moment when the Rada make themselves heard. I shudder as the three sacred drums penetrate my very blood. In sequence, all the great *mistè* that rule over nature are invoked, starting with Legba, the one who opened the primordial gates. Meanwhile, the children solemnly execute the ritual dances designed to honor the names of the *lwa*: *yanvalou* and *mayi*. The drums, however, keep up their beat, and soon, the children intoxicated with the Spirits, begin to whirl around and around one another. Likewise, Cocotte and I are swept away by the voice of the drums. Having nourished the Spirit of the *marasa*, a new vigor comes over us. We dance, only partially conscious of one another, yet our steps have the same rhythm and our gestures are identical. We are one and the same: subject and reflection. But which mirror can we call our own? The dance of the *lwa* continues to lift us up, and we enter into that gentle trance of the Marasa that makes our bodies undulate yet leaves our eyes crystal clear. There is, however, this dull, inexplicable pressure at the nape that makes our necks bend and our heads dangle like a corolla barely beginning to open. When the drums grow silent, we fall to the ground like young birds from their nest and at that point we are carried away into the night half asleep toward the big house, where Mama is waiting for us.

Gently she puts us to bed and, sighing, closes the door to our room.

Cocotte

Violaine's room! First, there is a big bed covered with macramé and protected by a large mosquito net. The spectacle is rather strange. Imagine the room of a well-bred girl haunted by a jungle cat: white furniture, a skirted dressing table with its silver toiletries, organdy curtains, but all this more or less topsy-turvy and cluttered with fruit and grassy plants brought back from forays into the countryside. Then the crudely made earthenware like the kind found in farmer's markets catches your eye, along with wicker beggar's bags with their outlandishly colored pompons, small cages containing all kinds of animals gathered up in the woods—birds, lizards, caterpillars, some remnants of a harvest from God only knows where, with an incredibly strong rustic smell that violently contrasts with the affected ambiance someone has tried so hard to give the place. As a consequence, it was driving Madame Delavigne to despair and, at wit's end, she would no longer set foot in this room. Violaine moved brusquely about her witch's lair as if she were in a cage. To no avail, I tried to put some order in all this, but by her sheer presence, Violaine turned everything upside down. Only in the fragrant refuge of this room, sheltered by its cool penumbra and scent of ambergris, did we honestly feel at home. We read aloud, endlessly whispered our little stories to each other, buried our treasures there and, later, felt it was the only place where we were safe from outside threats.

It was also a strategically well-placed observation post from which we could see everything taking place on the Plas Zam. I can still picture us, hiding as we often did in the afternoons, behind the railing as if we were attending the theater, watching the boys come out of their school. The large door creaked open, followed by the escape of an extraordinarily noisy but interesting horde. All the boys attending the Friars' School exploded into the square, their legs dangling beneath their impetuous shoulders. All colors mixed together: ebony, gingerbread, amber, cinnamon, bronze, honey, biscuit, gold brown, the color of whole meal bread, all the sparkling, Caribbean colors in one compact bundle—nuances reflecting the very hierarchy of the city.

In contrast to the girls, sheltered within the confines of a veritable bonbonnière as if someone were trying to make glazed fruits out of them, the boys were abruptly turned loose into the big wide world. I must have heard at least a thousand times the Delavignes and their peers proclaim: "Oh sure, a little aristocrat, growing up the hard way, his feet on the ground. Let's hope he gets to know the 'people' and rubs shoulders with the ones he'll direct some day!"

For the parents of kids from the lower part of town, the Friars' School was a magical place where the famous "bread of instruction" was handed out. All through my childhood, I dreamed of going there someday to taste it myself. I imagined it piping hot, very round, all golden and crusty on the outside, but soft inside, and tasty as sin. And to think that even to this day it continues to pass beneath our very noses, this bread of instruction, just like all white bread, for that matter. But, all kidding aside, even at that time, for my friends who came from the poorer neighborhoods, nothing was more sacred than school. Their parents would have given an arm and a leg for their sons to have a chance to escape the humiliation, the misery, the long days punctuated by the gurgling of an empty stomach that they calmed by drinking nothing more expensive than sugared water. They would have made any sacrifice for their sons to have, someday, the opportunity to leave those stinking alleys where the main sewer channeled its filth, dead rats, and greasy waters right out in the open. But, you had to see these boys making their way along the road to school every day, shining like new pennies, their foreheads reflecting the light of all the love, all the effort exerted by that valiant woman who awakened them each morning to the world. And of course, they made a clean sweep of all the honors. The distribution of awards at the end of the school year was their day of triumph.

Pale with envy, Violaine greedily eyed all the games of these turbulent youngsters, reveling in the virile camaraderie they openly displayed. "Look at them, Cocotte, just look how everyone leaves them alone, and how they are allowed to act! Ay, it must really be nice to be a boy! And that moron by the name of Philippe Edouard doesn't even begin to realize how good he has it."

A little off to the side of the noisy crowd, Philippe Edouard is engaged in an animated conversation with his best friend, Alexandre. I watch them, ivory skin contrasted with dark skin, confiding intimately with each other like true conspirators upon whom the very fate of the world might depend.

The friendship between these two is unique in Jérémie. Upon leaving school for the day, Philippe Edouard and Alexandre return to two worlds as fundamentally divided as a river splitting off into different directions at the fork of a hill. Alexandre is a child from the poorer part of town. Through the friendly guidance of Philippe Edouard, he is able to peddle his princely demeanor of someone from someplace else in the salons of the wealthier sections of town as easily as he circulates among the miserable houses in his own neighborhood, apparently without even noticing the difference. In the bourgeois salons, he's welcomed by the men with open arms, welcomed to those gatherings to which women and girls are not invited. His intelligence amazes and amuses. But when he's with his own kind, it's something altogether different. They love him.

Not one single time does Alexandre look in our direction. Does he even know we exist? He passes in front of the store without looking at us, his forehead held high. He's always so unapproachable, so unable to be playful. Sure, I know his father is dead and that he never laughs. Yes, a sad boy indeed. His mother, Sor Mélie, has two sons she's raising all by herself. Her tireless, pedal-operated Singer hums away from dawn to dusk. All the girls from Jérémie including the rich ones have her make their uniforms and everyday dresses. Often, when I was sent to run errands, I would stop to watch her. She seemed so frail, pushing the sewing machine's pedal back and forth, click-clack, click-clack. I also liked the little street,

Ri Fontenn Mango, where she lived. It was a small alley that appeared to climb all the way up to the sky, hemmed in on both sides by a swarm of wooden houses that looked like toys or matchboxes and were painted every color imaginable, like at a costume ball. The people who lived there needed to dress up their misery with joy, and I must say they had been rather successful. You felt good there, despite the smell of poverty. Even the women peddlers plying their wares along this street would suddenly break into a dance, humming a tune but always keeping their baskets balanced on their heads. My friend Anacréon, a cobbler who worked there, used to sing away even though his sole task day in, day out, was nothing more than repairing old boots. Yes, it was a happy street, brightened by Sor Mélie's gentleness. I also remember one shop as fat as a thimble that attracted every kid in town with its incredible assortment of candies. Lamercie, the lady who owned it, would artfully arrange them in round bottles. But I remember it too because of Solon, a parrot that spoke *Kreyòl* as well as French from France.

Once again I'm rambling, while Violaine is completely absorbed watching a fight take place below between two rival gangs, each following its leader. There are all varieties of punching, kicking, *pataswèl*, *ʒoklo*, screaming, individual battles with wooden sabers or spears. And even, here and there, you can see the *fistibal*, those deadly, outlawed weapons. They all act as if they are Zorro. You should see them! And Violaine, who wants to jump into the middle of this melee, can't hold back her tears of rage. When she gets those flashing, deep mandarin yellow eyes, she's like a wildcat. She can almost be frightening at those moments.

Philippe Edouard and Alexandre make their way toward the center of the market place, climbing up the steps of the small kiosk, as they continue to talk about prosperity like politicians. And that conversation seems to go on forever. Finally, shaking hands, they part company solemnly. At that point Philippe Edouard looks up toward the window in Violaine's room. He had seen us all along, the monster!

Violaine

Every Friday night Cocotte and I became euphoric. School was over for another week, and the weekend, the enticing weekend, unfolded before us brand-new, full of possibilities for exploring our freedom. Filling it with a few definite plans, we put off as long as possible the moment we would have exhausted its fascination as something whole, swollen to the point of bursting with all our dreams. Saturday morning, we were irresistibly drawn to the market, with its noises and strong smells. Once there, we would fill our eyes with the fried foods and fruit the women were selling that day. Ay, that divine aroma of fried plantains, the powerful, burn-your-mouth pepper used in the preparation of *kreyòl* sausages, and the delicious juice of grenadine snowcones that were always so soothing to our inflamed mouths!

Afterward, that marvelous escape to the Grandans. Overflowing with supplies, its lanky boatmen and talkative *madan Sara* taught us all about its perilous and secret passage. You had to know just the right technique for keeping your balance on those shaky rafts and for deserving those baskets filled with pearly *piskèt* and red fish. We jumped into the current of this maternal river like *saval*, swam about with our eyes wide open among the darting fish in that liquid crystal that still washes down rather lazily from the mountain in the distance. What a joy to feel that fresh, icy water on our deprived bodies, stifled after a whole week of being constrained, and the sensual excitement of our bare feet tramping through the silky mud along its banks or among the reeds growing there.

The weekend for us was also the vast, open hinterland, carved with valleys and dotted with warm, inviting cabins. Sometimes it meant getting together again with the carefree children of the countryside. In the radiant afternoon sun, we all used to wander aimlessly through fields of tiny, starry millet blossoms or those filled with shiny Congo peas. We used to raise up the *karabann*, woven traps from which we released birds of every color of the rainbow. The ultimate pleasure was to see them fly out of our snares, still quivering from the fear of having been captured. Then came a short stop at Aunt Cléante's, who was always surrounded by her latania baskets, those light hanging vessels she never stopped weaving. But when we appeared at her door, her agile fingers suspended their work for a moment in order to treat us to some savory sweet potatoes cooked under the coals of her fire and to some of the very best ground corn in the world, spiced with the aroma of salted cod and fiery red peppers.

At siesta time, we would pilfer a few mangoes and *kenèp* with the children who lived near the river, but then they would gently lead us away from the cabins in order to give the adults returning from market a chance to rest.

Finally, exhausted, we shared our friends' quieter games. It was in moments like these we played a game of mancala. Crouching, we let the black and white stones slip through our fingers into holes hollowed out in the clay earth. There were also sophisticated guessing games that Cocotte, who was very clever, always managed to solve ("After the wooden barrier, the iron barrier; I drink from the clear spring. What is it? It's a coconut!"), and of course the game of knucklebones those times that both Cocotte and I would try shamelessly to beat each other. As the day wound down, we set off together toward town, dancing about in little groups, sashaying our hips back and forth to obscene *rabòday* that we chanted at the top of our lungs. We all chimed in to our heart's content with the most licentious, most forbidden refrains we knew, laughing deliriously out loud in a way we would never have dared in town.

At the top of the last hill just before reaching Jérémie, we parted company with a lump in our throat at the very moment the sun was slipping into the bay. Filled with sadness, we made it back to our stuffy, gloomy home.

Cocotte

Violaine and I had grown up. At age sixteen, we were budding
young women, if not already what some considered "small fruit"
because of the experiences we had gained, because of the things
our four eyes had taken in together concerning the human comedy.
Our adolescence had been feverish yet calm, divided between
flights to the countryside, secret escapades to the *ounfò* at the edge
of Jérémie on the one hand and on the other the stilted, affected life
in the Delavigne house. Yes, that is a good way of putting it, "stilted and affectionate," because it was that kind of ambiance common
in provincial households, where the social niceties that were a little
too convenient, those ready-made truths and inviolable conventions with which we were bludgeoned at every turn of the road
were mixed with the warm tenderness and the pervasive sensuality
profoundly impregnating this bastard city. No one in the Delavigne
household suffered from a lack of human contact, whether kisses,
caresses, an occasional slap, or Nounou's vehement reprimands that
contained extraordinary mixtures of old French maxims and African proverbs. She never let us get away with anything. Throughout
the whole blessed day, she was always right there, drumming into
us the rules for a good upbringing and proper etiquette because, as
she often said: "You kids were born with a silver spoon in your
mouth, you little scoundrels, rebels in the making, muddleheads.
But never forget that, for you especially, the good Lord's pencil has
no eraser!"

The holy sisters of Saint Joseph de Cluny had returned Violaine
to her family with some stern and rather sobering recommenda-

tions. "Here you are, Madame. We're returning to your care the most intelligent, most original young woman we've ever attempted to instruct. But may God help you in trying to tame her rebellious nature. Such an undertaking will doubtless be a heavy burden. But, have courage!" Apparently, after observing Violaine for six years, the Mother Superior had a definite opinion on the possibilities of converting her into a "proper young lady."

Even at sixteen, Violaine still had this inimitable way of whispering, of hiding her laughter behind her hand or calling her friends "my dear child," an expression only acquired by those who have been trained by the sisters. For sure, they'd done their best to train her properly. But, good God Almighty, all that was soon to be lost in the powerful stream sweeping her unerringly toward us, toward that other bank, that other side of herself. Violaine had honey-colored skin, somewhat darker at the joints as well as around her finger nails. Her mouth with its wide, fleshy lips was the color of a fig blossom, and her hair, in spite of Nounou's vigilant care, was still wild, alive, frizzy, and copper-tinted, just like a lion's mane. What's more, she had immense, tawny eyes. Though slight of build, her limbs were powerful, and yet, she had wide hips and a superb rear. There could be no reproach whatsoever on that score: nothing skimpy back there. She had all the things that made her ours, all those things that in spite of lace and fine cloth, in spite of lessons in posture and piano playing, and training in deportment— all the good sisters could teach, she could not change. She was one of us and we knew it. At the slightest tremor of a drum the small of her back and hips began to quiver. Then she would walk as if dancing, approach us, shuddering and shimmying, heading for freedom.

That particular year, she was still having endless and impassioned conversations with her high school girlfriends. She wanted to love them, participate in their daily lives, help prepare their trousseaux, as well as do everything in her power to make them look pretty for receptions in those circles she personally despised. Yes, Violaine wanted everything. She was still unaware that she would soon be summoned to choose, to renounce something. Those months, after high school, were a period of grace, a peaceful islet in her tortured existence, a moment when she lived completely that blissful illusion of thinking she could be loved and accepted by everyone. It was still a moment when she believed it possible to live to the fullest all the rich potential she had within her, even if, in order to do that, she had to hide a part of her life from the eyes of those closest to her. Because, for Violaine and me, our parallel lives consisted early on of contact with that "other part" of town. This protracted impunity, however, had made her think that deflowering, that inevitably painful mutilation, would be superfluous. The poor creature! Madame Delavigne suspected right from the beginning that her daughter, her only child, was not entirely present before her eyes, but she had no desire to learn what she couldn't see ("What the eyes can't see will not sour the heart"). She knew that Violaine was not like other girls from Jérémie. From the day her daughter was born, she had accepted that, since "every Haitian family has its ring at the goldsmith's" (as the elders used to say, in sibylline fashion), Violaine was obviously this flaw, this pain to bear. But Madame Delavigne did indeed try to limit the damage. I can still see her face during Holy Week, when the *rara* celebrants used to wend their way down from the mountains. One of the woman would come to dance in front of our gate, and Monsieur Delavigne would always pick Violaine up in his arms, carry her like a little queen over in front of King Rara, who was predictably resplendent in sequins. Then, he would raise her at arms' length while presenting her to the four points of the compass. Whereupon the king, by means of some very fancy footwork, performed his ritual dance right in front of her. The crowd would also begin to dance as Violaine looked on, calm as an idol. Of course, her participation contributed to fulfilling family obligations, but everything about Madame Delavigne conveyed the firm determination to keep things within acceptable limits.

It's not out of line to say that Violaine always provoked something unusual happening around her. Tell me now, in spite of all we know about her, in this city corrupted by prejudices, in this city suspended like curdled milk because of its absurd hierarchies, tell me, how was it that a young girl from the "upper crust" could somehow manage to escape into the night perched on the shoulders of Salomon, the caretaker? What other young woman (even a *marasa* with

an equally strange way of behaving) perched on Salomon's powerful shoulders would have had the ridiculous idea to go to the *ounfò*,
where the common people were paying homage to their *lwa* while
her parents were fast asleep? We really do follow the paths of our
own destiny and what we don't know is always larger than ourselves. More often than not on Friday nights, as I trembled with fear
while Violaine was radiant and beaming, we danced to our heart's
content in the exhilarating mist of the Vodou ceremonies all the
while protected by the good men and women of Jérémie. Because,
as you might have realized, dance is our form of prayer. Each time
we arrived, we were met with a burst of joy, and then we would
lose ourselves in the undulating throng of people in the temple.

Violaine was the beloved protégée of Man Chavannes, the most
famous *manbò* from Grandans. With just a slight movement of that
perfect arch of her eyebrows, she could virtually do anything she
wanted with that mountain of flesh and wisdom. You had to see
firsthand how the priestess' eyes would light up at the sight of her *ti
kay*, the "darling of the sanctuary," as she affectionately called Violaine. From the start, she had done her best to teach the girl everything there was to know about the Spirits, about the plants and animals they had given us for our well-being and for their service: in
essence, all their magic. In addition, Man Chavannes had taught her
about the stars, their influence on our moods, about how some men
and women carry life in their clavicles and others in their stomachs
and about the passions that overwhelm the souls of the pitiful playthings we are. She had also washed her young *marasa*'s head with
the sacred leaves containing the necessary power to put all the mystical forces stirring within into their proper place. Thus, at sixteen
Violaine had all the calmness and strength of an initiate, but as Man
Chavannes used to say, she hadn't yet tamed the *chwal* within her
soul, and that was her guiding star.

Philippe Edouard was the only mulatto who knew about Violaine's double life. But we were confident he would keep quiet. His
avid gaze had accompanied all the moments of our lives, and we
had grown accustomed to the furtive palpitation of his presence
wherever we went. The more time passed, the greater grew this irrational love that possessed him. I remember overhearing Nounou

complain, while sighing deeply (because nothing ever really escaped her keen insight): "Ah, Holy Virgin Mary, something is wrong with that boy. He's got misfortune in his blood. He doesn't know how to love. He always carries it to an extreme. That kind of torment is no good. It only leads to all sorts of trouble, even to death. To be a good husband, you have to be at peace with yourself. But just look at his head, will you? It's from beyond the grave. Either a bad spell will come over him or he'll bring one on us. Good God, have mercy upon us!" Before anyone else, Nounou had sensed the death inherent in the febrile quest that possessed Philippe Edouard. Of course, to many it seemed that he was leading the idle and elegant existence of a young man of means. He was an excellent horseman, a good tennis player, and a consummate dancer. Moreover, that sparkle in his deep, black eyes didn't fail to drive the girls wild. But a mysterious sorrow seemed to haunt those eyes.

At eighteen, his father had taken him on his tour of Europe. He had come back with his head full of new things, somewhat changed, but with that pretentious speech pattern, that "northern accent" affected by all Jeremieans who have traveled. He had loads of funny stories to tell. Violaine, however, couldn't understand them because once in his presence she was always overcome by her own irrepressible lack of interest. Poor Philippe Edouard was on the verge of losing his mind, so great was his unresolved desire to capture, if only for a few minutes, the attention of the distracted young woman who tormented him so. He had even lost the advantage enjoyed during our childhood games when we spent long hours telling each other old stories at the back of the garden. Very quickly, he had fallen back into his distant longing and that unhealthy, clandestine participation in our life. It wasn't hard to see in his eyes the beginnings of that irreversible misfortune that was going to come crashing down upon us.

Violaine

Lurking (me too, just like Philippe Edouard) behind the climbing rosebush, I'm watching Cocotte, observing her intently; and even though she's a clever little so-and-so who knows everything I'm thinking or feeling at a distance, she suspects nothing. I should also emphasize I'm doing everything I can to appear as motionless as a corpse. Barely breathing, I have done my best to slow the blood coursing through my veins, the beating of my heart. I'm even trying not to blink because I don't want to take my eyes off her for a second. Cocotte, my sister, my other half, you're so much a part of me I forget to look at who you really are. Today is very important because I'm going to study you just as one might study a precious insect in a collection, with great care and precision.

Let's see. First of all, she's small-boned and appears taller than me, even though we're the same height. It's because of her legs, which are long and slender like sugarcane stalks. They seem endless, almost as if they were taking off into thin air, while at the same time her calves have no definition whatsoever. They're just long. No, let's say "very long"! And her thighs are the same way, very long. There she is, standing in her yellow dress. She seems to shoot up into the air with that youthful curve in her lower back. It's almost as if she were about to fly away, a little palmetto bird metamorphosed into an ibis. And her hips, how narrow they are! She has nice muscular buttocks, taut and protruding like those of an adolescent. Her back is solidly built, hollowed in its middle with a supple, rectangular furrow. Her small, full breasts are upturned, and her round neck, which she holds perfectly straight, is absolutely elegant. Perched on top of all that is the most adorable little face in the world with a rounded forehead, eyelids sharply contoured at the edges, and eyes dark as jet marbles. Her gaze is calm and kind, but also proud because Cocotte's serenity is the reflection of a perfect awareness of herself, of an assurance that is neither forward nor pretentious. And that is, without question, what her solemn, limpid gaze expresses. Her nose is small, well-constructed, its bridge precise and curved. Her slender, pointed chin displays a sovereign impertinence by the way she carries it. As for her pliable, sensitive mouth, it blossoms without any sign of sluggishness whatsoever. Dark and rimmed in beige, it unfurls into the color of ripe cherries. But it's Cocotte's smile that is truly extraordinary, a veritable sunburst. Her face teems with dimples, and her small white teeth shine mischievously, glistening like drops of milk. I watch her move about the garden. She's helping Nounou spread out the laundry, unfolding those long arms of hers, then her long skillful hands with their nimble, silken gestures carrying out each task with flawless precision. Suddenly, she appears very distant to me as if she had come from someplace else, like a princess uprooted from her native Africa or even a little Meroitic Pharaoh queen in exile. Her silhouette stands out against the moist linen sheets. And as she passes I can hear the bitter wail rising up from the slave ships of long ago. Africa, our secret wound, buried deep in our heart, we'll never heal from you, never get over you, never! Our past, molded out of fear, consists of uprooting and rape that has transformed us into a variegated throng, a people torn apart at our very core. Once again, my reverie has gotten the best of me, leaving me foundering on the banks at the other side of the great water. However, as I'm studying Cocotte, I know I'm approaching the very heart of that strange bond that ties us together. Yes, I now know why her and why me. People like us from the south of the island belong to the river, to the water. We're dreamers, and yet, at the same time we're peasants who have virtually sprung from the land. Logic is always hiding right there behind our most immediate and apparent dreams. We're always looking for a reason even for the most mysterious things. And I discovered all by myself, buried at the bottom of a trunk, my own family's secret, which is in fact the same secret all mulatto families from Jérémie fiercely hide at the bottom of a similar old trunk. The first clue I came across was a yellowed photograph taken back in the second half of the last century. Along with that snapshot were some letters and a newspaper. In the photo a young girl wearing a dress inlaid with Valenciennes lace exudes an undeniable charm, yet there's no smile on her lips. Instead, immense, feverish eyes seem to swallow her whole face. She has high cheekbones, a broad, fleshy mouth, everything just like me, everything exactly like me! However, the small chin, the slender neck and what appears to be an ethereal elegance, all are uniquely hers. Or rather, have I seen them somewhere else? But just listen now to the most interesting part of all. The girl is black, black as black can be. No doubt about it, she is completely black! And I look just like her! Victory! As you can imagine, my heart was beating as if it were going to explode! But here's the whole story as I managed to piece it together after hours of reading in the dust of our old attic.

CHIMÈNE'S SECRET STORY

The young girl in the yellowed photograph answered to the beautiful name of Chimène, because, instead of coming into the world like everyone else at the moment predicted by the midwife, this impatient little creature was in too much of a hurry. To put it mildly, she came into the world, burst forth into broad daylight at a turn in the *chimen* as her mother was coming back from the market. Since it was a question of a baby girl, *chimen* became "Chimène," a name which fit perfectly my fiery, paternal great-grandmother because that's who she was. No one could possibly have guessed it from the pale color of my father's skin! As for me, I call it bad faith. In actuality, it has to be intentional. But let's get back to the little girl. Like me, she had willingly lived hidden away, camouflaged. That's why I understand her so well, why she obsesses me so. Having come from a village in the mountains as a young child, she had been raised in the Delavigne family. At sixteen, Chimène was as pretty as a sunflower blossom, but also clever and cunning. Enthralled, my great-grandfather, while still a bachelor, had hired her as a house-

keeper to keep his home in order. Nothing was more common in
that era. Usually, this type of situation lasted until the young man
married a proper young woman "from his world." But, contrary to
tradition, my great-grandfather never married. In fact, he fell head
over heels in love with his young housekeeper. One could even say
she had purposely inspired this violent passion in him. What's
more, it was rumored in the salons at the time she had most likely
cast a spell on him. In all truth, she treated him like a king. She lived
her life like a recluse, closed in with her power, reigning supremely
over his large house, a genuine love *ʒonbi*, a scandalous guardian of
a secret that made the man she loved her slave. All the other women
suffered at the very thought of her existence. No one ever saw her
again. She lived closed off in the middle of the city like a buried
treasure. She was the secret dream of the city. Refusing to compete
with the other women, she had turned away from any kind of af-
front or humiliation and slipped into legend intact like a flame. She
had given my great-grandfather three sons, three superb-looking
sons the color of tobacco, all of whom proudly held their chins
high. The great-grandfather adored them and had given them the
finest education possible. Whenever they needed anything, no expense was too great. At any rate, his children were "sons of someone important," and he was sure that their striking looks, money,
their light-complected skin would open wide the doors of that new,
crossbred society in which he lived. Indeed, I still remember my
grandfather, the eldest Delavigne son, with his brownish-gray skin,
his white linen suit, sporting a panama hat and a silver-handled
cane. I can see him even now looking out over his coffee plantations, his broad smile exposing all his fine teeth, if not a certain
wolfish air.

Of course, to have peace and remain free, he had married a
proper young woman belonging to the Jeremiean aristocracy for
whom he cared about as much as he did a streak of bad luck. My
father was born from this marriage of convenience. Then, following the indomitable will of his grandmother, he was given the
responsibility of having to fulfill our obligations to the *lwa* of our
ancestral village up there on Macaya Mountain. He did it with dis-

cretion, quite naturally and full of piety, like all those things we are forced to do that are a part of life: breathing, drinking, eating, bathing, or even appeasing our ancestors while finding ways to commemorate their importance. My father willingly carried out all of this because he understood that the rigorous observance of the "rules" was the essential condition for maintaining prosperity in our family. In order to preserve his status, fortune, and even his health, he had to fulfill his responsibilities with respect to the *lwa rasin*. How many prosperous, proud families had fallen on the worst of times because they had forgotten this, because they had actually believed they had become white families? It was easy to call to mind several examples whose miserable offspring ended up insanely alcoholic and consequently were forced to survive by begging. Others managed to keep their fabulous inheritance intact but gave birth nonetheless to a horde of idiots, abnormal creatures, all of whom were either crippled or deformed. And all this was the result of having been ungrateful, of having rejected the African *lwa* who had originally been generous enough to bestow upon them their money, power, but also, and unfortunately, a skin so clear they believed it possible to do anything their hearts desired. As is their want, the African Guinean Spirits who have given us so many blessings, can easily, from one day to the next, send us back to the dung heap from which they have plucked us.

The source of our good fortune is in the earth, in coffee, in men working with the earth, and all that comes, needless to say, with certain obligations. My own father came down from that same hillside from which his grandmother, Chimène, had escaped like some regal bird of paradise with deep black skin, a diamond in her closed mouth. And that gossamer ease I now see animating Cocotte's movements in the garden is the same one swaying the winged gait of the people from the hills, those same hills from which we both come. We come from a people made up of maroons and coffee bean–pickers whose crimson cherries fill the strongboxes with gold. Our ancestors were rebels who escaped the whip and cane early on, fierce men and women who fled the flat plains and plantations of the colonists to find refuge in the freedom of the mountains as they ripped their *govi* from the hands of slavery, only to bury them in silence deep within the hills. Their blood, the blood that coursed through their veins back then, flows in us today. As I continue to watch Cocotte with every fiber of my being, I can tell you here and now that our bond is not just mystical. We are blood sisters through and through.

Cocotte

It's four o'clock in the morning, a very early morning with the purple haze still lingering even as it begins tearing away its veils as immodestly as a girl on a carnival float. I watch as the Plas Zam is decked out with all the colors from the countryside. Way over there, gleaming fruits and vegetables announce their presence, while close-by glimmers from bric-a-brac, *maldjòk* dresses, and *kreyòl* scarves catch the eye. But in addition to these visual delights, the aroma drifting from the market place goes straight to my head, a powerful mixture of peppery and sweet smells, along with the pungent tobacco fumes of peasants' pipes, the chlorophyll from fresh green leaves, all kinds of fruit, as well as their bouquet of distilled sugar, the earthy freshness of the vegetables, the profusion of spices, whose fragrances present a kind of delirium delineated in progressive stages. Added to this are the healthy, musky smells of the montagnards' sweat, the leather from their rustic sandals and, above all, the smoke from the small buccans used to warm the *akasan*. I'll never grow weary of becoming intoxicated with the fragrance of this market place, which is as addictive as a drug. And each time I go away from Jérémie I'll miss it, just as I would a drug.

Here comes Anaspa. He's what people call "disturbed," but the Spirits that constantly dance in his head sometimes say good things and sometimes predict the future, either the near future or the one further off in the distance. At any rate we shall see. He hangs around the market places like all the lunatics, clairvoyants, and "babblers" touched with insanity given by the spirits. All these poor souls are gently welcomed, clothed, nourished, even protected by the women in the market places who, in this way, perform an act of piety toward the Guinean Spirits. From as far back as anyone can remember, Anaspa has always brandished a palmetto frond that he shakes incessantly above his crazy head. It's because, as he puts it, if he were to stop, the sky would collapse and come crashing down around us, breaking into a thousand pieces like a gigantic, blue porcelain chamber pot. So, little by little, we're going to find out exactly what the *lwa* would like Anaspa to accomplish down here. Perhaps he will, in fact, have to shake that palmetto frond indefinitely because, after all, what do we really know? This particular morning he's talking, then talking some more like a wooden rattle as he paces along the market place with large uncoordinated strides, his palmetto branch gyrating frenetically in accompaniment to every one of his febrile steps. But it's more the "Word" coming from his mouth that interests us. You can always tell when the Spirit is speaking through him by the nasal tone in his voice.

"Oh yes! I can see him, Sor Mélie's little boy. He's coming back. Rage fills his heart and terror is in his eyes. He's coming back in search of peace, but he only brings disorder with him. Death follows him like the traces left behind by foamy waters!"

What is Anaspa saying there? Sor Mélie's child is coming back? Sor Mélie's son? That would be Alexandre, right? That quiet young man from our childhood, that tall distant chap who never laughed but managed to impress us a little! Even Violaine didn't dare talk too loudly in his presence! He left a good three or four years ago, perched on those long legs of his. I still remember Sor Mélie's eyes at that moment. They were completely filled with tears as she watched the old carcass of that huge sailing ship, *Sirène*, slip slowly into the distance, carrying away her eldest son in the bowels of its brightly painted wood. Could he indeed already be coming back from Port-au-Prince? Time continued on its way, forgetting us, as we languished along its shores. Here, everything seems to have stopped, frozen in its web of eternally identical gestures, of days that are all the same, or seemingly so. Despite Violaine's impetuousness, Jérémie remains Jérémie, a lethargic city, dozing in the dust and stench of mildew, bogged down in the pathetic memory of its own opulent past. No one gets excited here anymore except when it's a question of something insignificant. What's more, the slightest sign of something new is greeted with mistrust.

I hurry and put on my shoes, then dash out of the house. I've just got to race over to Sor Mélie's to see what's happening. Sor Mélie, my friend. As a little girl, I used to love to go and sit down quietly like a cat next to her sewing machine, riveting my eyes on her forehead as she leaned over her work. Those hours spent like that, literally in the folds of her dress, have always been associated in my mind with the sweet smell of vanilla. Her whole house was embalmed with this fragrance, and even her eyes seemed to resemble two brown, translucent pods from the vanilla plant. I quickly make my way across the market place, then proceed along the streets buzzing with commercial activity, down the alleys bottlenecked with workers who have just washed up for the day as well as coffee sorters as talkative as *madan Sara*. I push my way through, going against the flow. Everyone else is heading for the wharf and the factories.

"But where is the Delavignes' Cocotte going like a crazy person?" shouted a woman selling sesame. Finally, I clamber up Ri Fontenn Mango as fast as my legs will carry me and, at long last, stop directly in front of Sor Mélie's house. I don't hear the clickety-clack of her sewing machine.

"Yoo hoo, Sor Mèlie!" I call out, feeling a little worried at that precise moment. "Sor Mélie, it's Cocotte!"

The door opens, and Sor Mélie appears holding a letter in her trembling hands. She looks at me with glistening eyes and says in a voice drowning in tears: "Alexandre is coming back, Cocotte. He arrives tomorrow aboard the *Sainte Ursule*. My son is returning just like that, without delay!"

"Fantastic, and what are we going to prepare for him? All his favorite things, right?"

I try to redirect the force of her emotion toward the trivial activity of preparing for the homecoming. First, I take it upon myself to give her a large glass of cold water to ward off any kind of seizure. But no doubt, you have noticed yourself, seizures brought on by happiness are never fatal, whereas bad news can stretch out the most hearty individuals stiff as a board.

Sor Mélie and I begin to plan an elaborate effort to "refresh" the little house. First, we have to wash, then starch the cretonne curtains. Next, we lavish the place with flowers. After that, we'll start cooking all those special dishes served only on occasions like this. Everything has to be just right. Then, just like a little girl, Sor Mélie nimbly climbs up the three steps of her stool and begins to take down the curtains.

"But you know, I've been thinking," she says suddenly, interrupting her work, "what could have possibly brought you here so early in the morning, Ti Cocotte? I haven't sewn anything for your family. You haven't even had a cup of coffee yet. Let's see if we can lay our hands on one. Come along my child."

Anxiety tugs at my throat. Anaspa! It's only now his words come back to me. He predicted misfortune, disaster, even death to be a part of Alexandre's baggage, and Anaspa sees clearly, on that we can rest assured. Poor Sor Mélie, she's so happy her son is returning. Later, when I returned home, I stopped at the church to light a large candle on the altar of Saint James the Greater. May he protect and keep them!

The next morning, as handsome together as a young married couple, Sor Mélie and Jean-Jacques, Alexandre's younger brother, are front and center on the quay long before the *Sainte Ursule* comes into view. When the tiny silhouette of the ferryboat finally appears on the horizon, they know there will still be a good hour to wait, the longest one of all. But not long thereafter, the *Sainte Ursule* pulls into the dock engulfed in the commotion of its diesel engine, porters swearing and jostling one another, the women vendors hailing their cronies from the bridge, already getting involved in transactions of some kind or finding out how the market has been going (the "Never Sleep" as they are called). Sor Mélie is beside herself with impatience: "But where is that slowpoke, anyway? After not having seen his Mama for four years, you would think he could move a little faster!"

Just then, a long silhouette rises up at the top of the gangway. Alexandre! That adolescent with the endless legs and arms, the torso that was too thin, with all those knobby bones he had as a child, has become a man. He has become a very handsome man, I would say, as fluid and symmetric as a royal palm, though he still has his high forehead along with that impertinent chin of his adolescence. Yes, this one, without any possible reproach, is now a tall, handsome individual. I look at him bursting with joy, happy that Sor Mélie is so proud of him. I too am proud because Alexandre is a brother. Quickly, he hurries down the gangway, grabs his mother up in his arms, flashes a somber look, then a beaming smile seemingly as bright as the sun.

"Mama, my dear Mama, it's so good to see you again. Your vanilla aroma, hmmm. I've even dreamt about it! You're beautiful, so beautiful!"

Actually, at that moment Sor Mélie looked as if she had only just turned eighteen, stars sparkling in her eyes and a smile so radiant it lit up the whole wharf. Then, Alexandre turned to Jean-Jacques, who had been admiring his every move. "How are you doing, brother? Just look how tall you've gotten! It seems I should have simply stayed in Port-au-Prince, since you seem to be doing quite well here!"

Then at last, it was my turn, even though I had been trying hard to make myself as small as possible. "Cocotte, what a beautiful girl you've become! I bet you catch the eye of all the boys in Jérémie now!" And in a perfunctory way, I was granted two resounding kisses, the kind that make a loud smacking noise, the kind you reserve for sisters and children. As the reacquaintance ceremony on the dock wound down, we started moving off together, linked as if in a chain, silent from all the emotion, toward that house on the small street brimming with all the colors of the rainbow.

Once seated there on its porch, we sipped Sor Mélie's punch with some of the people from the neighborhood, but all of us had gathered together for no other reason than to celebrate Alexandre's return. He was everyone's child to some extent. This woman over here had taught him how to recite his multiplication tables, that man always used to resole his worn-out shoes (and God knows they had the heels worn off them often enough), another had stuffed him with gingerbread and *pirouli*, and still another one of the men seated amongst us had taken care of him when he fell and hurt himself one time, not to mention that big-hearted woman who, although the same age as Alexandre's young mother, had nevertheless relieved him of his virginity with a hug punctuated by tenderness and delirious laughter.

Everyone had come, curious to see him again, happy to see how handsome he had become, to have him so close by. You must understand: we have seen some come back from the capital city with such an urban air that they are incapable of recognizing their old friends. As for Alexandre, he had the same beautiful smile as before, a warm handshake, and an embrace as affectionate as ever. He went on endlessly about the big city swarming with so many people that in some neighborhoods they had to sleep in shifts in the same room so that everyone would have a chance to rest, about how the *taptap* virtually burst at the seams with a jumble of poor people, animals, mottled baggage, all of which is heaped and piled all the way up to the roof of the vehicle! He told stories about angry students, the new political regime, crime, scandals in the ministry and the *makout*. He gave us news of all the Jeremieans living in the capital city: those, for example, who had succeeded, had become wealthy and had forgotten about us altogether or those, to the contrary, who had lost everything and as a result didn't dare return home empty-handed with nothing more than their full complement of shame. He also told us about that group, far more numerous, leaving for the United States to try their luck. Yes, the exodus toward New York and Miami was in reality the last hope for those unable to find work in Port-au-Prince. They were leaving at any cost, sometimes even at the expense of their lives. The lucky ones who managed to obtain a visa took one of the regular flights out, the others, the impoverished, set out on that frightening adventure involving run-down sailboats and clandestine motorcraft. Countless numbers went off only to feed the sharks in the Gulf of Mexico. Ah! How many never reached Florida's inhospitable coast? Boat people, the *bwa debèn* of the twentieth century.

As Alexandre spoke, revolt filled his voice. I could feel his desperation. He had come back disillusioned by all his disappointment. "Remake the country," those were his words before departing, but obviously, he no longer believed in them. The political institutions had left us high and dry, and at a very crucial moment. He used to say the peasants were his only safe haven and now he was going so far as to declare that "they've always known they could only count on themselves." And as a consequence, he seemed to have no other recourse than to conclude "they're the only Haitians still standing tall."

I listened with all my heart as the eyes of his neighbors from Ri Fontenn Mango tenderly filled with sadness. They knew this story already only too well, particularly when you recall that this country has been in irresponsible and greedy hands since a very distant past. Alexandre wasn't the first to come back from the capital full of bitterness. The neighbors' glances intimated their recognition of yet another rebel fashioned by the system, yet another miserable soul from whom it had stolen his dreams. And he's so young! Will we be able to protect him?

The glasses of punch crowned with sugar continued to flow. The warm, fraternal buzz of the conversations had somewhat subsided. And as the light became softer, you could even hear now and again silent interludes filled with the happiness of people together, understanding one another or just being similar. Alexandre had taken out his guitar and, leaning against the balustrade, began to let his fingers run over the strings as he hummed: "Marabout of my heart with the tangerine breasts." He smiled at the memories this song brought to mind. The melody lingered on for a moment, then stopped abruptly, as if suspended in air. A silhouette we all knew well loomed up at the bottom of the slope. Philippe Edouard. Alexandre had already headed down the hill toward his friend. In just three large strides he had reached Philippe, then hugged him closely in his arms. Bronze muscles interlaced with those of pale gold, same jeans, same white T-shirts, young, powerful men, but oh so vulnerable. The older people looked at them somewhat pensively, while the youngest saw in them a real sense of hope. Nothing more to say than here were two superb sons of Jérémie the Spiteful. But they didn't realize yet they hadn't been brought into this world to like each other, that they were born on different sides of an absurd chasm. The older people knew, however, that they would soon learn all about it. But, after all was said and done, perhaps not, thought the younger set.

Philippe Edouard and Alexandre stand there looking straight into each other's eyes. Four years, an entire world separates them. They no longer know anything about each other. Their paths have taken different directions and they've been orbiting among entirely different planets from adolescence to adulthood. It takes only a second to contrast the pampered youth of Philippe Edouard, his travels, his apprenticeship as a young entrepreneur with the hard life Alexandre has led as the son of poor people, his solitary struggle far from his loved ones in the filth scattered on the sidewalks of Port-au-Prince. Nonetheless, Philippe Edouard extended his greetings to everyone, then came in under the porch swinging his arms back and forth while flashing that huge smile of his. The peaceful ambiance that had prevailed before was slightly disturbed as everyone greeted the new arrival. Oh, of course, all of us had known him when he was nothing more than a ragamuffin; but he had grown up in the meantime, and now we weren't quite sure how to approach him. I could distinctly hear the muffled comments of my friends from the lower side of town: "You have to understand that a child is a child, regardless of where he comes from or the color of his skin, but a young man of twenty-one already belongs to his own world. At that point, he's no longer 'Ti Phil,' as we used to call him around here when he was little. Perhaps he was even going to insist we address him as 'Monsieur.' But you know, those kinds of people are unpredictable because just when you think you can treat them normally, they begin to cloak themselves in their own importance, and then to the contrary, they sometimes extend to you an almost shocking familiarity, when, don't you see, it's better to demonstrate respect." Philippe Edouard kindly hugged Sor Mélie, who in turn complimented him on how good he looked, offered him a drink, a place to sit, all the appropriate things. The young mulatto politely sipped his punch, apparently in no hurry, and only when he had swallowed the last drop did he reveal his real reason for coming.

"Alex, as soon as I learned you had come back, I came looking for you. We're all gathering up at the house, all your old schoolmates, to celebrate Clériac's departure. You absolutely have to come. Everyone wants to see you. So, come along, old friend; perhaps we'll never have another opportunity to get together again. You're the only one missing. What a miracle that you arrived today!"

At any rate, the party here was drawing to a close and certainly Alexandre wasn't going to miss this opportunity. Just think of it! The old gang reunited once again, and on the very day he had returned home! He left alongside Philippe Edouard, joking around like a little kid. Have you ever noticed that, when two childhood friends get together again, regardless of their age, the little boys they once were reappear in their gestures, in their speech patterns, the tone of their voices, even their laughter.

I took all that in with my sixteen-year-old eyes, those eyes that recorded everything, believe me. But that particular day, I hadn't yet seen anything. The sunset seemed to linger for an eternity, bathing the whole town in a kind of irrational light. Our long shadows stretched way out in front of us. And it was in the phosphorescent light of this dusk, a light like the aura surrounding the devil, that something irreparable took place. No one, not even me, could have prevented it. It was written with India ink in the book of the Great Master.

Lost in my thoughts, I left my friends behind and set off toward the house, but not without stopping at Saint Louis Church on the marketplace. Once there, I knelt in the back in the most isolated corner, the one relegated to Saint James the Greater. Then, I prostrated myself, my arms out like a cross, at the foot of the altar, which was constellated with the trembling flames of what seemed like hundreds of candles. Impassive in his blood-red robe, Saint James listened to my prayer, his immobile glass eyes twinkling in the glimmer of the candles. I implored him to make the string of bad luck that Anaspa had seen closing in on Alexandre go away. When I had finished my invocations, I earnestly lit my little candle, then stuck it in with the others, nudging it as close to the Saint as possible: "Ay, Papa Ogoun Feray from Guinean Africa, you from whom all violence comes, Master of weapons and the forge, Protector of young boys, take care of him for me! You, my Valiant

Black Man, my All-Powerful One, my Taurus, extend to him your strength and keep him within your circle of followers, dear Papa!"

Despite this prayer, my heart was still aching. What's more, a swarm of butterflies was churning in the hollow of my stomach. As I left the church, my eyes were still dazzled by the constellation of all those flickering flames dancing around the statue of the Saint, as if the whole town had prayed to him that day.

I ran into Violaine on the stairs. She, obviously, was not going to a party because she was wearing her white dress, that old Sunday dress she loved so and used to traipse around in the whole blessed day. Her hair was flowing freely on her back, radiating its spontaneous and natural aggressiveness.

"Hey! Come on with me, Cocotte," she says, all excited, "Béa received lots of books when the boat came in today; I'm sure we can find something we'll like."

Béa was Philippe Edouard's younger sister. She and Violaine had been in the same class together at the Catholic Sisters; but, in contrast to my foolish *marasa*, Béa was a perfect little girl, well-raised, as nice as she could be. Though intelligent, she was nothing to write home about. As the supreme accomplishment of a Jeremiean mother, she had been so masterfully tamed by her upbringing that her manners, language, her straightened hair style, and that "exquisite" reserve in her bearing made you completely forget about any trace of cross-breeding, in spite of the fact that her skin was much browner than Violaine's. You only had to watch Béa and Violaine walk side by side to assess the extent of Madame Delavigne's misfortune. Béa ambled along sensibly, advancing one pretty, arched foot after another, and all this without putting the rest of her body into motion. Violaine, on the other hand, set out with a movement that started somewhere in the upper part of her thighs, imparting a sensual sway to her fully blossomed hips. She seemed to keep time to the beat of a mysterious drum. When Violaine took a walk about town, all the men shook off their torpor, began to daydream, if but for an instant, so carried away were they by the rolling sway of her gait, carried away back to that most intimate part of their repressed African nature.

Like us, Béa loved books. From childhood, we shared everything we read, but basically we just loved to be together. In addition, all three of us used to go to the movies every Sunday. Those were magical moments, three whole hours at the Magic Ciné. We would get all fancied up, skip off, arms linked together, then very consciously lick our ice cream cones only with the small red tips of our tongues just to drive the boys wild. First, there were the serial films, *Fu Manchu* or *Zorro*, ah yes! And then there was *The Invisible Man!* And, of course, the great films: *The Sea Hawk*, with Errol Flynn, *The Queen of Sheba* with Eleonora Ruffo (which was only for those over the age of sixteen, but no problem, we were in thick with Alvanisse, the hunchback who checked the tickets), *Anna* with Silvana Mangano (the same scheme as above because we wouldn't have missed Anna's famous dance for anything in the world), *The Black Eagle* with Rossano Brazzi (ah!), *Tarzan*—in short, all those old films that the rickety projector massacred as it hissed away, but all to our delight.

With that said, Béa would never have attempted to escape, even if only for a minute, from her well-worn rut to go off and poke her nose around someplace else. Had she known about Violaine's real life, it would have horrified her.

Like a whirlwind as usual, Violaine made her way toward the Rougemonts' living room. Evidently, she was unaware that Philippe Edouard was entertaining his friends. I saw her freeze like an angel in full flight on the tips of her toes right in the middle of the entryway. Her sandals no longer seemed to be touching the ground. I stood behind her and, as her double, I could feel the violence of the raging storm crashing down upon her. Directly in front of me at the back of the room, I saw Alexandre, as if drained of all his blood, standing motionless like a statue, one with fireflies for eyes.

"Jesus Mary the Holy Virgin, Saint Louis King of France, Saint Jude patron Saint of all serious matters, Guinean *lwa*, don't let those two look at each other. Don't allow them to get near each other, but above all never let them dare think of loving one another. It must never happen, it is forbidden. It's impossible, impossible, impossible!"

And yet, when thinking about it more intently, nothing was more possible, nothing more inevitable, more natural, more compelling, more understandable. Nothing was more in line with the fabric of life itself. Because, after all, customs, taboos, prejudices are one thing; but the secret laws decreeing that a man and a woman have been created for each other for all eternity, like the canary for clear water, are another matter altogether.

Alexandre

If my father were still alive, he would know what words of wisdom to share with me: "Alexandre, my son, get hold of yourself, get back on that road that was, until yesterday, clearly and unequivocally being laid out before you. Forget this insanity of yours." But my father is dead and his spirit has grown silent. Yet, I know his speeches by heart. In my terror, I try to take some measure of my weakness. I'm alone, terribly alone. Today is the beginning of my struggle with the Angel, I can feel it. Did you see her when she came in, as radiant as all the city lights, her hair crackling, sparkling with flashes here and there? A joyous fire. Yes, no doubt, that's what it was. She was ablaze in the door. Never had my eyes looked upon such a woman, upon such a fierce mixture of freedom, audacity, revolt, sensuality, tenderness, displayed just like that, in broad daylight, without any reservations whatsoever. To come across such a shocking specimen in a Jeremiean parlor is nothing short of miraculous. And yet, sure enough, there she was, her ravenous mouth seemingly made for me, her breasts searing through her white blouse, her incandescent skin for me, and there was even more, and it was all just for me. Having jumped out of my dreams, having come from somewhere else, without roots or a past, without any kind of stigma whatsoever, daughter of herself, she was a creature from the moon walking about in the sunlight smelling of Africa. But she also was from an unknown part of Europe, hybrid, absolutely unique, a magical boat pitching about on the edge of all my wildest dreams. Yet, I can't even begin to say this person is pleasant. And why not? It's because she's disruptive, wearing the disorder of her thoughts on her large forehead, while revealing the excesses of her deepest impulses in those feverish pupils of her eyes. I find her unbelievably desirable, yet I know she's dangerous, always ready to do anything. But tell me, what perverse destiny created such a woman, my kind of woman from all appearances, but a daughter belonging to the Delavignes? My kind of woman but at the same time captive of the most disdainful, most arrogant, and most mulatto family in town? What a sinister joke!

Obviously, I couldn't take my eyes off her dazzling presence. The rhythm of her blood became my own. At a distance I began to match her breathing. There was something almost obscene about what we were doing in this provincial sitting room that reeked not only of musty air from being closed off but stale perfume. It was a room where everything was a trashy imitation—even the flowers were fake. And it also was a room filled with puppets playing out a vapid scenario and certainly one that had been repeated a thousand times. Even the fervor of Philippe Edouard's schoolmates had faded away inside this tomb. The poor souls were awkward and self-conscious; I didn't recognize their voices. What's more, their laughter was phony as they held their glasses in an affected way to impress everyone with their worldliness.

And both of us were there, our blood on fire, looking deep into each other's hearts. Everyone else could see the insanity raging within us. You had on that passionate face of yours, my beautiful Flamboyant. Yes, it's that same face you'll wear when I move you to explode with pleasure, a face that'll be as radiant as it is now and will convey that same famished, listless, yet somewhat frightened expression. And there I was, planted in that damnable salon with my desire burning away inside my body and my heart racing along like that of a savage, like the savage I had become once again through the simple magic of your appearance in the doorway.

Violaine, you understand clearly, I'm sure, that if we let ourselves give in to this force magnetically drawing us together, we're going to head down that road of unrelenting torment. We won't be able to face it all alone. You know better than I the revulsion Jeremiean mulattoes have for that Negro they all carry within themselves and have desperately relegated to the most obscure part of their memory. You're aware of their very real fear, which is of course absurd, of falling back into original sin, of regressing to that primitive source, their accursed origins. We can't predict where their obsession might lead them. Even the simple act of my eyes caressing you constitutes a sacrilege. The big one, the one, true sacrilege, I've never spoken to you, Violaine, even though I know the same fever that makes me shiver night and day has also taken possession of you.

Cocotte

I, Alma Viva Jean Joseph, otherwise known as Cocotte, Violaine's *marasa*, can say in all good faith, before the *lwa*, that I saw the earth move. It happened, an explosion! Ay, by the Eternal One, words escape me as to how to describe that encounter between Alexandre and Violaine, their burning looks screaming love and desire, and that immense energy that seemed to be throwing them together. When I think of how those two had grown up side by side without, shall we say, ever actually taking a good look at one another. And, now today, there they are devouring each other with their looks like two famished people, preparing to drag the whole town into that deadly adventure of their incendiary union.

I'm beginning to worry. Early this morning, I heard Violaine slip away like the wildcat she is. I took refuge in our room, pacing back and forth, trying to put some order in this chaos infecting us, trying to see clear into this boiling kettle of emotions and danger.

The door swings open with a bang. It's Violaine! She throws herself into my arms, shivering, quivering like a tender heart.

"Cocotte, I just had to see him. It was like an itch that had to be scratched, this need to be near him, speak to him. I couldn't sleep for thinking about it. So, this morning I just went over and prowled around his house."

"Given the hour when you left, my dear, everyone had to be fast asleep."

"Yes, Cocotte everybody was asleep. I wandered about until Alexandre woke up. And then when he came out on the balcony with his guitar I couldn't hold back any longer because it was not a question of doing one thing or another. Suddenly, I was right there by his side."

"How foolish you were, Violaine. How could you do something like that? You're not a *jennès*, not at all. You're forgetting yourself, my girl!"

"I'm not forgetting anything, my dear. Alexandre and I know we have every right in the world. I can't explain it to you, but he knows what I'm talking about."

She was right. Nothing ordinary was taking place between them. They were outside of what others perceive as the common law.

"He raised his eyes up to get a better look at me. I thought he was upset and at that point was going to retrace quickly the path I had taken earlier. I had already turned around when he called to me, 'Wait, don't leave!' Then, slowly I approached him. I'm sure his heart was pounding as hard as mine. 'Did you get lost?' he said, in a soft but somewhat mocking voice. 'Are you looking for your way home? Can I help you?' 'No, I'm not lost,' I said to him, affecting the same tone he had used. 'I know this town like the back of my hand. But you, on the other hand, may have forgotten it after all those years in Port-au-Prince. I've lived here from day one and can take you anywhere you want to go, even with my eyes closed. What's more, I know everyone and all the stories about them.' 'Ah! So you know everybody! Then tell me, who am I, huh?' 'Your name is Alexandre, Sor Mélie's son. You've just come back from Port-au-Prince and from the time you arrived you've spent every moment hanging around the Blancard peasants who have been grumbling about the coffee exporters. You see, I do know!' 'But where do you come up with such stories? A young lady like you should be doing her best to keep on top of the latest gossip from the wealthy side of town, taking care of her pretty dresses and worrying about her next picnic, and not what happens over at Sor Mélie's place or with the Blancard peasants!' 'Alexandre, I was the one who came to see you, to speak to you at this early hour. Why are you wasting your time with these frivolous jokes? So, let's assume then I've heard nothing, that nothing has, in fact, escaped your lips. But as you see, I'm still the one who came to you. I'm not playing games.' 'Then go ahead and speak, Violaine, speak, my Flower, and

I'll listen to you with every fiber of my being. And, since we're no longer playing around, I, too, will tell the truth. I was waiting for you, yes, waiting for you. I knew you'd come. And if you hadn't come, I would have come looking for you myself.' 'Tell me what to do, Alexandre. I would like to get closer to you, come right up to you, even stand right next to you. Do I have to forget my name, Violaine Delavigne, in order to do that? After all, it's only a name. You can give me another one!' 'You guessed correctly. It's your name. What it represents disgusts me!' 'I understand. But Alexandre, you have to appreciate, too, that my name is part of me. It's closely linked to one of the first secrets I'll share with you. That is, no one could take it from me without also taking a tiny piece of what is genuinely me. And I swear to you, everyone has tried. All alone, I carry within me our countless complications. It's like that! I want to be loved and accepted just as I am! I've never known how to deny anything. Not even the rich bastard Delavignes who gave me life. I'm a monster, and I say all this to you as openly as I can, with two heads, two tongues, two hearts, and one eye, one and only one. Sometimes, my mirror no longer recognizes me! With all these dissimilar parts it can't seem to piece together something that represents one whole, single person.'"

"Intrigued, Alexandre had moved closer to me to look directly into my eyes. 'In all honesty is there a real Violaine in there somewhere?' 'I'll answer that this way, Alexandre. I was born feeling as if I'd been torn in two. My African soul suffers in a body that's too pale for it; it also suffers as a result of my turncoat family, and, needless to say, all of them want me to choose a side, but I refuse. From my very first day I have managed to hold out. I am Violaine Delavigne, of mixed blood but bountiful all the same. As you see, I deny nothing.'"

"Alexandre's distraught face hid the whole sky before me. 'I understand one thing, Violaine. You are indeed this land with all its discarded wealth; you are this soil of ours that proves fertile in spite of itself, laden with alluvium from the very heart of the world, our accursed soil as we call it. You are the one who refuses to deny or give up while the rest of us relentlessly tear each other apart.'"

"He had really understood, Cocotte! My heart was bursting with joy. And he wanted to know everything, wanted me to tell him all about it. And of course I told him the whole story: you, me, the *marasa* in the secrecy of the *bagi*, grandmother Chimène, her constant presence in my life like a small bell, the village in the mountains, my mother for whom I was nothing but pain and who hardly knew how to love me, Man Chavannes, my initiation, even the pleasure I feel living with the people from the countryside. I talked so much I was afraid of making his head spin. After a brief pause, he asked, 'Tell me, Violaine, is there some place in the world where you feel perfectly at ease, at peace with yourself, reconciled with others, in a word, happy?' 'Nowhere, Alexandre, or least not completely. There is always a part of me that suffers or seems to be exiled.'"

"At that point he opened his arms and I nestled up close to his heart. He cradled me next to him and whispered that it was there I could find peace. It was there with him, and only with him, because I belonged to him. Right there in his life, I had found my place."

And I, Cocotte, Alma Viva Jean Joseph, could only murmur, "Amen, my girl!" What more could I say?

Alexandre

And now it's my turn to speak to you, Violaine. To tell you what I've become, to take you to the edge of that hell that vomited me up all bruised and battered into your arms. I want you to know all about it, living as you do bathed in the innocence of your provincial existence. Listen and watch. But above all hear what I have to say.

Wandering aimlessly through the streets of Port-au-Prince, the tepid air still quite noisy from the frenzy that takes over each day as soon as the sun comes up, I cast caution to the wind. For one last time the city shall be all mine. I take in its strong smells as well as its thick, dark colors, commanding it for this moment out of rage, despair, and disgust similar to what one feels with a prostitute. The tropical night is the shade of blue petrol as it eases with a serpentine elegance into those side streets where reputations are not the best. They are exactly what I need tonight, these darkened alleyways, with all their stench, peopled by ghostly creatures, haunted by human wrecks and their nightmares. The pulsations of the city match my helplessness. One after another, the dingy bars' neon lights are switched on, punching holes in the obscurity of the night: Casa Blanca, La Vida Loca, Copacabana, Cita Latina, Esmeralda, blip-blip, blip-blip, blip-blip. Some Dominican women, perched on stools in front of an open-air counter, their legs crossed way up high, cast suggestive glances in my direction and then in throaty voices: *"Venga, hombrecito! ¿Que quiere, mi amor?"* They're cute enough all dolled up in their elastic skirts, but most likely they're just girls made up and tossed out too soon into the muck of the city. They spring up in the gutter silt like miraculous flowers. *"La vida, chica, buscando la vida,"* misery. The worn-out juke boxes echo either outdated *rancheras* that make these girls cry or the long-forgotten merengues that set their hips to swaying. Their large, bold, and very dark eyes, in which sleeps a strange liqueur, flutter after me like butterflies of misfortune. The bordellos in the red light district, the "Frontière" as it is called because of the *chicas* who slave away there, are hard to distinguish from any of the other hovels in town. You find the same stagnant water, the same foul-smelling fumes, the same facades whose candy colored paint is washing out, if not peeling away, the same dust that lingers like a tenacious sorrow.

Oh! Port-au-Prince is a monster all right—you'll never get to know the whole story. She'll offer you her sumptuous gardens and extravagant villas. But for those of us tossed back into her seediest neighborhoods by misery, she has both the gentleness and the rage of a whore. A female city, Port-au-Prince sometimes cradles you with an extraordinary tenderness and sometimes spits in your face without your knowing why.

Tonight, as is often the case these days, the streets are deserted. Besides the streetwalkers, only some impenitent revelers dare to be out and about. The macadam resonates with the sound of heavy boots as the armed *makout* patrol the city. Some of them seem so feeble you have to wonder how they're able to carry around those heavy machine guns. But of all of Duvalier's henchmen they're certainly the most dangerous, however, because they've betrayed us by spreading misery beyond measure and their shame has driven them insane. As a result, they shoot like blind men without regard for their target.

A *taptap* is cruising around with its lights off. Its name, "Funny Life", is written on the outside. Ah yes, you old clunker, you're absolutely right. These days, life is definitely "funny," but in a rather curious way. We no longer talk to one another, we shoot at one another. In his big white palace, a lunatic has taken over the reins of our life, and the country marches to the beat of his delirium. "You're savages," he said to his *makout*, "your guns seem to go off all by themselves!" And yet, the jails have slammed their doors shut on all who have committed nothing more than the misdemeanor of thinking or who simply dared to say no. And as for those of us filled with hope (because how else can one live without hope), we clinch our fists, then are mowed down in a hail of bullets. For me, there's nothing more to do. I'm going home tomorrow. Purity will have to be rediscovered in its refuge far from the corruption of the capital city, in Jérémie along the Grandans. I want to pick up the simple gestures of life again. In Port-au-Prince, everything is screwed up, guns spitting out death on every street corner. How can anyone fight weapons and money with just bare and inexperienced hands? Everything is for sale in this rotten city, especially peace. You have to be for sale, my brother. If you don't sell out, you die. Tomorrow, it'll be Jérémie for me. Inside my chest my heart reacts like a Cartesian devil! Jérémie, when I think of you, I become a child again, a completely crazy *pitit moun*, itching to kick up my heels and gambol about, to meet up again with the peasants of Laginode whose rough hands know how to make things, peasants who have been abandoned in this country but nonetheless are its backbone.

The Bar du Serrage's fluorescent palm tree is flickering bravely like a small green semaphore in a night spinning out of control. A brother, drunk as a macaque and slumped down on the sidewalk, shouts at me. "Hey, you generous fellow, thirst is in the air, it's one of those nights where you can really work up a thirst. How about treating me to a small *kleren*!" I push open the door of the bar and enter the smoky room. Two lonely-looking prostitutes are leaning their elbows on the juke box. My friends from school are at the back of the room, and they welcome me with a joyous commotion. No one seems resigned to returning at this hour in spite of running the foolish risk of being picked up by the armed patrols. The brand-new diplomas just received that afternoon are going to open the way to too many contradictory horizons. Finally, they can begin. But begin where? There's just too much to do, and the junta of "New Men," who monopolize everything, close off every crack and cranny where some inroad might be made. The real battle, the one against misery, ignorance, sickness, is occluded by the race for power and kickbacks.

"I think you have to make your way without drawing unnecessary attention to yourself," says Michel. "For the moment we can't fight them because we're unarmed. We have to put all our efforts into staying alive, and keep fighting for those no longer with us. I've accepted an opening at the university. We have to keep the flame burning. We can't allow it to go out."

As our elders say, the mouth is made for speaking. With the help of his beer, Michel was talking mostly to convince himself. And, after all, nobody really knew what to do, where to go, nor how to avoid being splattered by all this mud. At that point Jacques stood up—if you could only have seen his eyes, like daggers.

"You're a traitor, Michel. So, you're going to teach! But in what kind of university? One where they muzzle you! What flame do you want to preserve as people are gunned down around us every day." (Jacques was our resident specialist in dogmatic discourse. His grandiloquence and intolerance amused us because, as we all knew, he wouldn't have harmed a fly.) He rambled on in his Ciceronian way, "while this piece of filth by the name of Duvalier has attacked all our institutions, that is, those that have managed to survive the dictatorships throughout our history as well as the American occupation. Our self-respect, our culture, our very soul has been trampled underfoot, and you're talking about preserving some flame! But don't you see? It's dead, your noble flame! We have to fight, brother. We'll find the weapons. Cuba is right there within our reach."

A heavy silence has fallen over the small bar, which we hadn't even noticed, so involved were we in redoing the history of Haiti one more time. Three *makout*, hidden behind their dark glasses, have invaded the room. They are now settling in as their weapons rattle around them. One of them kicks over the old jukebox sputtering out a vague melody. Visibly frightened, the prostitutes take refuge behind the bar. And as we watch the *makout* without saying a word, anger slowly fills our eyes. Their arrogance fouls the atmosphere. Small beads of sweat begin to cover the shiny head of Gros Jo, the owner.

"Would you gentlemen like some rum, or perhaps one of our little *tranpe*?"

"That sounds good, fat ass, let's try some of that *tranpe* crap of yours!"

We recognized him by his pocked-marked face. It's Ti Boulé, one of Papa Doc's most savage torturers. His hatred for students is legendary. No doubt about it, he's going to give us a hard time.

"Hey you! *grimo*, come here, bring me my glass and hurry up about it!"

Michel, the *grimo*, gets up and walks slowly toward the killer with the glass in hand, looks him directly in the eyes, plants himself firmly in front of him, then deliberately lets the glass fall at his feet.

"Sorry," he mutters through his teeth, "you'll have to order another one."

The bully begins to choke, his face now nothing more than an arrogant snarl.

"Do you want to die, you dirty little café communist? You think you can get away with insulting Pierre Septembre? Do you have any idea why they call me Ti Boulé, huh? Do you know why? Because with *kamoken* like you, I hose them down with gasoline and have them set afire like torches. So, if you know what's good for you, you'd better lower your eyes around me, cockroach!"

"Show me yours, Commandant, I can't see them because you're hiding them behind your dark glasses."

Those famous dark glasses, a taboo subject when standing before the regime's killers! I'm trying to hold back Jacques, who is about to spring to Michel's defense.

"Back off, man, he'll kill you both! Wait to see his reaction. After all, he might just burst out laughing."

But on that particular night Commandant Septembre wasn't at the Bar du Serrage by chance, as we later learned. He was indeed looking for Michel.

"Run that jerk in for me!" barked Ti Boulé. His flunkies attacked Michel with ferocious pleasure, kicking him, pistol-whipping him with the heavy grip of a .45 caliber pistol, then pushing him brutally into the trunk of a big black Dodge, where there was already another man tied up like an animal. The glimmer from the flashlights reflecting off his broken glasses momentarily spangled the obscurity with stars. Ti Boulé didn't take his eyes from us. He waited. We didn't dare move, we scarcely breathed.

"We have all the time in the world. Your turn will come. You'll run into Pierre Septembre again, or may lightning strike and shatter me into a thousand pieces!"

Slowly, he turned around, slid into the front seat of the Dodge, but not without some difficulty. His insane laughter continued to resonate in our ears for quite some time. Now the beast had struck at the very heart of our little circle, carrying off in its ghoulish entourage all that remained of our childhood. We felt even more vulnerable than before, our helplessness overwhelmed us.

"They've arrested Michel Célestin!"

The rumor spread like an insidious stream of water. Michel was Port-au-Prince's favorite son. His broadcasts on Radio Caraïbe were enthusiastically received in all the shanty towns. From Brooklyn, Site Solèy, Lasalin, Bèl Lè, Bapedchoz, Kafou Fèy, Flè Chenn, and all the way to Sanfil, the transistors reverberated every morning at dawn belting out his famous signature song: "My heart doesn't skip a beat, my heart doesn't hesitate, my heart doesn't flutter. Ay my heart! This year our drums will beat more strongly than guns," and so went the song. The common people of Port-au-Prince, whose principal virtue is, perhaps, their mischievousness, had deciphered all of Michel's parables. He had become a master in the art of communicating dispassionately the most incendiary slogans all the while pretending to give commentary on the latest successes in the area of mini-jazz, a musical trend that had become the rage.

"They've arrested Michel, the dogs!"

Following an old tradition that entails playing the role of constituents of the men in power, Jacques and I have settled on a desperate strategy in order to tear Michel loose from Ti-Boule's claws. We're going to try to arrange a meeting with the Minister of Justice before the situation gets too far out of hand. Of course, we know that this man, like all of Papa Doc's close collaborators, lives in sheer terror of displeasing his boss and consequently spends his life trembling in fear for his unstable, though lucrative livelihood. Perhaps we will be able to persuade him that the commandant's actions last night risk putting him in an unfortunate situation. This is going to be a delicate negotiation, but not impossible. Violaine, you shouldn't be too surprised to learn we'll have access to his bedroom. A woman still living in Port-au-Prince, one of my older cousins who is well-acquainted with the minister's mother, is going to plead your case. And since no man can ever refuse anything his mother requests, it would be highly unusual if we weren't granted some time with him soon.

So, at the crack of dawn we find ourselves in the minister's bedroom, a cup of steaming hot coffee in our hands. A tall man in freshly starched pajamas, tilting solemnly back and forth in his rocker, receives us with a certain courtesy but not without a pompous air.

"Yes, I pay close attention to our youth because you represent the Haiti of tomorrow! And as a builder of the future, the President puts all of his hope in you."

Apparently he has no idea what brings us to his bedroom at this ungodly hour. Our old cousin must have really put one over on them. We explain that one of our friends, an agronomy student, was arrested last night by Commandant Pierre Septembre, that his name is Michel Célestin, and that the minister has probably heard of him. His arrest sparked quite a disturbance, but we emphasize it's still possible to avoid a riot of some kind because apparently there's no charge pending. Commandant Septembre took him into custody at a bar where he was just having a good time. Consequently, it should be no trouble to set him free. We're sure the President will appreciate how quickly he has acted upon the matter because we know he doesn't want any blood spilled.

Our naïveté deeply amuses his Excellency, who then tries, to no avail, to suppress a smile. Ah, ah! So, you still believe the President cares about the blood of the people, you poor imbeciles! The minister shakes his head and chuckles in a knowing way. Ay, so you've come here to tell me you still don't know who François Duvalier is! Then, a cloud passes over his face. It's a combination of terror and firm determination to stay in control.

"What you have said is in fact correct. I am, gentlemen, quite familiar with the situation. But perhaps you are not aware of the following: Célestin is a dangerous communist who has been under surveillance for several long months by the personnel at the American Embassy. We have tried to get them to be a little bit more patient, but all this was inevitable."

At that point this caricature of a human being starts to reek of cynicism and spinelessness. His soft lips contract and the peaceful man sipping his coffee while rocking gently back and forth is suddenly transformed into a vociferous brute.

"Communism will never take hold here as long as WE are in power! We have promised this to our friends in high places! As such, I'm unable to do anything for this young scatterbrained friend of yours, but he only has himself to blame. People just cannot be allowed to ridicule anything and everything with impunity at the expense of all our basic values. Ah, no! That is not acceptable. As for the people, if they get out of control, we will silence them. If a riot does occur, it will be the last one!" The minister looks directly into our eyes, and his sensual face suddenly becomes expressionless. One might even say he looked like a tomcat that had just eaten its fill. Then in a calmer voice he concludes, "You, ah yes! I know who you are! Out of respect for my mother who helped get you in here, I am going to warn you. You, too, are under surveillance. So, a word to the wise: back off and get out of my sight!"

Jacques and I execute a rapid retreat. Finally, we start to understand we are caught in the aura of a well-known figure. In order to receive a new delivery of arms or an "injection of fresh dollars," as he usually puts it, Papa Doc is preparing to furnish Uncle Sam his next piping hot ration of "young communists." This son-of-a-bitching minister is absolutely correct. There's nothing we can do other than try to avoid a bloodbath.

I smile today when I think of how stupid we were at that time. We had no idea whatsoever what the "new era" meant. In spite of the minister's explicit threats, we had a hard time imagining the *makout* opening fire on an unarmed crowd because, let's face it, we were reacting like Haitians from another era. We still believed we were free to speak, to persuade, to act according to the old customs. We hadn't fully comprehended that free expression had died, that Duvalier, out of hatred for his own people, had decided to decapitate them, strip them of their leaders, in order to brutalize them all the more. This is, perhaps, the reason we were unable to be more convincing. Oh, we still tried to prevent the demonstration. We explained that the *makout* were ready to shoot everyone, that Michel would never be turned over to us, but nobody really wanted to believe us. Some, the same vultures who had been following us around from the beginning of our struggle, even spoke of the cost of bloodshed one has to pay when overthrowing tyranny! We were too distraught to understand at one fell swoop what that meant.

Then, that afternoon of the same day, there we are, gathered with our friends, in addition to that sublime throng that Port-au-Prince only produces on special occasions: the young, the old, men and women. All of us swept along by the same surge, the same indignation, the same blessed anger. We head toward the National Palace. I'm walking with them, against them, carried along by them. And the pulse of the crowd begins to beat within me as the warmth of my blood merges with the love flowing from their hearts. I breathe deeply, filling my nostrils with the smell of their poverty and sweat while my arms cradle their ridiculous courage as well as their sorrow. It's not just for Michel's life that they're marching and shouting. It's their way of exorcising their misfortune, their wretched children, their prostituted daughters, their men without work, their brothers crammed into old people's prisons or the holds of death boats (making their way toward which Florida this time, which insane hope?). They continue to march and shout. We all push on together, unarmed and innocent, until finally, like the lunatics we are, we confront Papa Doc's armed, bloodthirsty horde. Shortly afterwards, bullets begin to whistle by.

"Give Michel Célestin back to us!"

"Free Michel Célestin!"

"We want Michel! Give him back to us!"

The Thompson machine guns tear a gaping hole into the advancing mass of people. All around me bodies are falling. A small woman who usually sells pistachios is cut down as she tries to escape with her pitiful basket of wares, collapsing like a dead bird. I offer my bare chest to the hail of bullets. It's all too hideous, we'll never find a way out of this filthy hole. Just look at our empty hands. Just look at us, pitifully poor, illiterate, starved! But we're not afraid. The cavernous voices of the Springfields blend in their intermittent rumble with the lugubriously staccato bursts of the Thompsons. The crowd now begins to scream its anger.

"Down with dictatorship! Down with death! Down with Duvalier!"

The gunfire continues to wreak its havoc. Jacques is struck in the thigh. He can barely walk and is losing a lot of blood. The crowd gathers up those who've fallen and then begins to scatter in all directions. I heave Jacques onto my back and head for Ri Kapwa. Once we are there, a doctor friend will take us in. For some reason the bullets didn't want anything to do with me today. I start to sink into a deep despair. Ah! He's going to end up killing all of us.

I put off returning to Jérémie because someone had to take care of the wounded, but more importantly we had to get organized to deal with this new brand of aggression from the beast. Indeed, the minister was right; there would be no more peaceful demonstrations. At last it had hit home. It was time to get prepared for a long struggle, one that would have to be waged in every way possible! Never again would we have the luxury of lowering our guard.

Michel was killed in the basement of the National Palace at the very moment the crowd was shouting his name. After recovering from his wound, Jacques left in the night for Cuba, but made clear that "It's over, Alexandre, we'll never allow ourselves to be slaughtered like a bleating flock again, and that I can promise you. We'll start over, but this time we'll have weapons." As for me, once my responsibilities were finished there, I set out for Jérémie as intended. Besides, since the poem I wrote on the massacre at the National Palace had caused quite a stir, it was just a better idea to get away from the capital.

I haven't mentioned hunger, Violaine, and yet I came to know it firsthand. And I haven't talked about the miserable shack on Ri Magloire Ambroise that my friends and I shared with bedbugs and vermin. From the moment I began, the most important thing was that you understand my reason for coming back to Jérémie. Because, in spite of all I've told you, in spite of my determination to begin the struggle again here with the peasants, ultimately I've come back, trembling, virtually incapable of drawing a breath without you, to place myself in your hands. You are, for me, a new life. And yet, if I had an ounce of sense, I would get the hell out of here, my beloved.

Alexandre

I'm sure she said "Wait for me at sundown under the cursed fig tree near Klere Spring." I'm not imagining this. I know she said it to me herself. And yet, for over an hour, I've been pacing back and forth from the spring to the tree, then from the tree to the spring. After that, my steps trace a circle around the tree, which is filled with birds at this time of day. My blood is coursing and a knot is starting to form right there in my solar plexus. I think my heart might stop beating from this unbearable waiting.

Suddenly, a meteor shower explodes before my eyes. Time vanishes. She's right next to me. I forget everything else except this smell of cinnamon surrounding her. Pressing her close to my body, I wrap her in my arms. Her wildcat eyes are wide-open right up against mine, while her eyelashes flutter against my cheeks like hummingbirds. The world begins spinning around us as I taste her purple mouth, a delectable fruit between my teeth.

"Are you afraid, Violaine, tell me, are you afraid?"

"I'm not afraid. I want you in me. I want you! Oh! how I want you!"

She begins to sway back and forth, a liana in my arms. Her whole body caresses me with a certain softness and violence as she rolls and rubs the bulge in my pants, that courageous, bashful friend of mine. My hands run up and down her thighs. She sighs deeply, as I set sail now on her desire, the swell of her hips making me lose control. Out of my mind, I raise her skirt. No panties, what a little temptress! Her naked behind quivers in the small of my hands as the music with which it beckons makes me tremble like a palm in a storm.

"I want you, too, my sweet Violaine, but I'm afraid!"

And yet, already my hand has been captured by that mossy fleece between her thighs. In that very hollow of her being, I begin to fold back a tender, fleshy flower, soft as a *kayimit* with its abundant flow of tepid liqueur. A pearl flashes between my fingers, and from then on there's no turning back because I've gone completely insane. Oh! Guinean *lwa*, give me back my sanity. I know I'm falling into an abyss at the bottom of which is certain death.

Although she keeps her devilish eyes open, Violaine shudders with pleasure as my fingers continue to explore every inch of her skin. Then she offers me her breasts, her nipples swelling and trembling at the touch of my tongue. Yes, she's giving herself to me.

"I belong to nobody, Alexandre. Nobody can keep me from being yours! I love you, and that alone gives me the right to choose."

You're the one who is unbuttoning my jeans, and I'm giving in as I imprison your hips in my hands, guiding you toward that part of me that can no longer wait to lavish its tenderness upon you. Delicately, the tip of my desire caresses your half-open, secretive cockle, which then bursts into flame from the heat of my fever. The tender moaning slipping from your lips is only interrupted when, with a small push of your hips, you plunge me deep inside, but not without a whimper like a child who has just hurt herself. Ecstatic, I slide in, penetrating your velvet enclosure, your crimson vulva, so fleshy, rich, unctuous, so mysterious and moist as it opens little by little, acquainting me with the virginal luxuriance of all its textures.

I'm doing it to you, making love to you, my sweet treasure. That musky scent of yours, your sunny fragrance is going straight to my head. You're dying love's death beneath me, a death both painful and pleasurable at the same time. Oh! My hot-bodied Violaine, my crazy lover. And I come into you with all my distress, release into you all the weight of my excessive, uncontrollable, and untamed love. And as you continue nibbling at my skin, I'll sway both of us back and forth. Come with me, Violaine, let's never turn back now.

Violaine

It's dark in my room with the curtains lowered. Stretched out on my bed, I'm filled with your presence, trembling, impregnated by all your vigor, still carried along by that wave that took us to the top of the world. I can honestly say I've come alive, Alexandre, that you've made a new woman out of me, washed me clean. Your Violaine has blossomed, hatched, and has been born anew that day she found herself motionless, unable to lift a finger or bat an eyelash, with her pupils riveted to yours, incapable of anything except loving you.

My cupped hand is still protecting that painfully tender, though delightful, butterfly that landed in the middle of me. I'm your wife, your woman, Alexandre! As I drift back to our dream, I soar off to the grotto where we were wed. Your hands set my blood afire while your ravenous mouth seizes hold of mine, but still not without an extraordinary tenderness. My consenting breasts nestle into the hollow of your hands, bursting into bloom while obeying the demands of your every desire. Your arms pull me close, and I can feel you beginning to get hard. You're on fire. Our hips begin dancing the same love dance as your volcanic skin singes against the hot copper of my own. Your teeth grind together as you subtly nibble at me, those same savage teeth of yours that wind pearly bonds around my defiant ankles with a magical power capable of transforming all the women slaves from *Ginen* into sultanas. Your tongue is becoming acquainted with the most intimate secrets of my body as you plunge into me, exploring every crevice and fold. It's all so insane, you'll be the death of me! And my fingers get lost in that burning bush of your hair, yes, completely lost.

You're resting now by my side, exhausted. You've closed your eyes, all of your strength drained from you. I listen to your breathing, perfectly content to die from this bliss, my love.

But then I want you all over again. Make love to me again, Alexandre! In the softest and deepest part of me I want to feel you explode with joy. Your voice murmurs ever so softly in my ear: "Violaine, my insatiable love! Violaine, my *kreyòl* sugarcane, my loving woman. Though still panting heavily next to me, I can see your beautiful smile starting to come back. I want to lick you everywhere all over as a cat does its kitten, bury you in my lair, carry you off someplace. You're my prey, my captive. My hands are crazy. They just can't get enough of that roundness of your behind. I'm breaking you in, riding you like a new filly. Gently, my beauty, my wild woman, my lovely mare, die love's death once again. I love you!"

Cocotte

The sky tonight looks like a nest of phosphorescent ants as stars by the thousands flicker indiscriminately over our heads. You can feel the *ʒobop* and *vlenbendeng* flying about in the air. As their wings brush by, it electrifies the animals that, instead of sleeping, are beginning to moo, bray, and whinny like spirits in distress. Overcome with anger like some wild spirit, Philippe Edouard is coming toward me, his large body shaken from heavy sobbing. The hatred blazing away in the pupils of his eyes has gotten the best of him, while his sorrow ferries him along like a river overflowing its banks. He comes toward me, words spewing from his mouth in poisonous bursts. Ay, he must have seen everything. He must know the whole story. And what he saw is too much for him to handle.

"Alexandre! He dared to touch Violaine. He dared take such a risk. How can I tolerate that? Just think of it from my point of view, Cocotte! How can I go on living after I've seen her give in to him, make love to him, in essence, pledge her love to him forever? It's just too much for me to take, even in my worst nightmares. I think my heart has stopped beating. I'm going to kill both of them."

"Phil, Philippe, Philippe Edouard, I know, believe me I do, I know! Your whole body is like a field laid waste, and your heart is aching, but for goodness' sake, let go, calm down. Come! Sit next to me, let's talk, just the two of us."

"There's no use talking. I've died inside, I'm telling you. So, don't talk to me anymore, Cocotte!"

He swept into the darkness like a *baka*, like a piece of human flotsam or a wisp of straw all ablaze, a spark carried off by the wind.

Violaine

The night was long. I tossed and turned in my bed so much I'm aching all over. Shivers ripple through my sore limbs while my whole body trembles like a leaf. For the first time in my life I'm really afraid. Ay, Papa God, chase away these nightmares taking shelter under my eyelids, especially the one where Alexandre's wrists are shackled in handcuffs as he is forcibly led away by armed men whose eyes are nothing more than large black holes. Chase away that frightening vision where he turns back toward me, his face shattered from suffering, then gradually disappears from view altogether! Or the one where my insides are being torn apart, as I lie virtually lifeless while a small monster springs from between my thighs. All these images are starting to make my head throb. But I know a place, the only refuge in Jérémie where I can find salvation, if it exists.

I slip out of my room, taking care not to wake Cocotte. The sun hasn't come up yet from behind the mountains. Nonetheless, I'm already starting to take in those early-morning smells full of flesh in bloom and moist earth. Everyone and everything is asleep. My old habit of furtive escapes guides me steadily through the various traps in the silent house: right here is where I have to avoid the creaky slat in the parquet floor, and there I have to go around the balustrade, which is so hard to see in the dark. Just like a cat, I creep along as quietly as possible. Without making a sound, the door swings easily on its hinges as I glide into the garden, where a milky haze still hovering over the ground suddenly springs at me. The heavy, dew-laden branches of the trees glisten silently in the gray mist. No sooner do I take a few steps on the moist lawn than my sandals become completely soaked. Then, pulling my large shawl over my nightgown, I head toward the edge of town. The hillsides are covered here and there with small cornfields that mount quickly in an assault on the sky, once freed of the weight of their *kay chanmòt*. There, at that juncture, the city blends in so well with the countryside that no one knows whether those who live in this intermediary zone are townspeople or country folk. Indeed, they don't even know themselves. Their dwellings made from rough-hewn, jigsawed lumber give the appearance of delicacies plopped into the middle of a miniature *lakou*, which nonetheless bears all the indications of its peasant origins.

Out of breath, I finally arrive in front of Man Chavannes's place, a large cabin of imposing proportions immediately distinguishable from all the others because of its lacy trim made from soft, green wood that lend to the whole structure the appearance of a large bouquet of horsemint. The well-kept, medicinal herb garden, surrounded by its basil hedge to ward off bad air, is right next to the *kay mistè*. Aromatic waves emanate from its *peristil*, and slowly the vice that has been tightening down on my skull starts to loosen its grip. With a sigh of relief, I look more closely at the animals beginning to stir in the predawn light. As is the case at the homes of most *manbò*, a veritable Noah's ark welcomes me. There are the sacred animals destined for the feast of the gods, always prepared at sunrise: Ogoun's red roosters, speckled hens destined for the Petwo Lwa, small black pigs that squeal as they plow up the ground with their snouts, Danbala's white roosters, Simbi's pigeons, kids with their coats of many colors to be used in sacrifices for the faithful of the temple, and then a sturdy steer gallantly waiting for the big *rada* celebration. I greet all of them, my throat taut with emotion:

"*Onnè!* . . . Yes, I say 'Honor'!"

But there's not a sound, not even a whisper to indicate that Man Chavannes is home, and yet she's the one who always gets up before sunrise. Jesus, Mary, the Holy Virgin, please let her be there! I need her strength and wisdom at this point. Selavi, the old dog with the pointed muzzle, kindly licks my feet to reassure me.

"*Onnè!*" Now it seems I'm shouting out this formal greeting almost like an insult, as my impatience starts to get to me.

"*Respè*, my *fi*, respect. Just look at how upset you are! Peace, calm down!"

A concerned look on her face, Man Chavannes comes out of her prayer chamber, waddling on her huge rheumatic legs.

"Man Chavannes, oh, how I need you! You absolutely have to help me! I'm dying of anguish and I don't know where to go or who to trust!"

I take refuge in the reassuring warmth of her massive bosom, snuggling more closely to her maternal breasts. Her steady, patient hand softly encloses my buzzing head.

"I know, my daughter, I know all about it. I was hoping I'd see you this morning. All night long the Spirits have been sending me dreams about you and, as a result, my mind is burdened with many thoughts."

She wraps her protecting arms around my shoulders as I close my eyes, forgetting everything for the moment, so lost am I in the soothing gentleness of her affectionate touch, in its perceptive strength, forgetting the black hole at the bottom of which I'm floundering. Then, Man Chavannes leads me into her *bagi*, has me sit in a low-slung chair, and forces me to swallow a scalding hot decoction with a strong, bitter taste that revives and comforts me. Only after observing the effect of her remedy is she willing to hear me out.

"So, my child, what put you in such a state? Tell your old Mama."

"Mama, you stayed one year and one day under water in the land of the Simbi and you came back purified like an incandescent firebrand that can fit in the hollow of one's hand. You saw me come into the world, grow up, and on numerous occasions you even washed my head! You know me through and through, you know how I am. The man of my life, the one destined for me from the beginning of time, could never be the son of someone in my family, right?"

She looks at me through her *manbò*'s eyes, those eyes filled with infinite patience, capable of waiting without blinking until the sun dries up the ocean, those penetrating eyes that have seen everything, now veiled by cataracts, but still able to peer into the deepest part of your soul.

"I'm listening to you, woman."

"Mama, this man came just for me. When he got off the boat, there was no doubt about it, he was mine and I belonged to him and him alone. We made love, Mama, we love each other. Do you understand? No other man will ever touch me or God will reduce me to ashes."

"But, my daughter, what you're describing is a very happy event. So, tell me, then! Who is this young man who's turned you on your head like an hourglass, my courageous, little woman?" asks Man Chavannes. But I can already see there's no need to explain, she has already understood everything.

"Mama, you want me to tell you his name, huh? Okay, I will, but get ready for a big shock." (Oh! it's so hard for me to say Alexandre's name, so hard to let it slip from my lips, from my heart, from my stomach, from that refuge where I have deposited it in the hollow of my being.) And then finally, drawing in a huge gulp of air, I blurt it out.

"His name is Alexandre, Sor Mélie's son."

I expected horrible imprecations of some sort, but Man Chavannes said nothing. However, almost immediately thereafter, I could feel her turning to stone as the flame of her gaze dimmed and disappeared in the shadowy light. Then all signs of life seemed to leave her enormous body, even though she's still right there before me, huge, massive, like an ancient goddess, the eternal feminine carved out of lava. Apparently, she can no longer speak. "When words are too powerful," so goes an old saying, "the jaw swells and becomes too heavy." Yes, Man Chavannes could indeed assess the extent of the scandal brought on by a loving relationship between Sor Mélie's son and the Delavignes' only daughter. But for the moment she remains silent, and this silence seems to last an eternity.

At last, she pulls herself up out of her armchair, briskly shaking her head.

"Ay, Violaine, what is done is done. No use wasting our breath saying empty words. I'm going to summon Papa Loko. At the very least, my child, we need his eyes to help us resolve this situation."

Firmly, one foot after the other, she makes her way toward the back of her *bagi*, toward the *pè*, the three-tiered ceremonial altar covered with ritual objects. At the top, is the cross for the Master of the Crossroads. Then, just below on the second level, are the *govi* decked out in all the colors of the great *lwa*. Finally, on the third and lowest tier sits a human skull for the cult of the *gede*, the spirits of Death, along with gourds containing offerings, playing cards, the *manbò*'s rattle and glistening *foula* bottles covered with multi-colored sequins. On the wall behind the altar hang all the raiments of the gods: Zaka's pompon covered satchel, his smock and har-vester's machete, Bawon Samdi's dark top hat and long, black dressing-gown, as well as *Ezili*'s wedding dress. Also, hollowed out in the wall are small nooks piously lit with oil lamps and in which those Catholic Saints (fixed forever in their theatrical poses) repre-senting the principal *lwa* of the Vodou pantheon are keeping a watchful eye: Saint James the Greater for Ogoun, Saint Lazarus for Legba, Saint Patrick for Danbala, Mater Dolorosa for Ezili Freda, the Black Madonna of Czestochowa, who has two scarifications on her right cheek, Ezili Dantò, Saint Cosmas and Saint Damian for the *marasa*. Suddenly, I'm starting to feel really good. The *ounfò*'s magic is definitely having an effect. A kind of delicious peace comes over me as I let myself slide into a world where everything is simple, where the gods, people, animals, plants, all live on good terms with one another. This sanctuary has been my refuge for as long as I can remember. Man Chavannes, Asoutini as she is known by her Valiant Name, is a bona fide *manbò asire*, one of Ogoun's most beautiful horses. To be his *fi kanzo* is an extraordinary stroke of luck as well as a great honor. Her temple is well-equipped, be-yond reproach, maintained according to regulations in the purest tradition.

Solemnly, Mama picks up Loko's *foula* bottle, the one that "gives eyes." Pivoting slowly, she presents the shiny object to the four faces of the world as she pronounces the word *langaj* at each turn. Next, she takes in a long, healthy mouthful of the magical liquid and spews it out over the top of her folded arms to the four corners of the *bagi*, closing her eyes and concentrating with all the intensity she can muster. Now, as her face starts to turn into a rigid mask furrowed with deep wrinkles, comes the dramatic moment when the Spirit appears. Little by little, the virile, imperious traits of the god are inscribed on her own features. In her broad face, shining brightly from the ecstasy she feels, can be read not only all our suffering, all our struggles, but that very ancient esoteric knowledge passed on by our forefathers from Africa-*Ginen-Gelefre*. Grabbing her rattle, the old priestess begins shaking it in a spasmodic and monotonous way while chanting Papa Loko's favorite sayings. And then suddenly, there he is! The Spirit mounts and begins to ride his horse. So familiar is she with the *lwa* that this hardly startles her at all. Seemingly from out of nowhere, the cavernous voice of Papa Loko, Master of all *ason*, First among *oungan*, speaks from her mouth: "Greetings my children, I say greetings, Valiant Women!"

I prostrate myself with my face down and my forehead pressed against the hard clay of the *ounfô*.

"*Ayibobo*, my dear Papa! Grace be unto you, oh Loko Miwa!"

"So how are you, my children, those of you gathered here before me?"

"We are here, yes Papa, to see you, the good Lord that you are."

"Why, Children of the Leaves, why have you summoned me to your miserable earth?"

"Papa, you know very well we need you to help us live through the trying and tormenting times of our lives. We are your children, Papa!"

"Hmmm, beautiful Violaine. You'll tell my horse later that I send greetings and that all her worries are in my hands. Do you understand, my daughter?"

"Yes, Papa. I too am in your hands, yes indeed!"

"Ah! My child, what problems, what a commotion, what a troubled head you appear to have! I won't lie to you, Violaine. You'll have to be strong and valiant. Do you understand, beautiful woman? And your life is going to seem even more frightening in the days to come. There's nothing you can do concerning the outcome of your destiny. Put your heart at rest and submit. Have you understood what I've just said?"

"Yes, Papa."

"However, Daughter of the Leaves, you were born with twenty-one lucky charms. Our ancestors wanted you to be an animal of seven leaps. This is what you have to do. You will tell my horse to prepare a protective bath for you and have you take it Friday as the sun goes down. Do you understand?"

"Yes, Papa."

"Now, Beautiful Woman, repeat along with me the following formula for preparing your bath: seven *langlichat* leaves, twenty-one from the sandbox tree, seven soft liana heads, three leaves from the cashew tree, a *wont* stalk, a handful of reseda, water fetched from afar, a pinch of red precipitate, along with a dash of some of the white. In addition, Asoutini—your Man Chavannes as you know her—will mix with all this a small decanter of your usual perfume, then lay you on top of an image of Saint Expeditus along with one of Dantò upside down. Then she will sprinkle the blood of a white pigeon onto the fontanel of your head after which she will bury the tender creature alive at the foot of the tree serving as my temporary altar. Did you get all of that, my child?"

"Yes, Papa."

"Very good, my daughter. Now, I can return to my own land, for the road is long. Come, say good-bye to me and receive my benediction, then you will of course convey it to everyone else. And especially, my child, remain calm in your heart regardless of what happens."

Papa Loko pressed his forehead against mine, blessed me by rubbing his sweat onto my face. He made me turn to the right, then to the left. I kissed the ground at his feet, after which he disappeared, leaving Man Chavannes unconscious in my arms.

The inanimate body of the priestess was heavy, but it soon lightened as I felt life coming back into her powerful limbs. She shuddered, opened her eyes, and passed directly from that mysterious world of the trance into that of everyday reality. In no time at all her head cleared, and she returned to her *bagi*, once again in complete command of all her faculties, although obviously troubled because she was already starting to question me about what had happened.

"So, my child, what did Papa Loko say?"

"He sends you his greetings and blesses you, Mama. He also said that my situation was very serious and that you'll have to give me a bath. I have everything he said stored away in my head."

"And you, my daughter, exactly what are you saying to me? There's still something else you have to tell me, right?"

My eyes did their best to avoid her unyielding gaze. But she grabbed me by the chin, forcing my stubborn head to face her directly, and then, looking deep into my eyes, into my very soul.

"You must tell me everything, my little hellion, if you don't, how do you expect me to help you? When you bathe in the nude, you can't expect to hide your navel! So let's get to the heart of the matter. What have you done, what have you two foolish birds been up to? Come now, out with it!"

"No, Mama," I responded vehemently, braving her stare without blinking. "I can't let you treat us like foolish birds. Am I to believe then that you agree with the other members of my family who would prefer to kill me rather than accept the fact I'm different? Please, not you too!"

"My daughter, denying reality serves no purpose. What we know, and even the passions inside us, only concerns us individually in the final analysis. Society either accepts this or refuses it. In reality, it takes its pick. And we have to learn to live with that. So, Violaine, let's talk now. Let's talk about what has weighed heavy on your heart ever since you arrived. Courage, woman!"

"You know everything already, Mama, don't make me speak."

Man Chavannes looks at me, impassive, without uttering a word. If I don't speak, she'll scorn me for the rest of my life. My God, by all the Saints, how can I tell her, In what words?

"Mama, listen to me with all your heart. I've never known how to do anything halfway. I love Alexandre the only way I know how, with my head for sure, but with all my body and soul as well. Ay, how my body aches for him, Mama. He has given me a child, that is, we made the child together. I'm so happy with this small part of him growing inside of me! It's a tremendous joy that has completely taken me over. I'm even beginning to wonder if I can think about anything else!"

What I'm trying to tell her in so many words, she knows. It's just that I actually had to tell it to her myself. She also knows about all those other things we don't bother discussing: my family, the inviolate proscriptions we have transgressed, along with all the dangers hovering around us. She watched more than actually listened to what I was saying. But I know that when she finally decides to respond nothing frivolous will come from her mouth.

"When was the last time you had your period, my daughter?"

"It was two months ago, Mama."

"Hmmm. Who else knows about this, my dear?"

"Only Cocotte and Alexandre."

"What does Alexandre say about it?"

"He's beside himself, like me, very happy. But at the same time he's scared to death. He isn't acting the way he usually does and seems to have trouble making any kind of sense."

"He must leave here, and quickly." Then closing her eyes and contorting her face, she utters those words that tear into my soul, words that burn into my body like the tips of red-hot metal blades or, rather, implacable truths.

"Listen to me, Violaine. Gird your loins with that belt that only courageous women wear. As for your baby, forget all about it from this moment on! It will never see the light of day. There's no place for a child in your life. In their infinite wisdom the *lwa* are going to take it back, and neither you nor anyone else will be able to do anything about it, my daughter."

Her hand starts closing in again around my head, which is throbbing all the more from what she just said: "There, there, peace, my daughter," she murmurs softly. My stomach starts to contract, then a beastly wail like that from a lost animal escapes from my lips. I have a taste of bile in my mouth and am feeling nauseated.

"Now, come along, let's go get everything ready for your bath. You have to take it tomorrow just as the sun goes down, right? Make sure your *marasa* sister accompanies you, my daughter. It's a good thing we'll have at least two people to take care of you. But, believe me, the hardest part is yet to come."

Cocotte

Man Chavannes performed all the necessary sacrifices. She anointed Violaine's fontanel with the blood of a white pigeon as Papa Loko had advised. Meanwhile, the *ounsi kanzo* recited nonstop the sayings of the all-seeing spirits, as well as the appropriate chants for the leaves. Seated in the middle of the *peristil* on a mat, shivering, a blank look on her face, her hair spread around her head like a flaming cloud, Violaine seemed to belong to another world. Her hands, which clung to mine, were dry and burning hot like pine needles. Man Chavannes made her ingest a gooey, putrid, dirty-looking concoction, if I judge by the spasms of disgust that shook Violaine. Then she bathed her in a blend of the juices from the prescribed leaves and massaged her stiff limbs vigorously along with her tense back and arched hips. Suddenly drowsy, the troubled young woman finally began to relax. At that point, though limp and swaddled in a blanket, we placed her astride Man Chavannes' old mule. The *manbò* accompanied us as far as she could. But once we approached the upper part of the city, Violaine had to get down. Since she was very unsteady, she leaned on me as we furtively crept back to our room. Intoxicated from the Loko's bath, she is now sleeping, breathing normally, as light as a breeze. At long last, she is resting. With tears in my eyes I look more closely at the violet hue of her long eyelids, her quivering eyes, and the childlike smile on her swollen lips. Papa Loko, my Beautiful Mirror, watch over and protect her for me in all your omnipotence!

Just then pebbles begin to clatter against the blinds. It's Jean-Jacques, Alexandre's brother. I race down the stairs and hurry to the front door. Jean-Jacques hands me a message for Violaine and whispers in my ear.

"Alex would like you to come to our house before daybreak. It's very important. Don't say anything to anybody. Not a word to anyone, you understand!"

I slip the message under Violaine's pillow and lightly touch my lips to her forehead (it's cool now; everything seems to be all right), then I scamper out the door. Once more, I'm making my way through that tangle of side streets that crisscross the city like a network of veins out of control. After dashing quickly across the Plas Zam, then continuing on beyond Gran Ri, I start to breathe more easily when finally within the shelter of the scaly facades found in the more densely populated neighborhoods. A dog is barking at the moon somewhere. You can hear endless whisperings through the thin walls of the buildings. These sections of town never completely go to sleep anyway. Slums are frenetic by nature, it's inevitable. Plans are continuously pieced together, schemes endlessly "brewing" in the stifling, rat-infested rooms. Extreme poverty overruns the place—impossible to defeat it, but you always have to try to bring it under control nonetheless. Every day, life has to be invented all over again. You have to be quick of mind, get up very early in the morning to survive on this slippery earth of disinherited tightrope walkers. Yet, in their dark streets you can move about in peace. Everyone there knows we all have our own problems and that the road to solving them is always fraught with peril. The dark lanterns lining these neighborhoods give off virtually no light at all even though their acetylene odor permeates the greasy mud below. All the same, the shantytown continues its subterranean life.

Finally, I make it to the small, friendly house. Sor Mélie pours a delicious-smelling cup of coffee whose aroma warmly greets me in the early morning chill. Alexandre, who has been standing watch behind the blinds, pulls me into the main room. The blue flame from the alcohol stove outlines our furtive shadows on the walls.

Marcadieu is there. A traveler from Dammari, he's a huge, calm man whose broad red face is lit by his small, brightly shining eyes. He drinks his hot coffee by taking small discreet sips, all the while blowing softly into his cup. He brings with him into Sor Mélie's *kay* that invigorating breath of sea spray and tides. His serene gaze settles momentarily on me, then questions Alexandre.

"Yes," the latter responds to the unspoken question of the tall man. "Cocotte is our sister. She's strong and silent. She knows the mountain like the back of her hand. But just wait 'til we get her dressed up like she's supposed to be. No one will mistake her for a city girl."

Alexandre leads me to the back of the room. "We have to act quickly, Cocotte. Our friends need us. They arrived this very night at Dammari in three rowboats. So you see, we have to get them out of harm's way. You'll have to lead some of them to your village on the mountainside while I take care of the others. Understood? Now, Mama Mélie, lend her some old clothes and transform her into a mountain girl. Quickly, we don't have much time."

Trembling, Sor Mélie helps me slip on a plain chambray dress, wrap the muslin scarf folded into a triangle around my hips, tie the *tiyon* of red satin on my head, and finally fasten some peasant sandals on my feet.

"Cocotte, take care of yourself," she murmurs, "and watch out for Alexandre, too—you know he never protects himself. God be with you, my children!"

Alexandre had swapped his jeans and schoolboy sneakers for a baggy pair of canvas pants and rough leather sandals. A dark blue smock and a straw hat completed his transformation into a mountain peasant. Perfect! Except for our hands, we'll look just like a young peasant couple coming back from Saturday's market. Walking briskly, we leave the city, angling along the beach. Once on the road, still thick with fog from the night, we come across a funeral procession. Two powerfully built young men are shouldering an enormous casket made from poorly hewn planks that are all out of square and blackened from use. It's an evil box, surrounded by nauseous fumes. My blood runs cold. This must be misfortune itself passing right before us. "My Suffering," as it is rightfully called, is the communal coffin from Jérémie's prison. The men are making their way toward the pauper's grave with their sinister burden. According to custom, they always follow the most complex route, panting heavily, huffing and puffing to the rhythm of their dance, three steps forward, two backward to ward off death, to throw it off the trail of the living once and for all.

"Damnation, what terrible luck this early in the morning!" complains Marcadieu, spitting over his shoulder. "What unfortunate soul did they snatch away from his miserable life last night?"

Two saddled horses tied to a coconut palm are waiting for us. Marcadieu mounts his as Alexandre lifts me up behind him, and then we are off, slicing through the dawn's blue air, toward Dammari. The horses make their way at a good clip along a path only barely visible to the human eye. The breeze whipping our faces is filled with unusual smells, fresh flowers and ripe tobacco, and all carried along on gusts of wind from Cuba, the big island not too far from us.

As we arrive in the small market town of Latibolyè, a rosy tint already fringes the early morning light. It will easily take us an hour to cross the Montagnac plantation, one whole hour just to ride through its narrow rows of cacao trees whose broad, polished leaves glisten under the rising sun's caress, as their long seed pods rattle like a thousand tiny bells. Visibly worried and, as a result, indifferent to the beauty around us, Alexander whips his horse on. At last we ride into Dammari. The sun at that moment is just rising over the crest of the mountains. The houses, faded and run-down, stoically exhibit the traces of their downfall as well as the remains of their glory, that grand era of cocoa. Steadily, they guide us toward the port, scarcely in better shape than they are. How could I have guessed that what I saw before me, as if in a crystal ball, was what Jérémie would become after the big massacre? Do you know, in those days, Jérémie was still a city full of life?

Dammari sleeps on. Not even a cat in the dusty streets. Marcadieu hustles toward an abandoned warehouse, where he calls out in a low voice, "Hey there! Va-Malere! Hey, are you there?"

"I'm here, my friend," answers Va-Malere in the same tone. "For God's sake get in here, and do it quickly. The sun is starting to come up!"

With just a slight hand movement Marcadieu signals us to follow him. We enter the musty darkness of a large room whose solid metallic framework is rusting away. A group of silent men is seated on the floor in the back. Their cargo has been unloaded and placed in one corner of the warehouse: boxes and bundles, all wrapped in drab, olive-green canvas. One of the men, a real live *barbudo* like you see in *Bohemia*, the newspaper for Cuban revolutionaries, breaks off from the rest of the group and slowly comes over to us. It's Jacques, Alexandre's friend.

"Here I am, brother. I told you I'd come back!" He whispers while warmly wrapping his friend in his arms. "I guess you realize we're going to fight!"

Alexandre closes his eyes. "Yes," he answers, "we will fight. But it'll be very hard, Jacques. They're strong, these sons-of-bitches, and heartless as well."

"We'll take them, you'll see. The country is with us!"

Marcadieu shakes his head. "We've already lost one, Alex. It was one of our fighters who didn't know how to swim. He jumped into the ocean as soon as he could see the shores of Haiti. The poor bastard couldn't swim a stroke. It was just because he let his emotion get the best of him, or so they say. You'll have to explain to them, my brother, that if they allow themselves to be swept away with that same kind of emotion, then there will be no revolution. Oh, none at all! The *makout* aren't children. They're everywhere, and believe me, they don't fool around. When they shoot, they use real machine guns!"

The rest of their palavering is lost somewhere in my memory. They continued to dream, rave on about freedom, about the national *konbit* and on and on. "Remake the country!" They were ready to die. But dying is not enough. Ay, to die like that.

So, Alexandre finally divided them into two groups. One that followed me silently up the mountainside with their mules loaded down with God knows what, and the other that he led off toward Les Irois, a small outpost inhabited by rugged men, smugglers, runaways as well as Les Irois fishermen with their red oakum dreadlocks and their salt-soaked skin, all gray and pickled from the water. These were men cooked under the Caribbean sun, tough men who never batted an eye.

Those who followed Alexandre walked behind a very tall, long-legged man, effectively a squacco heron. I saw him for only a couple of minutes before he left, but I have never forgotten his gaze, nor his voice, nor that powerful gentleness that emanated from his whole being. That day, he wasn't your run-of-the-mill man walking alone unto himself. In fact, one could even say he was mounted, inhabited, by a commanding *lwa*. Ay, Virgin Altagras! I watched them go off in the distance toward Les Irois through wisps of sunlight shimmering off the round backs of the waves. The sea was pitching and rolling as it glistened below, apparently as unsettled as the bottom of my heart. I spun around quickly and pushed my flock onward in the direction of the somber emerald green of the mountain, up toward the silent bulge of Mount Macaya.

Cocotte

Time has begun to haul windward. June is already here, along with its procession of first communions and the butterflies of Saint John's Day. A certain lethargy has taken over the city. The women rise at dawn, already stifled by the heat, only to collapse in the early afternoon, overcome by a heavy, troubled sleep. Sweaty children, their strident cries echoing throughout the city, race about, armed with long sticks, relentlessly chasing the butterflies that scatter in the sunlight like golden bubbles, nuggets floating off into the sky.

So, just another Sunday morning in June. Eleven o'clock and already the corrugated rooftops are crackling under the burning, yellow rays of the sun. Violaine is pacing restlessly around the room.

"Calm down, sister, try to be at peace in your heart. You need all of your wits about you, now! And with this oppressive heat, you're just going to make yourself sick. Give me your blouse so I can iron it. It's completely soaked!"

The day promises to be sweltering. Although Jérémie is exposed to the trade winds that strike the coast, it suffocates all the same just like one of those indistinguishable little villages found inland. There's not a cloud above in a flawless, blue sky. The tepid, stagnant air, devoid of even the slightest beneficent breeze, embalms everything, making it seem sticky like a pineapple liqueur. From our balcony, the city and its most immediate surroundings resemble a vast ant colony. Done up in their Sunday best, a crowd of people from the four corners of the horizon is converging at the red brick church. Little by little a festive atmosphere takes hold. Smells of simple holiday preparations waft from the houses: walnut chocolate (creamy and fragrant in its bird-sized cups), pralines, grenadine pastries, the powdered freshness of the dragées, and milk caramels, the sweet ones. With these childhood aromas, my mind takes flight on enchanted wings toward that time far away when we were queens for just such a day, Violaine and I. But today, the turmoil in our hearts clashes openly with the spirited formality of first communions.

Ah! Here comes Béa in a pink dress, her shiny black hair pulled back and held in place on one side by an orchid, her splendid brown skin playing hide-and-seek through the lacework in her blouse. Accompanying her, Philippe Edouard is dressed in a white linen suit, a blue shirt, and a straw-yellow tie. He listens distractedly to his sister's chatter. It's quite apparent that he, too, is ill at ease.

"Look, Violaine, just look at that furrowed forehead of his, his somber, blank stare. Something is smoldering in there, can't you see it? Ah! Take a closer look at him, my dear! Nevertheless, you have to admit he's a very handsome fellow, with his Clark Gable mustache, his golden skin, his black curls! Just look at him there!"

"Ay, Cocotte, spare me your silly ideas! I've told you before I just don't see the same Philippe Edouard you do. This image you've created of him doesn't make any impression on me whatsoever. Besides, I've got other things to worry about now, right?"

"Really? And what are they?"

Violaine looks at me with a horrified expression. "Cocotte! How can you dare ask a question like that?"

"Listen, Violaine, I'm very much aware of the fact you're in love, but in the meantime that doesn't stop the world from turning! And then, if you'd only listen closely to what I'm saying, I think you should take a trip, somewhere, anywhere, to the ends of the earth to get away from this curse. Once more, you've chosen the impossible, but this time, my dear, the impossible is truly impossible! You're a daughter of chance, yourself; and since the *lwa* are with you, everything can still be worked out! Give it up, Violaine! Can't you see you're both headed for destruction? You know how your parents will react. They'll kill you rather than accept Alexandre in your life!"

"Cocotte!" she sighed taking refuge in my arms. "Ah! Cocotte, I can't help loving him, I can't stop! Please, hug me close, give me some strength. Hug me tightly!"

I rock Violaine back and forth, feeling her quivering, withdrawn body next to mine. I refuse to let my mind wander. I don't want to think about anything because it's all too frightening. I continue rocking her as I watch the colorful garland of peasants unfurling around the square where the church is located. Each couple proudly pushes forward a young candidate for first communion, either a girl crowned with paper flowers or a boy dressed in white and wearing a large, knotted armband. Ah! And then there are those shoes for special occasions, outright instruments of torture. The people who've come down from the mountains and who are accustomed to the freedom of bare feet mosey along with an awkward, self-conscious gait. But today is a celebration and everyone has a certain dignity.

My friends from the lower part of town have gathered around the bandstand. They're wearing their Sunday best, the colors contrasting vividly with their fresh, healthy black skin. Even Anacréon has put on his best-looking (his only!) jacket. The girls taking communion are simply adorable in their organdy dresses. I know what these dresses have cost in late-night vigils, sacrifices, and hardships. But today all is forgotten. Pride beams from every face.

"Come on, Violaine, let's get dressed quickly, it's going to be our turn !"

She's right: first communicants from the upper part of the city are about to make their entry along with their relatives and friends. I won't abandon Violaine. She has to hold her own today without any incident. The second in line to the Delavigne estate, her cousin Gisèle, the daughter of her uncle Hannibal, will be the most celebrated communicant in all of Jérémie. The whole family will be dressed to kill. In double-quick time Violaine slips on her white tailored suit as I jump into my dress decorated with English embroidery. I arrange her hair at the back of her neck. She fastens some small roses into my chignon and then covers her head with that wide-brimmed hat of hers made from very fine straw. A spritz of L'Air du Temps and we're all set. I take her by the shoulders, looking directly into those big eyes of hers that seem to swallow her entire face.

"Come closer so I can put some pink on your cheeks, my beautiful sister, it'll make you look a little better."

"My dear Cocotte!" says Violaine tenderly as she kisses me.

We go down to join our relatives on the porch below. Once there, Madame Delavigne inspects her daughter's attire, which definitely pleases her, particularly the new suit. The straight cut of the linen jacket, almost masculine in appearance, significantly tempers Violaine's explosive femininity. Her high-necked blouse of embroidered batiste makes her look a little Victorian, but in the most complimentary way. She's absolutely beautiful beneath her wide-brimmed hat as it sows flecks of sunlight on her cheeks, nose, and chin. Yes, as pretty as a picture. And then where does this gentle expression of hers, a kind of distinguished pallor, come from? Madame Delavigne looks at her daughter and smiles. After all, life is beautiful!

"The Hannibals," as we call them in our house, make their entry into the square. We go to greet them. Gisèle is dressed like a bride, frumpy in a long, lace dress, a tulle veil, and topped off by a tiara. A pampered little mulatto, she observes from under dark, velvety rimmed eyelids her family bustling around, lavishing so much attention on her. She has milk-white skin (curdled milk, as they murmur with a disgusted smirk in the kitchens of the Hannibal house), pink cheeks, and glossy eyes like dark shellac. She too has inherited that rebellious, midnight-blue crop of hair, though a rather humble response to the auburn flow of lava tumbling down from Violaine's head. "Grandma Chimène's gift!" surmises Violaine, somewhat amused, "a heritage she left both of us. No one can ever mistake you for a white person with a mop of hair like that, huh, my mulatto? Right, my pretty Negro?" She continues to think about this, but still in a rather sardonic way. Violaine is trying to communicate with her eyes a kind of affectionate complicity to her cousin. After all, it's not easy being a Delavigne daughter.

While the Delavignes are congratulating and hugging each other, the Clériacs, the Villedraches, the Laforêts, the Desravines and some of the members of the Desrosiers family make their appearance, surrounding their communicants, all sumptuously dressed in white. Like Madame Delavigne, the other mothers are wearing pastel ensembles with their family jewels; and like Monsieur Delavigne, the other fathers are sporting their most attractive white dress suits, complimented by their finest panama hats. Everyone congratulates each other. So dazzled is Monsieur Desrosiers by the vision of Manon Clériac in all her finery that he begins to hum "Manon, here's the sun!" Everybody smiles benevolently at all this "white linen," at all this "candid integrity" (I'm telling you, people here are very literate).

Saint Louis Church is already filled with all the people from Jérémie and those from the surrounding areas. The time has finally come for all the beautiful people to move toward the front of the nave, where the seats reserved "for families only" have being waiting for them for generations, though ostensibly vacant. Six long rows of seats with crimson cushions, all empty. A murmur of admiration spreads through the multitude packed into the church. The first communicants from the upper part of the city, veritable extraterrestrials, like luminous monsters molded from impalpable flesh, slowly enter and begin down the main aisle, while Mademoiselle Aliette attacks the first bars of the hymn for the day on the harmonium. Then all in one voice, the congregation intones "I am a Christian, which is my glo-or-y, my hope and my salvation . . . !"

I let my thoughts wander, exploring this pious crowd. They are the ones who dance at the Vodou ceremonies, where they are carried away by the same mystical fervor. They securely yield to the sacred trance of the Guinean spirits. Indeed, isn't that Ogoun lurking there under the red cloak of Saint James the Greater, Danbala behind Saint Patrick's frock, Ezili Freda made up as Mater Dolorosa? And only time will tell what malicious spirit inhabits the pure visage of the little Saint Theresa of the Baby Jesus given by the Delavigne family in thanks for the miraculous cure of its sole male inheritor who was wasting away with typhoid fever (I've always felt there was something mischievous about her)? Everything is connected to everything else, as our elders say.

The ceremony drags on. The stifling fumes from the incense drift upward in deadly puffs as the sweltering air becomes still more oppressive from the powerful exhalations exuded by the ecstatic crowd. I'm beginning to suffocate. Suddenly worried, I turn toward Violaine. She's pale as a sheet and is beginning to sway from side to side as if she is about to faint. I know her; she's going to be sick, obviously unable to breathe in the closed atmosphere of the church. Like a robot, she heads for the exit, parting the crowd murmuring its prayers that closes inertly behind her as she passes. I follow her, with dread in my soul. The anguish causing my temples to throb for almost a week now takes hold of me once again. Virgin Mother, what else is she going to do, my foolish, out-of-control sister? I stop in the square in front of the church, momentarily intimidated by the sight of all the Jeremiean men who have gathered there to exchange serious deliberations concerning politics, the circumference of Chéa's sublime behind, the new recruit of the Vert Galant, or the square root of Lotus's boobs, that fallen queen of the bordellos. Violaine, however, continues straight ahead until she comes to an abrupt halt right in front of Alexandre, who is keeping his distance from the rest of the men. She speaks to him in a hushed voice. He listens, eyes gleaming. And then, like a scene from a nightmare, she moves even closer to him, as if walking in her sleep, until she's right up against his body, her breasts against his chest and her face against his, with eyes wide open and her arms dangling at her sides. Petrified, Alexandre doesn't move a muscle.

"Alex," she murmurs softly.

"Violaine," sighs Alexandre.

Already I'm on them, swooping down like a hawk. A mortal silence falls over the white clad men in panama hats. They remain perfectly still as if transformed into salt statues. I grab Violaine and drag her unceremoniously in the direction of the house.

Standing right behind me, Madame Delavigne, who had also decided to leave the church out of concern for her daughter's pallor, saw the whole scene. Jesus Mary! Only I can tell you about the typhoon that must have erupted inside her. She can barely walk. Philippe Edouard helps her, putting his arms around her shoulders as he leads her off toward the Rougemont residence.

Ay, I beseech you, all the Saints, the spirits, all my Guinean *lwa*, what kind of dance are you having us perform now?

Philippe Édouard

It was at that moment I understood my life as a voyeur had just ended. At long last my turn had come to play a role in this comedy I'd been observing rather ironically ever since childhood, biding my time, licking my chops, waiting for the day when finally.

It's true! For many years, I've been poking my nose into Violaine's life, sometimes amused or intrigued by what I found, and sometimes quite angry. But it's not just that. It was always her independence that attracted me, her complete unawareness of being so utterly different, of being woven from a fabric so distinct from ours, of being so enigmatic to the rest of us. She had always shown such tranquil indifference to all our "concocting," our "shaking and baking," as wretched, Jeremiean mulattoes, who consider ourselves chosen beings, while . . . In reality, we were nothing more than carnival kings. Could I ever have foreseen it? She used to drive me crazy, made fun of me and was constantly slipping from my grasp, but somehow I knew that one day she'd be mine, that only I could understand or protect her. That is, until the day I saw Alexandre take her in his arms. That day, every drop in Klere Spring began trembling, as I too trembled with all my heart behind the tree where I was hiding. I saw someone other than my friend Alexandre, because from that moment on "my friend Alexandre" no longer existed. I had to wonder if he had ever existed at all. This type of friendship, I now know, is often nothing more than a delusion in Jérémie. I saw only the dark skin of a man from the other side of the world, a man from that common night of ours filled as it is with hallucinations and taboos. I saw the tenebrous skin of that

Black Man we all faithfully try to chase from our very entrails. Yes, as troubling as it was, I saw that unfathomable skin envelop her like a dirty husk clasping a golden almond.

I kept my eyes open, although it made me die a little more with each passing second. The pain of seeing my love stripped of all hope was nothing in comparison to the revulsion that tore open my heart, nothing in comparison to that fury that took hold of me at the simple sight of this grotesque arrangement: my aristocratic Violaine, a mulatto girl from the upper crust of Jérémie, and Alexandre, a black orphan from nowhere, from the poor side of town.

I finally began to understand to what extent Violaine had escaped the laborious rearing that fashioned and molded us, the children spawned in this country of pain, and at the same time how much I was the perfect product of this complex alchemy of crossbreeding. Our turbulent past, punctuated by fratricidal struggles, suffused with the sounds of clashing weapons, the flow of blood, pestilence and tears, all this had made me into half a man, rigid and unhappy, whereas Violaine . . . Violaine was majestic, free as could be.

There we were, on that narrow, barren piece of land, hopelessly squared off one against the other: Alexandre (with his kind on one side) and I (with my kind on the other). Between us a dreadful magma of contradictory emotions was boiling: fascination and hatred, attraction and rejection, of a violence that our inability to express made all the more volatile.

Thus, that June Sunday, I thought very seriously about all this, thoroughly committing myself to imposing some type of order to the restlessness in my head, in my body, thoroughly committing myself to bringing it all to an end. This love, despite all the yarns the lesson-givers might spin to explain it, was against nature, damn it! And on my word as a man, I'll destroy it. Violaine, herself, provided me with the opportunity to do it today. Ah! Violaine, there really are limits to transgression, don't you think? My shameless Violaine, you openly flaunted your forbidden love right there at the front entrance to Jérémie's Saint Louis Church! But Violaine is a living provocation who can only keep on walking straight toward her own annihilation. Soon Jérémie was going to close its merciless claws on her. Somehow, somewhere in her carefree manner, she had to know it was going to happen.

. . .

I escorted Madame Delavigne home, sat her down in a quiet corner on the terrace while Elasie, our aging maid, fixed her some soothing herbal tea. Then I looked directly into the eyes of this woman, a strong woman like all Haitian women. She was ready to confront the truth (her husband never wanted to know anything about it even up to the very end). I told her everything, trying not to let my emotions get the best of me. When I'd finished my story, she remained silent for a long while as she absorbed the full effect of the shock. Then she took my hand.

"Violaine was promised to you, Philippe. Her natural place was to be at your side. Instead, she chose to go astray, down those forbidden byways where none of us can allow her to venture anymore. Regardless of the cost, we have to find a way to extricate her from this. And extricate ourselves as well because, as you must understand, there is a very real danger for all of us. Are you ready to help me?"

Of course I was ready to help her, and with all my strength! It has all worked out well in one respect, noted Madame Delavigne. Indeed, the whole family had already been called together, and as a result, she would be able to meet with the two eldest women and seek their advice. This was of the utmost importance for all involved since it was a situation concerning women.

"If it isn't too much trouble, I'd like you to be there. You know the whole story and can be useful to us. And then we have to find something, anything, without wasting too much time to remove Alexandre from the picture. This is crucial, if we really want to have a chance at stabilizing the situation."

"Ah, leave him to me, my dear lady!" I felt the deceitful mask of the traitor slipping over my kind, young male face at that very moment. Yes, in all truth, I was going to be as vicious as possible, even disgusting. I wanted it that way, without any scruples or feelings getting in the way. "Leave him to me! He's up to his neck in a messy story about an invasion. The police don't know it yet, but I'll bring it to their attention."

"Ah! Is that right? What a fool to get involved in that kind of nonsense! Please take care of the matter, Philippe Edouard, and don't dillydally."

Madame Delavigne seemed to be in perfect control of herself now, but I dreaded for Violaine the explosion of violence that would inevitably take place. Calmly, she got up to leave. Only a slight trembling of her hands betrayed how shaken she was in her soul.

. . .

Six o'clock in the evening. The night hasn't yet deepened into full darkness. A light breeze coming off the ocean finally begins to make the air somewhat less oppressive. I'm walking calmly toward the Delavigne house, but all the same, I have to confess that my heart is pounding away. In order not to attract the attention of the rest of the family, Madame Delavigne has me come in the back part of her house, which she uses for her boutique. She'll be pleased with what I have to tell her because, even though I really put myself out this afternoon, it wasn't in vain.

The room is dark. The first thing you notice is that aged, stately smell so characteristic of the offices of the big coffee exporters. Everything is made of expensive wood saturated over time from ink, green coffee dust, and musty old papers. The two women elders are seated around a large, mahogany roll-top desk—a kind of hollow presence, as well as a pompous, if not laughable, reminder of the absent master of this house. They seem to be captives of the halo falling from the green, opaline lampshade. Madame Delavigne was waiting for me. The hand she places on my arm is no longer trembling, only cold and hard. I bow respectfully before the older women. Nodding in acknowledgment but still quite formidable in their gray satin dresses, they look me squarely in the eyes as they set their long coral earrings in motion by their movements. No doubt about it, here are two beautiful specimens of provincial high society that you could even say were preserved given

the ceruse color of their skin and the fact that they'd always avoid-
ed the sun like the plague in order not to spoil it. Authentic store-
houses of traditions as well as prejudices, they wield an unexpected
power on any and all inclined to give in to the patriarchal appearances of Jeremiean mores. Rather impressed by so much venerable
attention concentrated on me alone, I let myself sink down into the
chair placed there for me and begin to study Madame Delavigne
more attentively. She is going to tell us about her meeting with Violaine that had taken place that very afternoon.

"Ay, Aunt Tika! To have children these days is unquestionably
to embark on a bothersome trail filled with many surprises. This
impertinent Violaine of mine, you should have heard how she
spoke to her mother, the tone she used! Ah no, there are limits to
what we can tolerate! I gather she is trying to pass off her shame as
anger. Alas, the situation is very serious, much more serious than
you might imagine. Brace yourselves, and don't forget I'm the one
telling you this!" A long silence followed, then she started again
abruptly. "Violaine's expecting a baby, and it was she herself who
insulted me with this news, yes! She's pregnant, thanks to her vag-
abond, that barefoot black peasant tramp! My own daughter! God
Almighty, are we put on this earth simply to atone for faults over
which we have no power? Ay, this burden, this very kind of burden
is just too heavy for our shoulders to bear!"

Madame Delavigne's beautiful face crumbles into pain, humiliation, and finally hatred. The two old women are unable to speak,
as their eyes bulge from their heads. Aunt Tika begins to shake con-
vulsively, while Aunt Frida, the stronger of the two, turns purple
from anger or simply from amazement. As for me, my heart sinks
to my stomach with what seems like a loud thud. Huge, silent tears
start to fall from Madame Delavigne's eyes. Then Aunt Frida explodes. "Stop crying, Clorinde! This is not the time for grieving.
After all, Violaine won't be the first to undergo an abortion on the
sly and then depart afterward for a long voyage in Europe! Calm
down, my child. There's a cure for everything. And don't forget,
we're the strongest. And if not, may lighting strike me down here
and now! If your daughter's blood is so tainted that she can go mix

with people like that, you understand of course that it's not a question of her splattering us! I know the perfect person for our situation, but we'll have to go up into the mountains to meet with him."

"Ay, Aunt Frida!" sighs Madame Delavigne. "You don't understand the full extent of our misfortune! She absolutely refuses to have an abortion. She's going to keep him, keep her little black baby. You know Violaine and how infernally stubborn she can be! This accursed daughter of mine is going to bring on a terrible scandal, incite rioting and ransacking, only to leave the ruins behind! What can we do? I'm telling you, she's going to drag us all into the mud with her. That's exactly what she wants!"

To look at Madame Delavigne, so crestfallen, so troubled, to hear her grating voice, I can only imagine the outburst, the fury of the battle that must have erupted several hours earlier in that room she decorates with roses and other assorted bouquets. I begin to imagine, as if I were there, this fiery woman lighting into her daughter, knocking the girl's head out of joint with every slap. I later learned, and it certainly was no big surprise, that she had even spit in her daughter's face and that Violaine, equally out of control, had done the same to her. I took a certain perverse joy in conjuring in my mind's eye this fabulous spectacle in which these tall, tawny females tore into each other, hair flying wildly about, with such reciprocal ferocity—the kind that only they knew how to inflict upon each other.

"We are left with only one solution; and as real women, we must not flinch, must not show any fear whatsoever."

The firm voice of Aunt Tika, who, obviously, has regained her composure rouses me from my strange reverie. "You understand, my dear Clorinde, that our shame must remain our secret. We have to act therefore before 'too late' sneaks up and surprises us. After all, we're Haitians in our own land, we shall return to our roots and take care of our affairs as it has always been done, that is, in absolute secrecy. Let's send for Eliacin and give him our instructions. His duty is to carry them out, ours is to command. It's our role. And as a result, things will return to normal."

What an old harpy! Though pale, the old woman, just like one of the mythical Fates, was still full of venom. Only much later did I come to understand the gravity of the decision she had just decreed. But, given the heavy silence that had followed her words, I sensed something deeply troubling nonetheless. Then finally, in a booming voice that produced a strange kind of resonance, Madame Delavigne spoke.

"*Ago bilolo!* I understand perfectly what you're saying, Aunt Tika. We have no choice!"

This African invocation coming from Madame Delavigne's mouth chilled me to the bone. I didn't know any of the cryptic words that had been uttered, but I was stopped dead in my tracks, struck with horror as they were pronounced. As they continued, I couldn't make out exactly what was being said, but they managed to rekindle in me familiar fears, those feelings of shame regarding what I experienced as a little boy, shivering from fright and hidden behind the bougainvillea listening to the stories told by my parents' servants about werewolves and *chanpwèl* throughout those interminable evening gatherings in December. But from even further back, there came surging out of the depths of my being the memory of an intense discomfort, the same kind that had gripped my throat when, as a child, I had discovered for the first time that anomalous, barbarous, incomprehensible "oratory" belonging to my mother. It was a hybrid accumulation of Western and African remnants, screaming out for all to hear in its strident colors, hidden away in the back of her closet, hidden away in the twilight of her subterranean life. During that time I had refused with every ounce of strength I could muster to accept this motley, bastard identity. Even today, the slightest reminder of my African origins (so far away!) burns me like a stigma that is too disgraceful to mention, like a fatal blemish or an ignominious mark of some kind. And here once again it was crashing down upon me with the weight of a crude reality—its magic, its obscurity and occult powers, seemingly with the whole weight of Africa, and all this from the mouth of Madame Delavigne herself. Had I suddenly been transported into the middle of a nightmare from a bygone era? And how many times have I heard it said that dreams and reality coexist indissolubly for us throughout every moment of our life? Africa for dreaming, the West for reasoning. In actuality, it's neither one nor the other, but both at the same time, a straitjacket for deranged people of mixed blood, in effect a curse. From what kind of humus is our soul made that it frightens us each time it's fully exposed to our scrutiny? In which language are we supposed to express our thirst? With which one of our hearts do we cry? And of what does the sunlight of our laughter consist? What about the sky that abandoned us? Which God, which gods dance in the heavens? With its incandescent cinnamon color, our skin covers, as best it can, that black sin we all shamefully bury deep inside ourselves.

In the thin light bathing the room, Madame Delavigne and the two old women seemed to be surrounded by deadly, poisonous fumes, so thick you could almost feel them on your skin. Yet they didn't budge an inch. Their very immobility conferred upon them a kind of malevolent grace. I was actually beginning to see them as they really were, stripped of their social vestment: Bizango, Gede Nouvavou, Marinèt Bwa Chèch, Gran Brijit, whichever *lwa* suits your fancy, but most assuredly powerful and feared. I swear to you, nothing I saw with my own two eyes was invented. These women are not your "safe-and-sound" types, I can assure you. They belong to an infernal, unstable world, a world between two worlds. Madame Delavigne is coming to life, but just barely. Then slowly she turns toward me, the features of her face firmly fixed.

"I would have killed her with my own hands, Philippe. Violaine is my daughter, flesh of my flesh. No one would have had to help me do it. I have within me more than enough love for her, but her mistake goes beyond the laws of the maternal womb. Now she has to atone for it herself. She still hasn't lived long enough, hasn't yet experienced real suffering. Consequently, she has nothing to give in exchange for the grace bestowed upon her. From this point on, Violaine's fate belongs to those Spirits in charge of repressing all forms of disorder. It is no longer in our control."

Madame Delavigne has her back to the light. Riveted on her every move, my eyes begin to blur. Tears? Or was it suddenly an immense fatigue, the result of all the confusion? At first her silhouette stands out clearly against the light, elegant, thin, and gracious, terribly Western and reassuring in her tailored Parisian dress . . . But then little by little, she starts wrapping herself in gaudy old rags, red silk scarves, *wanga*, gris-gris, multicolored feathers, and garish, glass pearls. Her face grows dark, her lips pasty and more clearly defined, as her eyes seem to congeal from the ecstasy of the trance coming over her. Ah! Her too, Africa hidden behind a fragile veil! The large, wooden blades from the fans above our heads whirl rhythmically in unison with the beats of my heart, in concert with the shooting pain that grips my skull.

"What are you going to do to her?" I yell, distraught from my anguish. Aunt Frida speaks without even a glance in my direction.

"Clorinde, don't answer this young man. Keep your mouth shut! It's over now. No one needs to say anything more. But it's also true that words would have little currency in the realm we're about to venture into. Have someone summon Eliacin and be quick about it. This isn't the time to fool around." Violaine's destiny has irremediably come to a stop. She's going to die, that's clear, but how it'll happen is another question. What kind of loathsome death will it be? I know enough about these things to ask the right question, but not enough to answer it. Or perhaps I'm just refusing to consider the inevitability of the horrific punishment lying in wait for her.

Suddenly, anger, a blind revolt, something rises up in me in protest. I picture Violaine walking once again in the middle of the Plas Zam. It's really the way she walks and nothing more than her sway that sets the city on fire. The simple fact is that she exudes life. And then, of course, there are those fiery Bengal eyes of hers.

"Don't harm her! Give her to me, she's mine!"

The three women look at each other in silence, their eyes searching one another. After all, by laying claim to Violaine I'm perhaps providing the very solution they've dreamed of. Their discussion rages back and forth for what seems an eternity. The two older women are in no hurry to be persuaded. My proposition entails some risk, but it's an uncommon solution. Madame Delavigne pleads my case, out of affection for me and also out of weakness for her own daughter. Apparently, she won the rest of them over after a hard-fought struggle, because here she comes now to explain to me quite gently as if speaking to a child.

"What you ask for isn't impossible, Philippe Edouard. There's a way of doing these things. Violaine was destined for you. We'll give her to you, if you wish. But think seriously about what I'm about to say. If we give in to your desire, your life will never be the same again. You'll be committing yourself to serve. You'll be the slave of a slave and will have to answer for it before some powerful Spirits. You'll be the guardian of someone who will sleepwalk through the rest of her life, which is certainly an ungrateful, solitary task. Once again, I encourage you to think long and hard about this. Are you sure you can handle confronting death on a daily basis? You see, from this point on, Violaine will always remain on the edge of Bawon Samdi's kingdom. You must have a pretty good head on your shoulders to deal with this kind of proximity because, as you have understood, no doubt, it will be a *zonbi*, one of the living dead, that we shall place in your hands."

Cocotte

Sor Mélie's eyes are dry now. She's sitting very straight in her chair explaining to me in a steady voice. "They came Sunday night, beating on the door like deaf people. Finally they kicked it in. You see, Jean-Jacques had left earlier for the hardware store to get something to repair it with and was supposed to be back any minute." I look closely at Sor Mélie, trying to hold back my tears as she goes on.

"They took Alexandre away just as he was, in his shorts. He didn't have a stitch of clothing on. They didn't even give him a chance to put on his shoes. They shoved him into their pickup and sped off. I could hear them yelling at him as they drove away. Jean-Jacques and I still haven't figured it all out. But I know my own son, Cocotte. Alex is a fighter. He won't kowtow to anyone. But, after all, are we nothing more than animals? Are we allowed no human identity whatsoever in this country of Ayiti Toma? And our life and death, shouldn't they have greater importance than those of mere cattle being led off to the slaughterhouse?"

"When will we have the right to defend ourselves? What about the legal system in this society? My children's father died with his civil code in hand. He said to his sons, 'This Book, this Book you see before you, as long as it is blatantly ignored in this country, not one step of progress will be made!' And in fact, it's quite true. So here we are today in a situation where they've taken Alexandre without a warrant, without anything. They just came and took him wherever they wanted. Like I keep telling you, it was as if they were taking an animal away! They'll do whatever they please with him. As for us, we'll never know anything about it. And our only recourse will be the right to keep silent."

I threw my arms around Sor Mélie's neck. "Mélie, oh! Mélie, oh! You have more courage than all of us put together! But, you'll see, we won't let them get away with it. We'll stand beside you. Alexandre belongs to us, too. We'll find a way to snatch him from their clutches!"

Sor Mélie looks at me shaking her head, a sad smile parting her lips, a smile coming from the heart of our sordid history of crimes and abuses. Unable to endure this any longer, I steal away like a thief. Violaine! What could I possibly say to her at this point?

I quietly open the bedroom door. There she is in the shadowy darkness. I see her bare back and think to myself: "This is not the back of a defeated person, not the back of someone overwhelmed, no, not her! She has a strong back. Ah! Violaine, it's truly you I see there!" She's seated on her bed, nude from the waist up, her hair all in disarray, her white slip spread around her. She turns around abruptly. Even the erect nipples of her breasts betray a certain pugnaciousness. Her eyes are dry, like Sor Mélie's. She hands me a piece of paper all wadded up on which Alexandre's large handwriting can be seen dancing about in every direction. The note was written in haste. "They're taking me away, Violaine. I don't know where. They won't kill me. I don't want to die. Just for you, I'll try to stay alive, I promise. I'll do my best to keep you informed. Be strong. Alexandre." Violaine doesn't cry because tears would be completely inappropriate in this situation. Alexandre is a fighter, and people aren't supposed to shed tears for them. Nonetheless, Violaine's eyes are filled with flashes of emotion. There is an anger deep within her that literally terrifies me.

"It was Philippe Edouard, Cocotte. He's the one who reported Alexandre to the police. The mousy little gendarme who brought me his note told me the whole story. It was Philippe Edouard."

Rage explodes in her as she throws the heavy brush she was holding against the ivory-framed mirror on the wall. It shatters into pieces, each of its shards bleeding from the purple twilight streaking the floor through the louvered blinds. Ah! Just look, the sun has already gone down. Threatening and as swift as can be, this day has flown by like a flock of crows. And finally Violaine begins to speak. She begins by telling me all the fisherman from Les Irois have been massacred.

"Alexandre's messenger told me the *makout* were searching for a communist leader, an exile from Cuba, hidden by the fishermen. They swooped down on Les Irois like birds of prey and soon found the rebel. They recognized him right away. People say he was a famous writer, very tall, very black, but also with that distinguished air of a leader. At first glimpse of him, it was easy to see what they meant. The *makout* stoned him, Cocotte, killed him just like that. The little gendarme told me he couldn't bear to watch this manhunt, it was so horrible. And even though a stone had struck the hunted man in the right eye, he continued to run, his injured eye dangling from its socket. Ah! Those savage dogs! Then they took out their machine guns and slaughtered the whole village. At least that's what this pitiful little man trembling from fear told me! In addition, he said they were now accusing Alexandre of hiding the rebel himself in Les Irois. This is all very serious. And to think that it was Philippe Edouard who informed the police about him! Death would be too kind for him, believe me! I promise you, he'll pay. He'll pay for Alexandre and for every one of the villagers struck down in Les Irois because of him! But let's take care of more urgent things. The little soldier explained everything to me: 'Listen, Manzè Violaine, at all costs he has to get to Port-au-Prince alive. You have to help him. As you know, if he dies en route, no one will even talk about it. Cut off from the rest of the world, the provinces are like a backwater that swallows everything. In Port-au-Prince they can raise a fuss about all this, try to get him released.' So, we have to see to it he arrives in Port-au-Prince alive. We're going to gather all the money we can to grease the palms of those helping escort him to the capital. At this point they should have reached Les Cayes. We'll send Jean-Jacques with the money to catch up with them. Cocotte, quickly now!"

Violaine then gave me a small box containing green paper bills, gold pieces, and assorted gems, all of which was to be converted into bribe money at the pawnbroker's, at the "business office," or the *plàn*, as it was called. After all, that's what it was for. All the desperate souls have had recourse to it at one time or another!

It's completely dark now around the Plas Zam, as if everything were plunged into muddy water. Only the window of our room, a small lantern in distress, shines in the night. I cross the square as quickly as possible, running straight toward the faint glimmer. Jean-Jacques has already left for Les Cayes. Mission accomplished!

"Violaine, he's gone!" I blurt out, opening the door in the same burst of energy.

Ashen white, she's there stretched out on the parquet floor. Jesus, she's white as a ghost, right there, lying on the ground. As I examine her more closely, I'm taken aback. From her thighs, between her legs, flows a blackish, somewhat lumpy, liquid, which is still spurting out. Ay, her very life is slipping away as this dark, gooey stream continues to gush from her. Violaine! I lean over her. Her eyes open and desperately look straight into mine. As I press my ear to her mouth, she murmurs: "In the drawer, Man Chavannes's bottle." Sure enough, in the drawer, I find a small blue vial. I have her swallow the entire contents because I know Madame Chavannes always distributes her potions in fixed dosages: a bottle, a pinch. Slowly, Violaine starts to recover. But all the more terrifying is the fact that this black blood full of thick clots continues to trickle from her. My God, what can we do to stop this deadly flow?

"It's all right," she whispers, "Papa Loko warned us of this, right? I wasn't supposed to keep this baby. It just didn't belong to me, Cocotte."

Ah! My sister, now I recognize this expression on your face. It makes me remember my childhood up on the mountain when we used to go help the little goats give birth to their kids. You have their look, one filled with a strange kind of questioning, a look into which all the suffering of the world would ebb, in spite of the love and care we gave; and then deep in their eyes was always this sense of waiting, an endless waiting. It's that look of all female creatures from time immemorial faced with the mystery of their womb.

Finally, I understand. Now, I know what to do! Without a moment's hesitation, I climb up and straddle her, pressing on her stomach with all my strength. Courage, valiant woman, everything has to come out! Because of the sheer pain, Violaine bites into her wrist as tears fill her eyes. But not a whimper slips from her lips. I push again and again, oof, on this fertile stomach of hers, which now only spews forth death. I murmur "Violaine, steady now, we'll get through it together, take heart!" Yet, at the same time, I think "We're going down, sinking further and further into misfortune!" (Life is also sometimes *marasa*. And in that regard there had been two seeds from which our life had sprung.) And then again you know what else I'm thinking? "Ah! And the others? Those that I hid myself, the others, are they still there on the mountainside?"

Yes, even at the very moment I was struggling to keep Violaine alive, I was also, in a sense, on the hillside with the half-dozen young fools Alexandre had entrusted to me. And all these thoughts swirled in my poor head at the same time.

. . .

I open my eyes. Dawn is unfurling its tattered orange colors around me. Violaine is already at the window. Just like every morning, she's always there, at daybreak singing away watching the sun rise. The golden globe of the sun climbs high behind the woolly, frizzy-topped hillsides that surround the bay of Jérémie, glazing and then spreading over them like a luscious guava jelly. The air at daybreak smells crisp and fragrant, its perfume of leaves and pine wood filtering all the way up under my warm sheets. And the marketplace below keeps purring like a cat as it dishes out its unrelenting morning litany.

Would you believe it? Both of us are serene, quite tranquil, or even, as some might put it, back to normal. The predictions of the *lwa* have turned out to be right on the money. What more can we do now? Despite the suffering, we are at peace.

Violaine's hands are at rest, calm like sleeping birds on her thighs. She's seated on that window ledge completely surrounded by ocher. Though a little pale, her face has a soft texture, rather placated at this moment of grace. She's savoring, somewhat blissfully, the early hour as it slowly inundates the room with its smells and light. Soon, she's going to have to marshal all her strength to face the day, yet another day of struggle. Ah! Merciful moment of abandonment!

I jump out of bed and bound toward the office where I help myself to a basket of coral-pink island mangoes. They're sun-drenched and small like eggs but with a fragrance that intoxicates you right on the spot. Then I climb back upstairs with my booty and sit cross-legged on the rattan carpet to eat my fill at leisure. "Hey, Violaine, here's some for you. Tell me what you think of them!" Solid food has always had a positive influence on our mood.

We devour our mangoes, delighting in their saffron-colored juice that sticks to our fingers and mouths, while the clear morning air fills the room with its crystalline quality. Violaine finally stops her daydreaming and slowly turns her head toward me. I'm struck by the fact that she seems unusually sluggish, sort of drowsy, and reluctant to make any movement whatsoever. But it's because she's storing up energy, absorbing through all her pores the life and strength vibrating around her.

The pain of the baby's death, that pain straight from one's entrails, a woman's pain, the pain of love, a pain so strong it takes your breath away, has shaken Violaine to the core. But you shouldn't forget she's also a courageous *marasa* before the *lwa*, an authentic *ounsi kanzo*, definitely a stormy head, yes indeed, but that's just the way it is. Each new torture purifies her, draws her closer to her primitive truth. Each little death makes her grow all the more. The Spirits wanted it that way. When they choose you, your life (no mistake about it) ceases to be a bed of roses. So, my little salamander has learned to grit her teeth all the more to be reborn just that much stronger.

"You know, Cocotte, tonight's the big dance at the Excelsior Club. Did you see? My gown arrived from Port-au-Prince two days ago. I haven't even looked at it yet. But I've already decided I'm going to go to this dance. What do you think about that?"

Violaine is showing signs of waking up. Ay, my lioness has begun to stir, watch out!

"Of course I saw your dress. It's magnificent. But do you feel up to going through with it? All of the important people will be there tonight, and you'll just cause a huge scandal."

"That's exactly what I want to do, Cocotte. Those people aren't that important, despite their numbers! And then again, what do I have to lose, tell me?"

It's true! She has nothing to lose, the poor kitten! Outside our window, the sun is already standing high over the church. The heavens are sky-blue, and the intensity of the blazing light of dawn has begun to subside. A new, gentle day has spread out over the city of Jérémie . . . Nothing bad should ever happen when the weather is so beautiful! But if life corresponded to the color of the sky, we would have been the happiest country in the world for quite some time, right?

. . .

Partially clad, her towel around her neck and dangling at arm's length a bag filled with her toiletries, Violaine crosses the garden with that dancing gait of hers. A golden mist rises from the grass as the morning light filters through the luxuriant foliage of the mango trees, transforming the vegetation into a sparkling display. She walks into a day filled with the smells of mint, moist earth and lush verdure. The intense jubilation coming from the very earth under her feet lightens her steps. She seems to float like a pink flamingo feather, a humming bird, or a tiny puff of down tossed about by the wind. She hurries toward the back of the property. There, crouched under the lacy canopy of some bamboo trees and surrounded by tiger-striped cannas, a green cabin shelters an ornamental basin . . . Hmmm! From the outside you can see nothing more than a scrupulously clean facade, a very sensible and well-kept exterior of a large Jeremiean house, behind which one would never suspect anything out of the ordinary, especially a secret hideaway just perfect for parading around in the nude. When we were very young, mischievous little girls ("rascals" as Nounou used to call us), Violaine and I were already drawn to the calmness, the mystery of the fountain. We used to sneak in there, our clear voices twittering away. We loved the darkness that smoldered within its confines like the light from an alcove. The mere presence of the enclosed water filled us with a certain seriousness of purpose and our childish laughter quickly faded away as we transformed ourselves into strange aquatic beasts. Without saying a word, without a sound, we'd let go, float freely in the cool water.

Violaine is now crossing the dark mass of foliage in which the fleshy pink of the Indian canes pokes holes here and there. Shortly thereafter, she directs a powerful spray of ice-cold water over her head and down her back, while energetically thrashing about.

"Lustral water, living water, purify me, make me smooth and solid like a stream-worn stone. Simbi of the waters, Simbi of clear springs, you who make the water flow anywhere your heart desires, lead me to the doors of life, strong and full of courage. Open my eyes and arm me to the teeth," murmurs Violaine as she rubs her sore stomach, numb arms, and aching back. She rubs herself all over as if her very life depended on it. Her skin begins to redden, as a lather spreads over it. And when the water finally carries out its full effect, she'll be shiny and hard, fresh as a newborn baby, supple and silky smooth like a freshwater fish, Violaine at sixteen, miraculously transported for a moment to that somber future that awaits her.

Seated on the bare ground, she follows as if in a dream the twists and turns of blue and green birds, the whorls, and the ornamental foliage on the tiled bottom of the basin while pulling a large-toothed comb through her tangled, copper curls. Then after putting on some silver earrings, she adds a touch of perfume just for courage.

"Alexandre," whispers her heart, "Alexandre, I haven't gotten you out of my system, you know. You're still there, very much alive inside of me, grafted and bound to me, a part of me!"

And she mournfully rocks her absent love child, swaying back and forth, right to left, then all around in a circle. "Oh! Alexandre, how I loved your eyes, the fire of your lower back! How I love your courage. I'll follow you to the very end. You'll see, I'm telling you the truth, they won't be able to do anything to us!"

Ay, my friends, words can also be used to exorcise fear. And Violaine is afraid like an animal, indeed very afraid. She feels death all around her and tries to chase it away as she feels it circling in on her like a deadly shark.

· · ·

The Excelsior Club is overflowing with people. The evening gowns and white dinner jackets hide, as well as can be expected, the poor quality of the decor. Inside, there's nothing more than a row of skimpy rooms, filled with heavy, unattractive mahogany furniture, the purest 1930s style imaginable, along with beige walls and glass light fixtures. But the waxed parquet floor shines like a mirror and the buffet table sags under the weight of the food. Hmmph, at least they're aware of how ugly their club is. All these people from the upper city. Just look at them, they've done the same thing they always do for everything. They've camouflaged their insignificance under a cascade of flowers! They've put them everywhere, tumbling down from the ceiling in long clusters, wrapped around all the columns and creeping along the handrails, and strewn over the tables.

In contrast, the women are effortlessly gorgeous. They couldn't be more attractive with their bare, velvety smooth backs, glistening shoulders exhibiting all the infinite nuances of the golden color of mulatto skin, as well as their divine breasts quivering in tiny strapless bras. Yes, they're really beautiful, all these mulatto women from Grandans! And if you only knew how much time they devote to their beauty, always coating their skin and hair with the crushed pulp of every kind of fruit known to the Caribbean region! What's more, they swim like fish in the cold waters of the Voldrogue, which gives them arms and legs like ballerinas, well-muscled yet slender.

Everyone has already arrived when Violaine makes her grand entrance on the arm of her cousin, Dantès Delavigne. Poor Dantès felt obliged to provide this service, but his heavy heart is unmistakable as he escorts his rebellious cousin through the various salons of the club. After Sunday's scandal, people can thoroughly appreciate his lack of enthusiasm. The old women, lined up like a row of onions against the wall in the first room, scrutinize every little detail of his young companion. They alone have tongues still swift and responsive enough to give running commentaries out loud. A privilege perhaps of having lived a long time. But all of them are more or less senile, so their words are worth next to nothing. The others, however, are struck dumb from astonishment. No one could ever have imagined that Violaine would have the audacity to show herself at the big dance tonight. Good Lord, is she ever worth seeing, my beautiful Violaine! You can definitely put your trust in her on that one. Her white tulle gown surrounds her like a sparkling halo, while her moiré satin corselet clings to her slender frame, making her honey-colored skin quiver as she walks. For the first time she is wearing her grandmother's diamond necklace, its oblong stones sprinkle her throat with a string of blue-tinted droplets. Her long hair, rolled in curls for the occasion, gives her the look of Queen Sun. Little by little, as she makes her way further into the crowd, a discernible silence spreads throughout all the rooms. Violaine continues on, even though escorted by all these threatening looks bristling with hatred. And, need I say, her wildcat eyes are her most attractive feature, lighting up her whole face. Her small chin is defiantly thrust forward. Of course she refuses to lower her eyes. To the contrary, she brazenly peers into the throng of people, seeking out her prey, or so it seems. She keeps coming. Then, suddenly she stops. She's right in front of Philippe Edouard. This is what she wanted all along.

"Come, my beautiful angel, come dance with me," she murmurs to him, right against his mouth, her spellbinding eyes looking deep into his. You might even say they're the eyes of a sorceress, or better yet, a she-devil. Philippe Edouard obeys her. The orchestra is playing a polite version of "Caroline Accao," Lumane Casimir's most beautiful song. Violaine drags her unfortunate cavalier into a wild, indeed obscene, merengue, certainly nothing comparable to the syrupy rendition being distilled by the musicians. Into her ball gown has slipped, as if through a magic spell, an energetic mare of the gods, animated by all the passion of the Vodou Olympus. It seems so strange and violently out of place in these ceremonial salons decorated with their pretentious flowers and high mirrors. Philippe Edouard begins to stiffen and turns quite pale. Violaine is now dancing faster, spinning around him, encircling him while frenetically shaking her hips, as well as undulating her shoulders shamelessly to the point of having her bare breasts escape from their satin sheath. What shocking behavior!

Some of the well-to-do guests on the dance floor begin to form a noisy, disapproving, and even threatening circle around her. It's a circle that will eventually close in and engulf Violaine. But for the moment, the magnetism of her dance is holding them at bay, like iron fillings can be repelled by the force field of a powerful magnet.

There! Finally, she stops, planting herself directly in front of Philippe Edouard and begins shouting at him. The orchestra dies down. Violaine's voice is loud and full of vengeance, like that of Ezili Jewouj in all her fury.

"You've been walking over dead bodies, Philippe," she screams. "You smell like death! Like filth! Open up your eyes! They're all around you, the bullet-riddled bodies of peaceful women, children, and men who have been massacred because of you!" She turns to face the others, who are transfixed with amazement because, my God, none of them had ever taken part in a scandal like this at the club before. "And the rest of you people, all of you! For once, flowers won't cover over the horror! This time, you're going to look at it squarely in the eye. I'm going to make you face up to it! That's right, no one else but me! Enough of this deception, you bunch of hypocrites!" At first Jean Maximilien Laforêt, a man who's respected, "respectable" as they say, certainly a restrained man, tries to reason with Violaine, then loses his patience and forcibly attempts to subdue her as quickly as possible. Ay, but she escapes from him! Then she begins howling like a Fury from hell. "Yes, you're all hypocrites! Everyone knows you, knows you're very skilled at putting your pride aside in order to jump in the same bed with all the corrupt politicians, criminals, and thieves, particularly when they're in power! You figure out how to cover up all their dirty tricks, or even end up using them to your own advantage!" Suddenly quite calm, she turns to glare straight at Monsieur Tilaire, who is standing nearby, and then soaks him with a magnificent gob of spit. Apparently, he wasn't a bad choice since without even waiting for anything else to happen, he rather sheepishly wipes his face with his handkerchief and lowers his head amidst the uncomfortable grumbling beginning to rise from those around him. Obviously, having decided to go all the way this time, Violaine continues. "Just look at how exclusionary you are, how your idiotic prejudices with respect to color come surging back as soon as it's a question of protecting the innocent or recognizing the value of a courageous man!" Then edging right up to Philippe Edouard, directly in line with his somber stare. "Especially, when he is all alone, right? Ah yes! In that kind of situation the color of his skin really bothers you, and you become quite bold!"

I let the silver platter I'm carrying and all its goblets of champagne fall noisily to the ground. Madame Delavigne collapses, falling in a faint. Everyone gathers around, trying to revive and comfort her. Like the wild, stray cat she is, Violaine escapes through the large bay window opened out onto the garden and vanishes into the darkness.

"It's nothing," says an older gentleman who's a little distracted—or, perhaps to the contrary, quite astute. "We just have to let youth run its course. She'll fall in line, you'll see, you'll see!"

"Ah, no!" yelps a beautiful lady, completely beside herself, "No! That would be too easy to accept! That crazy girl has to pay for this! She's a dangerous lunatic! We all know how to shut her kind up for good, the dirty communist!"

The orchestra goes back to its soporific zum zum. Small vehement groups begin forming, only to break up shortly thereafter. Throughout the whole club an intolerable uneasiness has set in. The Delavignes have slipped away. The party tries to play itself out as best it can, but, of course, the heart is no longer in it, as they say. Philippe Edouard has also disappeared.

. . .

The night sky appears diaphanous, like a ball gown sewn with stars. A strange crescent moon continues to display its sharp silhouette, and yet it's quite mild outside. It's that moment when night begins to tilt slowly toward the break of day. One feels it in this elusive glimmer shimmering just beneath the surface of the darkness. Aunt Tika is still rocking away. Slowly, she changes direction, her weight causing her chair to creak. Her eyes are wide open as she looks straight off into the void before her, the old harpy. She's waiting.

Nighttime is never really peaceful in Jérémie. In fact, the Jeremiean night is but a long sequence of chirrings, shushing sounds, jingling, and jangling here and there. These mica nights of ours are filled with the frenetic life of animals, with the brush of mysterious, humming wings, and dry, hoarse whispers, so strange that no one wants to know what it really is.

In a corner of the terrace one can make out the shape of a body rolled into a ball lying on a mat. It's a man sleeping, a man from the countryside clad in his dark blue smock. Aunt Tika rocks back and forth without even looking at him. She's still waiting.

Attentive to the slightest sound, her ears detect almost inaudible footsteps at the other end of the walkway. She sits up straight. Madame Delavigne emerges from the shadows and kneels at the feet of the old woman, silently placing her head on her knees. Aunt Tika lets her niece rest for a moment, then lifts her up. Madame Delavigne whispers softly, but her hurried words go on for quite some time.

"You're absolutely right," replies Aunt Tika in a decisive tone. "It's time. Your daughter has gotten way out of hand. We have to put a stop to it." Then she turns to the darkest corner of the terrace.

"*Madyawe*, do what you have to do."

The human ball unrolled and quietly disappeared into the darkness.

. . .

I had run ahead and been the first to arrive at the house. The main sitting room was extremely quiet. I bumped into Madame Delavigne in the hallway, where a strange odor lingered in the air, but I didn't pay much attention to it. Madame Delavigne looked me over carefully, then questioned me with that very concerned look of hers. She wanted to know where that crazy Violaine had gone? I assured her Violaine wouldn't take much longer, not at all, and then in passing asked if she needed anything. After all, I felt bad for this woman who had raised me and was, in her own way, suffering as a result of Violaine's fault (but also, by the same token, of mine as well). For sure, I was on Violaine's side! Both of us lived on the fringe of their useless rules. Because, as we all know, true feelings, those which make us legitimate human beings, are a powerful force and often transgress what is considered taboo. These feelings have neither country, color, nor social rank. Violaine and I, *marasa* before the Guinean *lwa*, had miraculously escaped the Jeremiean ferule, that leaden cover brutally clamped down on everything that somehow managed to overcome its mediocrity. Our destiny belonged to nature's dominance, to the stars, I believe, or perhaps to those forces that govern the flow of fresh water as well as the tides in the sea. But all that remains a mystery. Nonetheless, I understood how one could actually suffer as a result of these difficult, though frivolous things, these prohibitions our parents had drummed into us, images, winds blowing from all directions . . . Thus, Man Clorinde suffered the only way she knew how . . . She answered by saying no thanks, indicating she was going to lie down after all these emotional events. I couldn't help thinking that she was acting a little peculiar . . .

But here comes Violaine now, her ballroom slippers in hand, dancing along next to the railing. She's quietly humming a mournful song, what seems to be a monotonous chant she's making up herself as her dancing feet barely touch the parquet floor. She glides along ever so lightly like a bubble or small cloud of white tulle. She has undone the curls in her hair. So, there's our Violaine, the way she always ends up, wild and disheveled. I wait for her at the door, smiling and shaking my head. Ah that, yes of course! Manzè Pimba, obviously you must have had a good time tonight! That's right, everyone has to clean out their system from time to time, purge their soul. It's good for us . . . But she's crying. "Are you crying, Violaine, are you really crying?" She buries her face in her hands, shaking as she sobs her heart out.

"You know, Cocotte, it's no use. What I'm doing won't bring him back to me, even if I'm very bad, even if I were to howl like a Gorgon, my Alexandre has been taken away and tied up like some animal. My dear Alexandre will never be returned to me. Even if I were to kill Philippe Edouard! But they don't know me! In fact, I'm a bomb, whose fuse is lit and waiting to explode in their faces, ready to blow up this damnable city! Ah! Don't let me hate you, my fellow Jeremieans, because I'm dangerous!"

"Calm down, Violaine, hush your mouth, they know what you're saying all too well!"

· · ·

I undo one by one the fasteners to this infamous gown, this dress made for one and only one night. Violaine squirms out of it like a snake shedding its skin. The gossamer tulle corolla sinks to the ground with a gentle rustle, then Violaine leaps out of her corselet like a newborn colt, stubborn, her back defiantly arched yet quivering up and down. Ah! It's true. Yes, just looking at her, you had to know Violaine was not made for misfortune, not made for deception either, for that matter.

She slips on her housecoat and trudges solemnly over to her bed. Violaine, you've always gone barefoot from the beginning, it seems, even when it made your mother furious. What's come over you? Why are you putting on these slippers? Some beige satin mules with small heels placed knowingly (by whom? who did it?), some might say innocently, on the bedside rug? Violaine walks excitedly about the room. Back and forth, to and fro, her heels clicking across the parquet floor. But now she's beginning to whirl in a circle like a mechanical toy whose key has been lost. Violaine is out of control, unchained, spinning, just like a top thrown out of kilter. I hear her sigh deeply, as she continues to turn around and around, trapped like a flower in the swirling grasp of a violent wind. In a split second I understand everything at last. It's all true what our elders say. This is indeed the way they punish those who rebel, who refuse to give in or dare to be sacrilegious! Violaine, take off your slippers. Get them away from your feet. They'll be the death of you, because someone has dusted them with an evil powder! (Perhaps you've always known it; you've conveyed it to me through that submission, that grace you've always displayed as you've moved closer to your own death.) Still sighing, Violaine's head begins to roll on her shoulders, while her eyes stare blankly off into the distance then turn completely white inside their darkened sockets. And still she twirls round and round like a wild flower. Then, I hear her call to me.

"Cocotte, ay, Cocotte, I'm plunging into the blue, I'm sinking, bathing myself in star dust, blue, blue, blue everywhere! And drums by the thousands are pulsing like my blood. Don't cry, Cocotte. You see, I'm dancing, I'm dancing, I'm dancing my own death!"

Finally, she falls across her bed, smiling like a fresh flower cut down in full bloom. I rush over to her. Violaine, Violaine, why did you do that? Why did you put on these poisoned slippers? I rip them off her feet, which are already completely cold, but she's no longer breathing. Ah! My sister, the *madyawe* has passed this way! You have to go away now! And then out of the depths of my pain, I scream. "Jérémie, you evil city! You're nothing but a city filled with sorcerers, blood-drinking werewolves, an accursed city. You've finally succeeded in annihilating her, my *marasa* sister. But it's your great loss and sorrow, for she was a mere splinter in your venomous heart! A curse on you!"

Completely purple now, Violaine is lying lifeless on the white tulle of her first ball gown, across her childhood bed. Oh Guinean *lwa*, what have you done to the most beautiful of your *ounsi kreyòl?* And you, my impetuous sister, there you are all stiff and lifeless, suddenly a captive of death like a dormant body of water!

It's over. Madame Delavigne quietly enters the room as I continue to cry. She leans over her child.

"Sweet Death," she murmurs, "you've taken her from me; yes, I have given her to you. Life no longer stirs within her. All the suffering has taken wing."

The Gravedigger

It was just before sunrise. I was under the muscat mango about to drink my clove tea with my old straw chair firmly braced against the trunk of the tree. Above me, the mango's leaves, small green and violet-colored horns, trembled in the breeze's caress. What a pleasure all this was. The beauty and untouched delights of the countryside surrounded me in all directions. There I was, Brisius the gravedigger, all alone outside my *kay*, taking in the richness of the fertile plain before me, drifting off from time to time like a well-fed cat, breathing in all that invigorating air the sun would soon overheat.

I was there, clear-eyed in the gray, misty twilight, just like every day at the same time, when I heard the first cries. I pricked up my ears to listen more closely. It sounded like a chorus of lamentations, of women's screams tearing through the silence, noisily disturbing the absolute tranquillity of those precious moments just before sunrise. At first it was the unintelligible moan of a very young girl, followed by the powerful contralto of a middle-aged woman calling out to her child, "Ay, *pitit moun*, my child!" At that point I said to myself, "well, how about that—today someone is grieving for a little angel." Mercy on us! Death has desecrated youth yet again, and this time even before daybreak!

Soon the sorrowful voices of the two women were joined by the strident racket of the paid mourners. As true professionals, these women took turns passing back and forth the ritualistic clamor of a well-ordered canon. Their wailing is designed to escort the soul at the instant of its departure. The soul should never be abandoned at that precise moment because the loneliness would be too much to bear. Such is our custom. By dint of having listened to them, I've learned that this prescribed grieving was useful for the living as well. It helped deal with the sorrow, with that insufferable stab of pain inflicted upon us when someone dear is suddenly taken away. As for me, I know all this only too well, since death is my trade.

The chorus of paid mourners grew louder. It seemed like all the women from the city were rebuking death at the same time. I said to myself, "Papa Brisius, move that old carcass of yours. Apparently, an important burial ceremony is taking place down at the Plas Zam." A teeming crowd had already gathered in front of the De-lavigne house by the time I reached the square. Everyone mingled together, from the market gossips to the women selling fried foods, fruit, bric-a-brac, or *akasan*. They were shivering even though wrapped up in old rags worn over their dresses, their scarves pulled up around their eyes. All were standing alongside servants from neighboring houses, their hands held to their faces while shaking their heads in disbelief. "Ay, why Jesus, why, Virgin Mary of the Seven Sorrows, Saint Mary Magdalen, patron Saint of girls in full bloom, why?" Nobody understood yet what had happened. Ah! no question, it's quite a shock to learn about a young girl in perfect health dying like that.

Without saying a word, the *gwo zouzoun* from the wealthy part of town, accompanied by their wives and children, threaded their way through the crowd, slowly climbing up toward the big house. The sitting room was silent, and even in the street you could hear the clanking sounds of small silver spoons against porcelain coffee cups from inside. Out of the corner room behind the drawn cur-tains rose the polyphony of paid mourners. The loud voice I'd heard from my garden belonged to my old friend Roselie, Vio-laine's Nounou. Her plaintive song went straight to my heart, so powerful was the sorrow it conveyed. Do you think this woman will have the courage to continue on with her life after the death of her child? But then, I wasn't actually hearing the real mother. In the rich neighborhoods of our town we all know that they don't actual-ly mourn their dead themselves. They have it done by someone of lesser status. So, Madame Delavigne, instead of protesting to the high heavens, was probably off in her corner stifling her sobs to such a degree she would eventually make herself ill. I knew of one woman who, upon the death of her husband, had worked herself into sprouting large green blotches without ever opening her mouth. She stayed like that, like some spotted cow, to the very end of her life. Ah yes! What's more, that class of women always seems to have bad skin. They'd be better off if they followed the example of our women who live by their entrails, their flesh and blood, by the joys and misfortunes that life brings naturally, instead of stiffening up like white women, whom they hardly resemble. But after all, it's their business!

To tell the truth, little Violaine's death ate away at my insides. Nobody in all of Jérémie had ever seen such a child. It's hardly an exaggeration to say she belonged to everyone. Her smile, the warmth of her golden eyes, the energy she conveyed just with the movement of her arms, her tender heart, all this was a part of each and everyone of us. She was our little queen, our party favor meted out on a daily basis, in short, the delight of the whole city. But in thinking more seriously about it, did Jérémie deserve such a reward? Could this city in fact, so pickled in its own hatred and ill-feeling from times gone by, deal with this perpetual gift, this joy offered up to everybody without exception? Ah no, not at all! My friends, Jérémie has stopped laughing. Instead, it has become a city of furrowed brows and tight lips. It was only at the burial ceremony that I finally understood how they had taken out their revenge on her.

At that moment, the crowd that had gathered under the windows of the Delavigne home began to digest the news. The shouts from the street became a response to the clatter coming from inside the house. A lament in two voices slowly rose, swelling to its full volume, ultimately melding into the crimson dawn. Yes, dawn had come just like all the other mornings, indecent and gratuitous. And just to greet Violaine one last time, all the odors wafting from the market place unfurled their fragrances, all the songs usually born in those early hours mingled with the concert that sprang up around the news of her death. It was just at that moment when the great Papa Sun rose over the hillsides, dapper as ever and, as always, with great fanfare.

In the afternoon, they buried the child. Such haste should have appeared strange, yet it was a good bet everyone had understood what was happening.

They called me when it was time to close the coffin. I put on my best shoes, the ones that make my feet hurt so much, the same ones Mayor Saint Surin had given me last year for Christmas (oh! of course, they weren't really new; moreover, there wasn't enough room in them for my big toes, considering Saint Surin probably wears at least two sizes smaller than me). As a result, my feet were killing me. *Komabo!* It really hurt! My gait must have resembled that of a crab as I walked into the large funeral room in that condition. Violaine was there, lying in her casket looking like a little bird swaddled in cotton or like a mute liqueur bottle in gift wrapping paper. She was so beautiful I forgot all about my feet as I remained standing in front of the casket to get a good look. It intimidated me a little to stare at her dead face, which seemed so serious. Where were the mischievous air and the curled-up lip of a defiant *ti moun?* Vanished with death, woy, woy, woy! Violaine! Oh, Violaine, my little palmetto bird! Uncle Bri is going to pick you up and take you a little ways away from here so you can sleep in your own little tomb. What sorrow! While I was planted in the middle of the room murmuring under my breath, I took a look around at the others. Some well-dressed people in attendance, ah yes, no doubt about it! All the upper crust had come, six rows of closed, expressionless faces. No glances, no tears, but quite a few eyelids cast downward. I could feel the uneasiness oozing from these people. It was a malaise you could cut with a knife like they'd just committed some kind of horrible deed. That must be it! You bunch of phony whites! You still have the stain of her blood on your hands. You killed her! You wiped away all trace of this life that had neither guile nor arrogance because it tarnished your inflexibility! I wasn't quite sure how they'd pulled it off. But one thing was certain. The burden of this death weighed heavily on all their shoulders!

I picked up the mahogany lid to the casket and with help from Ti Capitaine, my "secretary," I moved closer to nail it down. The Delavigne children, all dressed in black like tiny crows, rushed forward to kiss Violaine one last time. And then their mother. Madame Delavigne positioned herself close by, right next to her daughter. She placed a waxen hand on the child's head, all the while refusing to look at her, her eyes staring instead into the distance, almost like a body without a soul. Monsieur Delavigne began to weep uncontrollably, which after all was a very normal display of grief. My God, he was burying his only daughter, right? Danton, the head pallbearer, was quickly dispatched to whisk him away, help him into another room because this display of sorrow seemed inappropriate, clearly out of place in this fancy, stuffy, but nonetheless distinguished sitting room. There was an overabundance of flowers, and their strong perfume made me feel a little sick. It was time to finish up. Ti Capitaine and I put the lid on the coffin. Violaine was now all alone in the dark inside her casket, the poor little devil. And so, off we shall go, all of us, one of these days, alone, completely alone as if we'd never belonged to this world, never loved anyone, never suffered. What torment, what a strange way of departing!

There was a rustle of fabric from the back of the room. Cocotte, Violaine's companion, collapsed onto the waxed parquet floor without saying a word. Like Monsieur Delavigne, she was escorted out as quickly as possible. But in her situation, it was much more serious because it seemed clear to me that a part of her very being had perished. But the intentions of the *lwa* are unfathomable.

Monsieur Dantès Delavigne, Monsieur Philippe Edouard Rougemont (some say he was Violaine's betrothed—hmmm, we'll have to see about that!), and four more of his gentlemen friends grabbed the casket, three on each side holding onto the bronze handles, the shiniest objects in all of Jérémie. Even in death, she was still making them march to the beat of her drum. This is all the more remarkable when you consider that many girls, even while still alive, have never had a right to so much respect. Pale, their jaws tightened, the young men began descending the long, mahogany staircase with the casket.

Upon reaching the door, the funeral procession was literally swallowed by the crowd. All the people of Jérémie and its neighboring villages had come. And the others, all those handsome gentlemen and ladies from our high society, were completely surprised. Never would they have suspected that so much love surrounded Violaine. People were actually crying in the streets, calling out her name. They were trying to put her good angel to rest so it wouldn't suffer too much.

"Ti Violaine, mama, take heart! How are we going to get along without you, apple of our eye? Yes, little queen, hold on as best you can. Don't go away! Don't leave us!"

People could be heard crying out, saying how much they loved her, how they mourned her passing, and how that was good news for her little soul as well as her big one. Since, like all true Haitians, she had two souls, one in her head and the other in her heart. Man Chavannes, *manbò asire* before the Eternal One, was there, leaning against an electrical pole, her eyes closed, her broad face streaming with tears. She was praying with all her might, and that too was a good sign.

After the first wave of astonishment had passed, the procession of beautiful people tried to elbow its way through the crowd like a gang of thieves. As for the coffin, it had been spirited away, lifted up at arm's length by all those the city considered able-bodied men, but perhaps not much more. They carried her aloft in triumph. They had Violaine dance one last time in the warm sea of our tenderness, before returning her to the cold, grim hands of the wealthy following her procession. We had all been deeply affected by it, but the death of our young friend had caused them to organize themselves in this way. We were certain they had taken part, one way or another, in this horrible crime by their tacit encouragement, their conspiratorial silence, or, in fact, their direct participation. In the end we all understood what had happened. They had cast out the foreign body. And (evil does exist!) we'll just have to wait and see what other kinds of calamitous conspiracies they found within the collective heart that beats within us. Nothing takes place in Ayiti Toma without the participation of our country's two political parties, the Blue and the Red, both always stuck together like on our flag. Always ready to oppose one another, but irremediably linked, incapable of accomplishing anything by themselves. And that has been the case going all the way back to the time of the French, when our fathers were slaves. Violaine's death, therefore, was the whole city's crime, despite the deep suffering it provoked especially in our own little community. I knew nothing for certain, but one thing was sure. The entire crowd shared my sentiments.

Later, a contingent of the wealthy from the upper part of town gathered around the small white tomb erected that very morning by the Delavigne family. Once again, no one bothered to wonder why Violaine, her father's only daughter, was not being buried in the family vault. They all stood there, stiff as a board, tight-lipped, but as dangerous as evil beasts.

Ti Capitaine and I had pushed the coffin into the grave, where there was just enough room, sort of like a knife's sheath; that is, if it isn't too tight! The priest had muttered his last rites in Latin. Violaine's classmates had placed white flowers on her tomb while continuing to sob and, then, that was the end of it. Ti Capitaine finished closing off the opening of the vault. Just one more row of bricks and then everyone will be going home. The day was ending, drenched in sunlight and tears and all bogged down in that dreadful malaise. May the Devil disrupt their cowardly sleep until the day they all perish from this earth!

Nounou

Violaine, with your tiny closed fists as soft as campeachy flowers about to burst into bloom, I helped you come into the world. Your little, red ebony face went straight to my heart that day and forever after. Even then, your golden eyes were already wide open! Venus deposited you in the cradle of my arms, *pitit*, and my insides shuddered as if I'd pushed you out myself into your first morning. Today, once again, I'll be the one to follow you to the very end of your sad destiny. God willing, and with all my soul, I'll watch over this strange half-sleep into which you've fallen; and may the Virgin gouge my eyes out, if ever I abandon you!

It was pitch black, my little one, a very dark night indeed. It was shortly after dusk. The combination of the hour and the serenity of the night chilled us to the bone. Yes, it had to be done, I knew it; but rebellion boiled in me as it does in a bottle of *mabi*. Why, my little girl, why my she-devil, ay, Manzè Pimba in a fit of rage, why could you never learn to keep quiet?

There he is, Eliacin, the *oungan* from Là Haut on the slopes of Macaya. He's prostrating himself before your tomb. Only tiny red glimmers of light illuminate the dark night. They're coming from the ritualistic candleholders, half orange peels filled with sacred palm oil, flickering at the five main points of Bawon Samdi's pentacle. The impenetrable silence of the cemetery is now suddenly replaced by the pounding recitation of calamitous magical formulas bursting from the lips of the *oungan* like a rare form of water. He does his work with both hands since the Great Master has provided two for him. He's summoning your Good Angel, Violaine, the one who'll trace your image amongst the stars, the one who'll wander in the sulfurous liquid amongst the tombs. And as for his rattle, it never stops either, filling the night air with the call of metal filings, snake vertebrae, and Guinean Africa, all with the intent of making you rise. And the *madyawe* is always there waiting at his side. The *oungan* lies down flat, face on the ground before your tomb, his eyes closed. All of his strength is in his stomach, which he now presses against the earth to make you rise up.

And he invokes Bawon Samdi, Bawon Simityè, Bawon Lakwa Divizyon, the Master of Tombs and Cemeteries, the Emperor of Death. He demands, he begs Bawon to surrender you, to give in to the idea of handing you over. His *ason* continues to rattle on its own, as if moved by a spirit in turmoil. At that point, my child, Bawon himself appeared. Without question this was a night full of spirits. Suddenly, I could hear his tremendous voice rise from behind a tomb, over there, to the right of yours. Indeed, it was the Bawon's voice without any horse to carry it. First, he politely greeted us. You know how they are, Violaine, the ancient spirits, those from the other side of the water. Even at the most tragic moments, they continue to insist upon their never-ending rituals for the proper way of doing things. Even Bawon Samdi, the Enigmatic One, is no different. His voice rose from the world of the dead, beyond the darkened waves. "Ladies and Gentlemen, to those gathered tonight, good evening! Good evening, my children, I welcome you. My Shadow is on you, O African Son . . . You invoked me, and, as you see, I have come! Tell me, *gangan* Eliacin, what are you doing here in the midst of this cold night, what are you doing in my domain?"

As if he had no idea whatsoever, this *lwa* who is always filled with mischievousness and tricks! Bawon Samdi is like that. Truth will never come directly from his mouth. But playing his game always requires some kind of trump card. And as for us, what else do we really do ourselves, as living, breathing Christians? What else do we do all our livelong days other than play with death, always cheating it at every opportunity we can find? That's just a rule of thumb. Bawon asks Papa Eliacin what he intends to do at the foot of your tomb. Eliacin begins to explain everything the crafty, old *lwa* already knows. He explains it all, relying heavily on ritualistic language, as well as lots of swishes from his *ason*.

Finally, he concludes. "She no longer belongs to you, O Bawon. The Woman Violaine now belongs to us. She transgressed our laws, and as such, it's up to us to punish her, to wash her clean before placing her once again in your hands. O Papa Bawon, her mother, who brought her into the world, has entrusted us with this task. Have mercy on her. Do not condemn your child to wander without end. Give me the Woman Violaine. I'll be responsible for her. Please, let her do her time here below, I beg you, such that some day her spirit might rest! I have spoken, Master Bawon, and I have spoken well!"

Meanwhile, the *oungan* had stretched out to his full height on the tomb itself. Then he embraced it with all his strength, the same way a man holds a woman when trying to get her pregnant, shielding her with his body, trying to seduce Bawon, trying to catch him off guard, or even to intoxicate him with his magical incantations. Bawon said nothing. Taking advantage of his silence, the *oungan* knocked three times on the entry to the tomb with his *ason* and boldly pronounced those all-powerful words from which there was no return.

"*Madyawe*, do your job!" he said.

With blows from a sledgehammer the *madyawe* began knocking down the thin brick wall erected that very afternoon to close off the vault. His work progressed quickly because the cement hadn't yet had time to harden. Ah! If Bawon had forbidden anyone to touch the opening of that tomb, the man would have fallen right there, bam, with the first smack of his heavy tool! It was apparent, therefore, that Bawon had decided to let you come back, my ghostly turtledove, and already my arms were stretched out toward the black hole from which we were trying to pull you.

I can still see him, the *madyawe*, solidly braced with his feet firmly anchored on the ground. Using all his strength, he tries to haul the casket where you've been resting out into the open air. Sweat begins to bead on his forehead, and the veins in his neck swell from the effort. He makes three tries at it before the heavy box finally lurches into motion, accompanied by a grating squeal. The man is breathing heavily now as he extracts it from the burial vault. Finally, the mahogany casket, braided with copper, is resting right there on the pentacle. Even though dimly lit by the five candle-holders, it still appears massive. The two men solemnly open it. You're lying there in your tulle gown and look very pale. But you're just sleeping, my Pearl! Indeed, it even looks as if you might break into a smile . . . Oh no, you'll never smile nor cry again. Alas, Papa God Almighty, alas, *zonbi* don't do anything of that sort!

The *oungan* has recovered his breath. He rattles the *ason* freneti-cally all along your open casket while continuing to mumble his magical words. Suddenly, he lifts a dark bottle to his mouth from which he spews a burning vapor into your face. *Foula!* You start to tremble. A long rippling motion passes through your entire body. But the *oungan* doesn't stop there. He carries on in the same way, only becoming more and more frenetic. And then you stand up, Violaine. Ever so slowly you stand up, very straight and tall in your gossamer gown of white tulle, which is spangled with silver sequins and surrounded by what appears to be a translucent cloud. Some might even say you look like a sacrificial dove, planted right there with your feet in your casket. I can't believe my eyes! You're so stiff and sparkling, like the blade of a new knife! Your eyes are closed and you're swaying slightly, as if rocked to and fro by the voice murmuring the incantations.

The *madyawe* then slips between your clinched teeth a silver spoon containing the seven drops of anti-air that are supposed to bring you out of the world of the dead. I hold you close to me, your head resting on my heart. Then I wrap you in a white sheet and we hurry away like thieves from the Jeremiean cemetery. But what's most important, I now have you, my precious burden, nestled in my arms.

A sturdy, mountain mule carries us up into the mountains to a house near Bordes that will serve as your new sepulchre. There, Eliacin and I join forces, devoting ourselves to bathing you in sacred oils followed by massages and fumigations. In addition, we give you those potions that are supposed to bring vitality back to your poor dead body, my Violaine. Then *oungan* Eliacin has to leave again, leaving me exhausted next to you. Little by little, you've started to get warmer; you're slowly beginning to stir on your mat, moan a little, although ever so faintly.

From that moment on, my dove, my dead child, I've continued to talk to you nonstop in hopes of snatching you back from that frightening void where you're now suspended, in hopes of pulling you back toward life itself. Your eyes look straight ahead and, though wide open, are saturated with nothingness. You don't seem to recognize anyone or anything anymore. You only obey, my once rebellious Violaine. But you'll come back, you'll see! I'm making you as pretty as I can because I don't want you to look like a dead person, like some sort of fallen waif. I want you to come back to us. And, I'm convinced that one day you'll smile at your old Nounou. That's the reason I'm looking after you with all my heart and continue to love you as always. And if for nothing else, I have to believe you'll come back just for that.

And I'm rather frightened, Violaine, as I watch this man possessed by you and whom you're unable to see. He's a man who leans a bit more each day toward insanity. I watch him cover you with his huge quaking frame, lavish your sleeping body with passionate kisses. I watch him coat your inert limbs with your favorite perfume without ever seeming to tire. He calls out to you like a madman, sobs over you with his head on your stomach, and squeezes you so hard it could smother you. Despite all this attention, you remain inaccessible, beyond his grasp. You don't even make an effort to defend yourself. I see him trying to love you all alone, so completely alone. I suffer with him, feel sorry for him.

In spite of our pain, neither he nor I (and this is without even speaking to each other) dare transgress the ultimate taboo, the taboo of salt. Each day, I put into your obedient mouth some rather bland nourishment which is virtually tasteless because, my little one, as you know only too well, *zonbi* aren't allowed to have any salt!

Philippe Edouard

Fresh water from the moon is falling on the crest of the mountain like a blue rain. The deep solitude of the night is all around, immersing me in that fervent darkness when not a living soul stirs. There are only the furtive steps of rodents searching for something to eat in the woods. Off in the distance you can hear the lull of the ocean. First, it's powerful, then gentle, like a very ancient cantilena of a cradling mother. Even as far up on the hill as I am, the sea can still move us with that rocking motion of the incoming tide followed by its never-ending retreat. It never fails to carry me away into its Caribbean reverie.

It has been going on now for days, weeks, nights, and more nights, endless nights that seem to go on forever. But, of course, the pain never really subsides. It just won't go away even though I hug her tepid, inert body in my arms so tightly sometimes I think I'm going to crush it. When Violaine was alive, she drew attention to her sweet little face by frowning (like a cat's muzzle curling up, mischievous and deliciously greedy). She also got attention with that face that was like a broken mirror and out of which life exploded into a thousand shiny, sharp slivers. But now that she's dead, her face is frozen in a mask with the pupils all clouded over. They resemble bubbles floating in the troubled water of her gaze. My Violaine just isn't there anymore. Please, somebody help! Ever since her soul departed her sumptuous flesh, her head only rolls around on her neck like a fruit too heavy for its stalk. Although her eyes seem to sparkle, they're nothing more than dead stars. It's impossible to imagine the horror of this empty stare from which all emotion has been drained. No one will ever have any idea of the suffering caused by this mechanical docility that still refuses to submit. If only I could possess this desecrated, uninhabited body, take my turn at desecrating it, too, this body I loved so! But how can you desecrate an absence or an unconsciousness—or for that matter desecrate yourself?

You're getting your revenge, Violaine. Despite my efforts to discover something of you in that deserted body of yours, I find nothing. You died on purpose to get away from my vengeance; you died in order to belong to him forever. This thorough annihilation of your presence sends a cold chill up my spine. Even now the dull, dry irises of your eyes continue to defy me. I swear to you on my own blood, the day will come when I'll inhabit them, these distant stars, these frozen green crystals, even if I'm forced to strike you, bite you, shake you until your eyes pop out of their sockets. They never seem to stop injecting their abominable immobility into the very heart of my being.

Violaine, my Violaine, my foolish multicolored love, finally I'm able to undress you. As I touch your opaline skin that seems to have been rubbed with gold, I'm starting to tremble. My hands are running wild all over you as I powder your body, brush over it like the gentle caress of a tuft of swan down. Now I'm slowly skimming over your protruding, yet velvety stomach, as well as the tender and secret insides of your thighs, your round breasts, which even yesterday were still jutting out, impertinent and hardly hidden beneath your blouse. The subtle aroma of face powder goes to my head! Your body is aglow, but you show no response whatsoever. You don't even try to defend yourself. Where did you go, disappearing with your flashes of anger, your dazzling smile and that fire that used to smolder just under your ripe mango skin? Are you abandoning me to my old curse, tell me? You never wanted to look at me, Violaine, and even now you keep on . . .

Your jungle hair, your huge mane still sticks out. It's as magnetic as ever, charged with electricity, crackling as it fills the teeth of the comb I continually brush through its phosphorous mass with bits of grit like a plethora of gems. Drawn to the vitality surging through it, I'll never grow weary combing your Simbi's fleece, in which some might say your whole life has taken refuge.

Just look at yourself—you look like a limp doll. Go ahead and die, if that's what you want!. No, don't die! Look, my beauty, look at me, look at my manhood pointing toward you, immense and warm, swollen with all the folly screaming inside my head. I'm going to fill you with pleasure now, and then life will come flooding back into you once again, I promise. No greater desire could possess me!

Nothing! You didn't move a muscle! Listen, Violaine! Even as a *zonbi*, you belong to me, do you understand, to me alone! No other man will feel the tree of his desire starting to rise while watching you sashay down the street, no one else will dream of loving you again, no one else will touch you or kiss your mouth. Never again. I'm going to take care of you now. You're one of the living dead, someone who's been mutilated, but mine, all mine, finally!

Nounou

I got up very early and put some stew on to simmer, a little braised kid smothered in eggplants and tomatoes. To this, I added a nice hot pepper, bright green and crammed with plenty of seeds and aroma to give the whole thing a little soul.

All night long my head wouldn't stop turning the same thing over and over. What kept coming back was the idea that it's no longer tolerable. It's over now. That is, if they'll just treat her half-sleep with a certain tranquillity and respect. Ah no!, Lord above, it's not written anywhere! No one condemned my little one to this kind of torture. Initially, I thought this macabre comedy wouldn't last, but little did I know it had only begun! My beloved Violaine, I want you to know this crazed demon will never come around you again, do you understand, as sure as I know my name! But what in the world has gotten into him, this Monsieur Philippe Edouard!

From my bosom where I'd stashed it in a secure spot, I took a good pinch of salt and let it drop into the boiling kettle on the stove. It disappeared into the creamy sauce with a delightfully pleasurable swish. Of course, the hand I used to pour the salt was trembling like a leaf because, in all truth, to break a taboo is very serious and who am I but an ignorant, old woman. But, despite everything, my heart was at rest, I'd definitely made my decision. During the night I informed the Spirits, warned them I would no longer accept the treatment being inflicted upon my little one. I'm an honorable woman and can say what I please to my *lwa*. They listened to me, I'm sure of it.

Besides, as you'll see, they're going to guide me like a candle burning brightly in my mind to the bottle in which Eliacin enclosed Violaine's Good Angel. Because it isn't enough to have a *zonbi* consume salt to return it to a human state, you still have to liberate the captive soul. If not, the wandering of the cadaver-body never ceases.

My goat stew was happily simmering away, filling the house with its tender aroma. It already represented a little courage entering my soul through my nostrils. Actually, just the smell of real nourishment is enough to give us heart, to help us get our head in the right place! And I began to search throughout the house, carefully exploring all the possible hiding places, even Philippe Edouard's closet.

Nothing, I didn't find a thing! Where in the devil could he have hidden that damn bottle? And what did it look like? Damned if I had the slightest notion. However, I was sure that when I finally came across it, I'd recognize it. Let's think about this . . . In their situation what would I have chosen, myself, to protect Violaine's soul? Not a fire-baked earthen pitcher as in the case of a peasant, nor a Coca-Cola bottle as if she were a common slut, nor a champagne bottle for a full-time, professional *awona*. No, without any hesitation, I would have selected one of her perfume bottles. That's it! Yes, it's the best choice, especially for a tiny seed of a woman like Violaine who always had a strong star shining in her eyes. As a good daughter of Ezili, she loved to be surrounded by perfumes and they loved her as well.

Pay attention to what I'm about to say because it concerns something very important regarding that subject. Through its fragrances, our favorite perfume always communicates a small part of our being. It blends with us intimately, mixes with our perspiration, with the very substance of our skin. It becomes the odor of our soul. Did you know that even the gods themselves consume huge quantities of aromatic essences in order to communicate with their initiates? Myself, I would have chosen an empty decanter of that eau de toilette Violaine always wore and that resembled her so much, that bouquet of flowers, fruits, and vanilla, that fragrance of a bold little girl which seemed to precede her everywhere she went. Come along now, let's look some more.

I turned the house upside down. For sure, the thing isn't here, otherwise I would have found it. It's now noon and I've been bustling around wasting my time since daybreak. After sitting down on the doorstep, I let my gaze wander to the venerable branches of the True Tree, right there in front of me. Just like that, without trying to force myself, I count some fifty breadfruit. Well! We'll certainly never be able to eat all that. And then, a small ray of sunlight a little brighter than the others catches my eye, inching its way between the leaves only to dive rather impudently headfirst into the grass. Along its trajectory at the fork of one of the branches, it shimmers like the glint from a tiny mirror. Huh, what's that all about? A mirror in the True Tree? My God Jesus, Holy Virgin, Saint Antoine, patron saint of lost and found objects, Oh my Guinean *lwa*, what is it? But you know (and I realize it only now), it's possible to hide a bottle containing the essence of one of the living dead in a tree. For sure, you can also bury it (no, by all the Saints, spare us that; that would be too much bother!). Indeed, the ideal spot is in a tree. It's a locale where the soul is bathed in nature more gently than anywhere else. Ah! So that's where they put it! A ladder, quick, I need a ladder. If not, I'm going to end up breaking my neck! However, on further thought, I believe I'll wait for the night mist before going to remove it from its perch.

The heat of the day has subsided, although a pearly sunlight persists. You can no longer hear the singing of the farm hands, their huffing and wheezing, or the muted thud of their hoes digging into the hard soil. Everyone has returned to their cabin. Without fear of committing any indiscretions I can now lean my ladder up against the gnarled trunk of the sacred tree and inch my way up to the main fork. The lacquered, dark green leaves, wide like the hands of a giant, provide umbrellas of freshness. I raise up as high as possible on my tiptoes, peering into the moist shade. There it is! The perfume bottle, securely wedged between two huge branches! Ah! Papa Loko! It's there, all snuggled in, filled with a bluish vapor. Two small crystal pigeons with their wings unfolded watching over the fragile breath of life of my sleeping daughter close the decorative mouth of the vial. Teetering back and forth, I clutch my treasure, pulling it in closely, and then climb down the ladder. Out of nowhere, my head is filled with thousands of colored lights.

I open the door to the bedroom. In the darkness, sheltered behind the curtains, she's there! Violaine is seated in her rocking chair. Her listlessness freezes my blood; but even when she does move, it's extremely slow. Only a slight motion of the chair indicates she's alive. I take her by the hand, even though it doesn't seem to have any weight whatsoever. It's almost like an empty glove. Obediently, she follows me just like a shadow. I sit her down on the terrace. With their large pupils her eyes look straight ahead, while her arms remain motionless. I start to do what has to be done, yet the seriousness of the moment makes me feel a little awkward. I arrange a large plateful of the ragout I'd cooked earlier along with two beautiful green bananas. This will be Violaine's sacrilegious meal, the one that will give life back to her dead limbs, the one that will resuscitate her deserted body.

As on all the days before, I gently force her lips open to feed her, slipping a bite of food into her mouth. And as on all the days before, she perfunctorily swallows it.

The first mouthful, I watch her closely.

With the second, her whole body begins to shudder, her nostrils start to quiver, and her eyes seem to light up as if in a frenzy.

The third spoonful she greedily slurps down, making loud smacks with her tongue, swallowing it as fast as she can, and then opening her mouth for more.

The fourth, she savors, growling with satisfaction. The salt, the salt is having its effect!

Deeply moved and with tears welling up in my eyes, I watch Violaine. She took the spoon from me and voraciously gobbles down everything on the plate. A new kind of energy has come over her that she puts right back into this miraculous act of eating, eating this fine food that brings life back into her. After the dish is empty, she looks up. Though terribly indifferent, her gaze does, in fact, settle on me, but only for a moment, then drifts on to something else. How painful! She doesn't even recognize her old Nounou! Suddenly, she jumps to her feet, stands straight as an arrow, and, with rapid though shaky steps, rushes toward the kitchen where my fragrant stew continues to simmer. At last, she's moving on her own! Like a doll that has been packaged too tightly, she has at least come out of that lethargy of death.

Oh yes! It's an absolutely dreadful vision for me because I raised her with such care. Just look at Violaine, my delicate princess, pouncing on this food like a beast on its prey, wolfing it down in six, four, then two bites, snorting, belching from beginning to end without even using the spoon in her hand.

She gulps down the whole pot of stew. An entire baby goat! Then, wiping her mouth with the back of her hand, although her face is still all spotted with sauce, she blissfully lets out a loud burp, Violaine, my Violaine who used to be so discreet, so charming! Ah! it's true, grace and the soul do walk together! Regardless of the pain we suffer, we have to live with our eyes wide open, take in all the mirages, the turns, the multiple facets of this grand comedy of life, because anything can happen. Yes, nothing is impossible.

The Violaine in front of me, licking her chops like a sated beast, isn't the one I know. My heart is breaking. This is definitely not my Violaine; it's only her body that has regained a certain vitality. But then my beautiful animal sets off on the hunt once again. Overcome with frenzy, she begins to pry into everything in the room, sniffing around everywhere, her nose turned up as she whines like a beaten dog. She knocks up against the walls, overturns the furniture. Lost and distraught, her arms flail all around her like the antennae of a giant insect. She's searching, yes indeed, searching! Ah! You can't handle it either. You too can't stand yourself like this! Calm down, calm down, my beautiful daughter. I have it. I have what you're looking for. Come, come here to me!

From the pocket of my apron I pull the bottle with the two crystal pigeons on top. Very slowly, I shake it under Violaine's nose. With her eyes closed and her eyelids trembling, she follows, as if hypnotized, the comings and goings of the flask moving back and forth before her, sniffing it a little bit at a time, pitiful little bird. Then, I pull on the stopper. It's very tight, and I have a hard time working it loose. I make it turn a little bit at a time, first to one side, then to the other. Finally, it comes loose, the crystal doves remaining in my hand. Violaine's ravenous nostrils breathe in the formless blue vapor coming from the mouth of the bottle with the same fitful fervor that compels a baby to cry out for the first time. Standing before me and rising to her full height, her eyelids open slowly, exposing the mobile flecks of light deep within her pupils. A raging inferno is smoldering in there. Who would have believed it? The same tenderness I used to bring her back to life is beginning to show on the surface of her moist eyes. All the torment has been forgotten. I don't dare touch her since she has just taken possession of her Good Angel. I sense she's still very fragile, like someone only tentatively put back together. But she's the one who leaps into my arms beaming ear to ear, her little-girl smile exploding like an immense flurry of stars. She doesn't say a word. Her forehead tenderly brushes against me and, while feeling its way around, searches for that place it nestled as a child. Ay, my baby goat has reappeared! Her arms encircle my neck, and I can feel the dewy warmth of her tears on my shoulder. Life has returned. A long soothing silence I wanted to last forever settles over us. Our joy is too powerful, our words too feeble.

Finally, Violaine moves away from me. Never has her gaze appeared so radiant, virtually ablaze with all that life has to offer. She says nothing, only staring at me intensely, as if to speak without emitting a sound. Somewhat uneasy given this dramatic change, I make an effort, however, to speak to her. "Violaine, my little girl, have you really come back, is that you there, huh?"

Her fingers wander over my face, exploring the features of my cheeks. She smiles, but it's a very sad smile. She is unable to answer me. And so, there we have it. She can't speak at all! They've stolen the words from her mouth. She can't speak!

But, am I crazy? All this will come back. It just takes a little time. Unfortunately, we don't have much. We're going to have to draw this outpouring of emotion to a close. I give Violaine a little bundle I've prepared for her containing some provisions, old clothes, and a little money.

"And now, little woman, your life is in your own hands. You have no one else to depend on other than yourself. Get out of here. *He* is going to arrive any minute now. Off with you—you'll survive, you'll see. Keep moving, keep moving toward the east, toward Port-au-Prince. That's where your destiny lies."

Light as a feather, tall and slender like a young cabbage palm, Violaine hefts her small bundle onto her head and escapes as quickly as her feet will carry her without looking back. The very evocation of Philippe Edouard shook her with fear. Yet, at the same time it seemed to get her going, seemed to carry her away swiftly toward that fading golden line over in the heart of the valley.

Violaine
on the Trails of Loko Miwa

Running, even flying, disappearing, dissolving, or melting like a piece of candy into the liquid light, I make my way along the trails. Yellow and round like a large pumpkin, the sun is about to fall into the bay. Fragrances from a soil filled to bursting with sap, a glutted soil, a red soil, and all of them go to my head. A light mist begins to rise across the plain. The day is at last coming to an end. Here I am, Violaine. I've come back to the world and I'm finally exorcising that ankylosis of death that took hold of me. My body is a hellish machine because I seem to be like a crazed animal staggering around the four points of the compass. The turmoil of my coursing blood, as I try to hold myself erect, whisks me along an impetuous course.

I throw myself onto the grass, inhaling as much of its powerful aroma as I can while filling my mouth with its rough, sweet-tasting stalks. I shiver, so smooth is the touch of the earth's flesh against my skin. A delicious fever begins to awaken between my thighs, and I compel it to rise within me like a tender, warm column. For what seems a very long time my lower back and hips undulate up and down. Again and again. This fever invades my whole being, forms small pearly beads at the end of my breasts. I'm on fire. I'm trembling. Slowly finding its way, my hand remembers as it slides toward that epicenter where I'm as hot as a small stove. Ay, my secret mandorla is my own softness opening up between my fingers, fleshy, melting, and warm to my touch. I begin to moan. At last, warmth is returning to this body of mine frozen in death for so long. Indeed, it is life itself returning, sensuous life, painful by definition. Then I press myself up against the tamarind tree growing right here in the middle of the plain, rubbing my whole body up and down its hard, wholesome trunk. And the tree begins to fill me with its veiled pulsation. As I continue pushing against it as forcefully as I can, my own silky sap moistens my thighs. Then, I explode. I'm alive again.

. . .

Darkness falls quickly. I find shelter under the protective wing of the last, rocky overhang on the edge of the plain. There, water has hollowed out a grotto in the mountain. I'm a wildcat with eyes that glow in the dark. I crouch silently in the dead calm of the rocky buttress. The huge plain before me extends as far as the eye can see. It's very dark, but strewn here and there with small buccans just like a field full of will-o'-the-wisps. I remember it's the time of the day for storytelling and soursop tea. The people who live here have gathered around glowing red embers safely placed between the three base stones of the fire pit. The night sky is very high and bursting with stars, and the Milky Way, which seems so close you could almost touch it with your finger as it teems with its countless stars, scatters them like so much dust into the night. The countryside is blessed with only a single breeze, but it's peaceful and melodious. Its breath, saturated with the smells of all types of vegetation, comes over me like a sweet liqueur. I say to myself deep in my heart of hearts, "This is good!" It's a strange voice beginning to speak inside me now, a voice that speaks distinctly, although the words never pass from my lips because I'm unable to utter a single word.

But after all, what a marvelous thing to be able to remain silent!

Besides, I have nothing to say. I barely know where I come from. My memory is full of black holes and fleeting, confused, even preposterous visions. The only thing that persists is an obsessive, haunting memory of having dragged around a heavy, dead body, of having felt mortal pain even with the slightest movement, of having carried the whole world on my shoulders, of having been weak and defenseless, empty, and ultimately uninhabited. But this evening I let myself be invaded by the sumptuous peace of the night, by the shimmering effects of all its mysteries. Life, all its intensity, juiciness, and flavor, is in the process of reestablishing ever so gently its hold on me through its magnificent procession of sensations.

Murmurs
around the Children
of Corail

At first you hear the trills of their laughter, the buzzing ring of their happy tittering, then comes the marvel of their eyes, creased into their tiny glowing faces, sprinkled with dimples. After that, there are the milk-white teeth, greedy teeth that love nothing better than to bite into sweet mangoes. The children from Corail fly about in flocks like wood pigeons, singing

> Pass three times,
> It's the last one who'll remain

Oh! And the sight of those brazen, little, plump backsides, completely bare under tattered bits of a shirt that brushes up against their belly buttons and sometimes exposes rather innocently (compared to the look on one's face!) their wriggling little penises! The little girls have cute legs, though somewhat skittish under their colorless or faded blue skirts . . .

> I lost my daughter.
> Get up Maria!

Corail, Pestel, and Barradères are the last remaining villages having a fertile plain, the last havens blessed with abundant springs where the tops of the tall trees still protect the fresh air. But after that, you won't see anymore chubby children, after that you'll only run into desolate lands, lands that have been devastated, lands belonging to men and women worn out by extreme poverty, a country charred like a piece of charcoal. But in the meanwhile, the little devils from Corail come charging down from high up on the cliff, shouting

Open the door wide
For the queen to pass.

Suddenly, they stop dead in their tracks, then fall silent. A very strange person is sitting there on the edge of the water hole. She has taken off her dress! Yes, she is naked, naked as a *pwa kongo*! A large shock of tangled hair surrounds her face. Her eyes are rather peculiar. Wow! They look something like quarter sections of an orange, opaque and with a fixed stare. She's eating a *kayimit*. She must be a voracious beast because she doesn't even take off the skin or cut it in half! Hmmph, this is no normal person, this one! Then she jumps into the cold water and slithers along like Danbala the snake or Simbi the eel. What is she? An animal? A person? A Water Spirit?

"Idiot! It's Queen Simbi. Don't you see how white she is? We'll wait until she finishes her bath, then go steal her comb. We're in luck,friends. Underneath her comb, we're sure to find gold, silver, diamonds, some kind of treasure!"

"Oh! She sees us! We've startled her. Now she's looking straight at us without moving a muscle. We're hidden behind the water lilies, but she still saw us. Let's get out of here! Quick, we're easy prey, like turtledoves!"

Violaine's eyes follow the frightened children. Oh! Come back here, *ti moun*, come back! If they'd only come back just for a little while, so I could hear them laugh some more and whisper with their hands held in front of their mouths, or hear the pounding of their little bare feet on the rocks flashing their pink heels as they race by like a pack of mice!

Violaine climbs out, the water dripping from her skin in small, round droplets. A rivulet flows down from the nape of her neck and rolls into the furrow of her back, only to get lost further down in the crevice between her buttocks. She twists her unruly hair, even more disheveled now because it hasn't been untangled for some time.

Tiny orchids, trembling at the end of their slender stalks, cling to the rocky walls around the water. Violaine plucks a few and sticks them into her hair. She really does resemble a water sprite, half woman, half fish, with nothing of that young, provincial city-dweller she used to be. She finally belongs to the spring, like one of its sedimentary rocks, or one of its roots bathed in water. At last she is a natural element belonging to the landscape, part mineral, part aquatic, part vegetable, and ultimately a part of something no one will ever know for sure. Her eyes are freshwater algae, her mouth a coral sparkle. The murmur of the spring mingles with the fundamental flow of her thoughts. So she has indeed come back to life in its simplest expression.

. . .

Now I have got to get dressed. Ah! here's a good possibility. Nounou included in my bundle an old dress folded with loving care. It'll do just fine. Violaine slips nimbly into a dress that must have been pink a long time ago. Anyway, its roominess and starched cotton fabric suit her more than she might have imagined.

A frightened scurrying can be heard from behind the ferns. Ever so carefully, the children have come back. Let's see what happens if I remain perfectly still. You little rascals, so there you are again! She turns calmly in order not to scare them off. Her old, rather unpretentious dress reassures them. Thus, Violaine looks like a tall girl with uncombed hair and not much else. The oldest girl in the group, probably ten or eleven, shows a little more spunk than the others.

"*Onnè!*" she says, her voice clear as a bell, her nose held high.

" . . . "

"So what's your name, huh?"

" . . . "

"Don't you have a name?"

" . . . "

"Are you a baby? Can't you talk?"

Violaine shakes her head. No, I don't know how to talk, that's the problem. She smiles at the insolent little girl who's looking straight into her eyes. What impudence! You don't stare directly into the face of a grown person like that. Didn't anyone teach you any manners?

Violaine stretches out her arms.

This is immediately met with a frightened movement to withdraw. The children pull back like a flock of wild guinea-fowl ("How bold cowards pretend to be!" goes the proverb). She looks at them with eyes in which can be found her entire tender but befuddled soul. A tiny guy barely as tall as a *rara* drum approaches, observes, and though hesitant, decides to touch her with the tips of his fingers. Violaine very gently caresses the palm of his hand. Completely reassured, the little boy takes hers and begins to turn around triumphantly toward the rest of the group as if to say, "look at me, I'm a pretty important fellow!"

Violaine doesn't budge an inch. The little ones confer amongst themselves.

"Yes, that's what we'll do. We'll take her to Uncle Dodo's shop, but we'll have to wait until our parents have gone home. Otherwise, they might be mean to her. You have to admit she really does act like a *mistè* who has lost her way, or a dead person, perhaps. They say that just like that, sometimes, the dead walk around aimlessly in the woods. Perhaps she's a werewolf? Or a bloodsucker? She doesn't even know how to speak! And then she moves around like a sleepy snake, like a *zonbi* . . ."

A shiver passes through the little group. Violaine, who has suddenly turned quite pale, can only look at them in despair.

"Is it true?" she wonders to herself. "Do I indeed seem so strange? And all along I thought I had come back, come back among the living, among my own! How long then am I going to wander like this on the fringe, on the threshold between life and death? How long am I going to be different? This solitude is just too much!"

Bitter tears stream down her cheeks.

"Calm down," murmurs a little girl. "Don't cry, do you understand? We're going to bring you something to eat. So stay there, don't run away. We're going to take care of you."

Obediently, Violaine sits down on a rock at the edge of the water and waits.

The children returned with two beautiful, crunchy *kasav*, some peanut butter, and fruit. Violaine gulped it all down. She escaped from the world of the *ʒonbi* with an all-consuming, uncontrollable hunger. Voraciously, she pounced on the food and devoured every last bit of it like a ferocious beast. The spectacle of all this thoroughly impressed the children.

They had departed now, and the waiting had begun once again. A wait that required no effort from her whatsoever. To remain inert without any movement at all had become a habit for her. She still lived in a cloudy universe, a kind of twilight zone where all perceptions, all sensations (once the explosion of the reawakening had passed) came to her either attenuated, filtered, or deadened altogether.

Whispers
on the Road to
Petit-Goave

"Jewelry, Cabaret,
Business Office"

The sun has brutally disappeared into the bay, leaving behind a deep purple trail and a strange glimmer of reflections the color of coagulated blood. Ever so insidiously, night spreads its wings, swallowing any and every sound in its path.

The water from the spring is sleeping in its hollow, motionless yet threatening like a love potion. The children are still there, chattering endlessly. Their murmuring voices whisper against the rocks. Standing in the middle of them, Violaine does not move. She's still waiting. The children take her by the hand, cling to her dress, surround her with their babble.

"Come with us, you're going to meet Uncle Dodo. You'll see, he knows everything. Only he will be able to tell you . . ."

One after the other, all along the winding path, the little troop cautiously pushes on with Violaine still in the middle. The local people, having come back from the fields or the marketplace, are gathered around their huts and have already begun starting their fires. You can hear the volatile, sticky resin from pine twigs gently crackling and popping as the flames engulf them. That smell of something being roasted or smoked on country hearths is always an indication that a village isn't too far off. You smell its presence in the air before seeing it.

The first house at the edge of the hamlet, the one a little off to the side of the others, is a small wooden shack daubed with paint, like a *taptap* that had just come to a halt right there. The children hurry over to it, then call softly.

"Uncle Dodo, hey, Uncle Dodo!"

"Calm down! You scandalous pack of *ti moun*," scolds a gruff, irritated voice. "Calm down! What could you possibly want with me in the calm of the evening?"

An old man, all dried up in his heavy, dark blue smock, is seated behind a table lit only by the meager glimmer from a *tèt gridap* lamp. His black face with its hollow cheeks and protruding cheekbones is laced with an extraordinary network of wrinkles. A sparse, gray beard runs the length of his jaw. With an appearance like that, coming out of the darkness and into the reddish halo of the lamp, he resembles a mischievous old devil. Violaine stares straight ahead, her gaze avoiding the old chap's sparkling eyes. Nor does she notice, lying on the table, the butterflies, flowers, or brass dragonflies his clever fingers have produced. You see, Uncle Dodo is part jeweler, but also somewhat of a magician. He braids bits of brass wire retrieved from crates used to ship smoked herring and cod in order to make baroque, rather affected, or some might even say ridiculous jewelry from them. As such, they'll end up on the blouses and fingers of unknown young girls with creamy skin, up there in New York, the destination of countless airplanes that endlessly plow the sky above our heads. Each month, in fact, an American white man comes searching for Uncle Dodo's jewelry but only pays him a pittance in return. However, after all is said and done, it's good, good for the American and good for Uncle Dodo as well. He has a sign on the wall.

JEWELRY, CABARET, BUSINESS OFFICE
ISIDORE DUCASSE
WELL-KNOWN JEWELER, TAVERN KEEPER

All this means that not only does the wily old fellow manage a rundown bar but carries on the very worthy trade of a pawnbroker, in addition to his art. Everyone has to make a living, right? Isidore Ducasse and Uncle Dodo are therefore one and the same. Everything, or so they say, has to come into the open in the end! Stiff as a board, her eyes staring off into the void and without batting an eyelash, Violaine sits right there in front of the old man. He looks at her with his clear-sighted gaze, all the while shaking his head and continuing to weave together his jewelry. The children speak, all at the same time.

"We found her near the spring. She can't talk. No, Uncle, not at all! We thought that you would know . . ."

Without saying a word, Isidore Ducasse approaches Violaine and studies her closely. Violaine lowers her eyes. The old man examines her carefully, walks all around her, and then finally brushes his callous hand across her face. Violaine shudders.

"Ah, that's a good sign," murmurs the old man. "Ah yes, a very good sign, she will indeed come back, all is not lost!"

On the porch of the small house, a young man bustles along, limping from one end to the other. He's arranging the gambling tables, organizing the "bar," which in this case amounts to nothing more than a rickety counter that he's supposed to stock with bottles of *mabi, tranpe, kleren,* and cola. Isidore Ducasse turns toward him, then calls out.

"Bonheur! Hey, Bonheur! I'm going to leave you in charge of the shop tonight, do you understand, my son? You'll close up the jewelry section all by yourself, but continue to serve customers even though I won't be here. When it gets dark, I want you to light the Coleman lantern and conduct business as usual. If anyone asks what's going on, just tell them I had to go away because somebody died, understood?"

"Yes, Uncle Dodo," answers Bonheur, swelling with pride. "You can count on me!"

"Another thing. I want you to continue to do this for as long as I'm gone, because I have no idea when I'm coming back. Off you go now, and try to be serious about all this, OK?"

Having said that, Isidore Ducasse hastily drags Violaine inside and carefully closes behind him the front door to the shack. He seemed to have completely forgotten about the children, who, slowly emerging from their silence, begin to make themselves heard.

"Uncle Dodo, Uncle Dodo, what about us, what should we do?"

"You? Ah! Go home, children, off with you! Forget all about what you've seen. It's too much for you. But above all, not one word of this to your parents. Off with you, get out of here! Scoot, scoot, scoot!"

And off they run, disappearing into the night. Isidore Ducasse goes back into the house. Grumbling unintelligible words while shaking his head, he grabs his hat, his sisal bag, his favorite *kokoma-kak*, and goes out the back to saddle his mule.

"Gee up! Patience, gee up, you old he-mule!" Isidore Ducasse clicks his tongue and prods the animal on the back where he has perched Violaine, wrapped up in a sheet to protect her from the cold chill of the night air. And he continues to ramble, mumbling between his teeth, carried away by his anger.

"Ah! What wickedness in this pitiful world, Lord Jesus, what ill will! Look at what they've done to this unfortunate child. Ah! There's just too much darkness in the human soul, my Lord God. Just look at this pitiful creature in distress. The poor *pitit*! Her Good Angel has been taken away from her, and she's left all alone to wander the highways and byways like a dog without a master. Ah! Now we shall see if it's possible to undo what evil has wrought. Come to me, my Gelefre Lwa from Ginen!"

. . .

Clippety-clop, clippety-clop. They've really covered some distance! Clippety-clop, clippety-clop. They've walked and walked and walked. For four days now, tugging his old mule along by the bridle, Isidore Ducasse has commandeered Violaine across hill and dale toward the sanctuary of his godmother, Clermézine Clermeil, a famous *manbò* renowned especially for her success in healing desperate and purportedly, impossible cases.

First they crossed a small banana field. Isidore Ducasse proceeded with caution, avoiding as much as possible the villages and small hamlets. He feared the reaction of those closely tied to the earth. He feared these types of men and women, for they are very quick to judge and can detect without much effort individuals heavily charged with the magnetism of the Spirits. These humble souls are frightened by such individuals and might stone them to death in a heartbeat. It's not a question of wickedness but rather an irrational panic that drives them to such things. But we have to acknowledge that for whatever reason, their fields are often invaded by grasshoppers, when it's not weevils or caterpillars. What's more, their harvests spoil, rot, or dry up, as well as produce inexplicably overripe fruit. If they had to run the risk of seeing their plantations sterilized by dead souls adrift, all their fruit going bad, or even worse, their own children being drained of their blood, then it isn't hard to understand.

Next came the cane fields, vast languid expanses, a soft, delicate green plain swaying in the wind.

At the end of the day, they crossed paths with some *kabwèt* loaded down with sheaves and pulled along by enormous, bellowing zebus with brass rings through their nostrils. The huge wooden wheels could barely turn, grinding laboriously in the furrowed road. Isidore Ducasse had to affect greetings enough for two as he jabbed Patience with his stick. Gee up, Patience! He had placed a large straw hat on Violaine's head similar to the ones worn by cane cutters so she would look like an old worker drifting off to sleep as she returned to her hut.

Every night he gave Violaine long massages with ointments he'd concocted himself. Gradually, her body hardened and visibly started to come to life. Only her eyes were still dead, giving her face an impassive look. Isidore Ducasse didn't become discouraged, however. He slept out under the stars. It was at the height of the dry season, December, the month of magical powders, leaves, and talismans, the red month of the Petwo Lwa. The nights were serene and clear, the mornings the color of cinnamon mango. At sunrise, the air seemed as soft and smooth as a mucous membrane and Violaine filled her lungs with it, purring like a cat.

On the eighth day of their journey, Isidore Ducasse awakened his protégée before dawn. They had spent the night on a hill overlooking the small town of Petit-Goave, where Clermézine lived. Their early rising revealed above all a desire to knock on her door before sunup. A little feverish that day, Isidore Ducasse, poor old man, was busy saddling his mule when a timid hand touched the back of his neck. Startled, he wheeled around only to have Violaine snuggle up against him like a baby goat. Visibly moved, he grumbled in his beard. "There, there, come along now, my daughter, there, that's enough!" He gently pushed her back to look at her more closely. There was a new gleam in her eyes.

"Ah!" observed the old fellow. "It appears my leaves have started to take effect. That's a good sign, little woman. Sister Clermézine will have less trouble than I expected!"

And he patted her back with his wizened old hand, a hand dried and wrinkled like a piece of parchment—his fine, rugged, healer's hand.

. . .

Clermézine positioned Violaine on the hard-packed soil of her *peristil*. Clumps of dried herbs are placed around her as she sits motionless, her legs stretched out straight in front of her. First, there's a little *asowosi* for making her eyes brighter, some vetiver to clear her head, followed by those leaves known as Three Words to loosen her tongue. At that point Isidore Ducasse begins uttering a series of magical sayings, a special incantation for bringing each type of leaf to life. Then he strikes a match, setting fire to the piles, and soon small blue or orange flames are popping out everywhere. Gently fanning their red glow by blowing on them, he calls upon the soul of the leaves to perform their task. After a joyful blaze flares up, the flames subside. Wisps of smoke, however, continue to rise from their embers, red smoke from the bitter *asowosi*, blue from the vetiver whose strong fragrance quickly spreads everywhere, and some gray from the powerful Three Words. Violaine is surrounded by these colorful, dancing columns that burn her eyes, make her head spin, and little by little hide her altogether from the looks of others. As the smoke grows thicker, she is completely isolated, all alone behind a filmy, vaporous curtain. She is obviously drifting now somewhere beyond this time and place, drifting toward the land of dreams, to the other side of the water, where we all seem to wander without end.

The odor of the burned vegetation grabs the throat. As Violaine fervently blinks her eyes, burning tears start to fall. Yet somehow she manages to stay perfectly still. Clermézine begins shaking her *ason*, calling to the Spirits, letting the language of timeworn rituals crowd into her mouth.

Suddenly Isidore Ducasse begins to stagger, hop on one foot, and spin around in a circle. A Spirit is descending upon his back, and that Spirit is Agwe, Admiral Agwe, Master of the Seas, the roaring god of storms, Agwe who helps feed the rippling waves, Agwe who makes them swell like huge sails or cradles them like tender, well-behaved children. It's Agwe Woyo, Master of the *lanbi*, Master of all Fish, of all Mysteries of the Sea, Agwe, majestic under the tattered mantle of an old man speaking with his thunderous voice.

"Hey, my Siren Violaine, beautiful freshwater Woman, you're torturing us! Yes, indeed! You come and go between life and death! You're always coming back, then going away. Damnation! What do you want, anyway?"

Standing tall, her legs spread wide, Clermézine answers him while blowing her cigar smoke directly into his face. Isidore Ducasse, the *lwa*'s horse, takes the full brunt of the smoke without flinching.

"*Ayibobo*, oh Chief!" Clermézine calls out. "Greetings Admiral Agwe! I am Clermézine Clermeil. I ask you to give up this woman whom you've seized just like that, in the flower of her youth, wanton spirit that you are! You have no sense of shame, you *lwa* from Ginen; in fact, you're completely shameless. To allow such deeds to be carried out in your name is downright scandalous. Therefore, let this child live among us, since she has that right. Master Agwe, I, your servant, hereby promise you a ram with horns aflame and three bottles of French champagne if you grant me the power to return speech and life to this woman!"

Emphasizing her authority as a valiant woman, Clermézine keeps pleading Violaine's case. Agwe listens to her as he pitches and tosses on the bridge of his invisible boat. He appears irritated, but that's just the way he normally is. However, abruptly losing patience, he interrupts Clermézine.

"Enough, Clermézine, that's enough! What a tidal wave of words! How about closing that mouth of yours, you gossipy old *manbò*. Good Lord, you make my ears hurt! My good friend Loko has really pulled something off here and only he knows why for certain. When you don't understand something, don't say anything about it, you damn hothead! But as for me, Admiral Agwe, Minister of the Seas and all within them, I have the power to open a door or two, but only just a little. I'll do it for you because I like your boldness, Woman of my Heart. Moreover, I'll do it, and don't forget, because somewhere in the not-too-distant future you'll give me a beautiful, fattened ram along with some fine French champagne! As for everything else, time will take care of it. You'll see, my beautiful *manbò*! Take this child to Iron Market in Port-au-Prince and abandon her in front of Bèl Antre. There, at long last she'll find her way. And now I say enough is enough. It's time for me to return to my kingdom!"

Then, it's true. Yes (may lightning burn me to a crisp if I'm lying!), incomprehensible *mistè* come to Clermézine Clermeil's sacred *ounfò* because now speech is going to come back from that secret, dark abyss where the gods have imprisoned it. With her deep forest eyes Violaine looks at the *lwa*, bows three times to him, pressing her forehead against the ground each time.

"Papa Agwe," murmurs Violaine. "Lord Agwe Woyo," she utters once again in a voice that can barely be heard, "all my respect, venerable *lwa* of the Oceans!"

Cocotte

As I woke up that morning, I was already sure something would happen. My heart had begun to race, my eyes were starting to see silhouettes from someplace else, from out of the haze of my memory, which no one else could possibly have seen. As I dressed in my little room, I was very impatient and had ants in my pants because I knew that day would not be like any other.

I plastered brilliantine on my hair and braided it into curly plaits, letting them dangle over my ears. To protect them from the dust of the city, I tied on my head a scarf that appeared to be dyed with every color imaginable and decorated with all kinds of birds. May they carry away all my sadness on their feathered wings! And so off I went with my stock of goods and bric-a-brac toward Iron Market.

Like every morning, the women from Bèl Antre are setting out their displays. At that time, Bèl Antre was an area located just at the entrance of the main market and was reserved exclusively for the vendors of *pakoti*. Ah! What charmers these women were: high-spirited and garishly dressed to boot. The daily game was always to see who would have the most attractive golden rings hanging from their ears, the prettiest scarf, or the slip with the most lace. So, we would toss some sequins to the nearby vendors, particularly those selling fruits and vegetables. And then as a result, we would have enough space to arrange our goods to our liking. We would lay out our scarves, fluffing them into flashy bouquets, spools of thread in every color piled into clever configurations, jars filled with buttons, rickrack, English embroidery, bars of soap, Florida and Cashmere Bouquet perfume, all kinds of lotions and that gleaming red chrysocolla that all the women from the working-class neighborhoods love to wear.

Gossip running rampant, the women are chattering away, calling back and forth from one end of Bèl Antre to the other.

"Well, ladies, tell me now, how is your body treating you this morning? How's life?"

"Not any worse than usual, my fine sister! We get along as best we can. We wrestle with the good Lord! Hey, Cocotte, what's the matter with you this morning? Did you have a dream last night? You're looking at us but don't seem to see us!"

"You know how it goes, my sister. One day it's okay, the next not so good. That's just the way life is!"

I stop listening to Céliane, who always has to put in her two cents. Besides, I know by heart the story of these bright-eyed women who've struggled like lionesses to raise by themselves and in their own way the children that some good-looking guy conceived with them one tender evening. It always happens the same way. Some handsome but disreputable man with teeth more dazzling than the sun comes into their lives, then runs off at the first wail from the starving child his loins engendered.

My head is swimming from images and tears. Two years ago today I lost my *marasa* sister. As survivors, our duty is to continue on, but how hard and cold life is without Violaine! Her absence is not a void but rather an insistent pain like that from a boil. I haven't been able to get rid of the idea that she's suffering, wandering, and being harmed, my Violaine. My head is haunted by all the torment she must be enduring. Methodically and rather mechanically, I spread out my wares as my thoughts drift back to Jérémie, to the day of my departure, the very day Violaine was buried.

. . .

Madame Delavigne had sent for me. When I got there, she pointed out with a rather harsh tone in her voice that I had failed all my responsibilities, that I had not taken the necessary steps to protect Violaine and, as a result, was no longer welcome in her house.

"Go wherever you like, my girl. But I would rather not see you again."

In tears, crestfallen, I had run to Sor Mélie's house and was shaking so from my sobbing I couldn't even tell her what had happened. But Sor Mélie already knew. She rocked me back and forth like a little child to calm and console me, to appease the violence of my sorrow. More than anyone else she knew I was crying for my departed twin soul, my other self. She knew that from now to the end of time I had lost that spark essential to my being, that henceforth I would have to live as if amputated from the luminous part of myself. I was going to have to learn to live like that, like a bird without wings.

At sundown, she had given me some money and the address of one of her husband's cousins in Port-au-Prince. Then she took me to the boat that was leaving that night for the capital.

"Once there, take a *taptap* and give the address to the driver. Everyone knows Bapedchoz. You'll see, Aunt Loulouze is a good person. She'll be kind to you. And don't forget you have a very important mission because I'm handing Alexandre over to you. You'll be the one who frees him from his prison. Go, my daughter, and courage be with you!"

The old sailing vessel, loaded down with its assorted cargo of living Christians, animals, and provisions of all kinds, had put out to sea. My heart was heavy. I felt completely alone in the world, aching all over. Why live any longer? You tell me: why go on? Where could I find the strength, now that my *marasa* sister had been wrested from me and I was forced to flee my home like a thief? I couldn't stop my tears.

"Poor girl! You're too pretty to cry like that! Tell me, why are you so unhappy?"

It was an old gentleman whose face was filled with kindness. He wore small, gold-rimmed spectacles and a stiffly starched, white suit. No doubt a country lawyer, I thought to myself, noticing his black tie and silver watch chain.

"Monsieur," I answered him, "I lost my sister. If I don't cry today, I'll never cry for the rest of my life. So, please, just leave me alone."

"My poor child, you have undoubtedly suffered a great loss. And where are you going to stay in Port-au-Prince?"

"I don't even know the woman!" I replied, starting to cry all the more. "I'm supposed to go to the home of a friend's cousin."

I really did feel like a tiny cork adrift on an immense ocean. The old gentleman, adjusting his glasses, examined the address I had thrust toward him.

"That's easy, my child. Bapedchoz is a well-known neighborhood and also very interesting. You'll see. There are more people in the streets there than you've ever seen in your life. And then of course I'm sure your friend's cousin will adore you. I'll take you to her place. My son, who lives in Port-au-Prince, is coming to meet me at the wharf. So, no need to cry anymore!"

To this very day, I never found out that old gentleman's name, nor his son's, who gave me a ride in his beautiful Chevrolet and deposited me at Aunt Loulouze's front door, but every night I pray to the good Lord to watch over them.

Sor Mélie was right. Aunt Loulouze was a "good person." But what a character! With her two daughters, she occupied half of the ground floor of a large house made from lacy pieces of handcrafted wood that had seen its best many years ago. The whole house was swarming with a group of restless people repeatedly coming and going at all hours. Most were well-dressed, though poor and somewhat feverish.

When the beautiful blue Chevrolet stopped in front of number 6, Ri Vyèj in Bapedchoz, it was eight o'clock in the morning. Everyone came to the windows or positioned themselves in the doorways to see who was going to get out of the vehicle. As a result, it was easy to get a sense of the unbelievable variety of the occupants of the house. There were students who were flat broke, employees of some of the finest stores ready to leave for work, numerous *restavèk* in rags, seedy-looking schoolmarms and masters who taught in the poorer neighborhoods, small-time seamstresses working out of their room, crooked and fallen lawyers, "businessmen," and parasites of all shapes and sizes. Everyone was crowded into the huge rooms of this former home of the wealthy. Today, it was nothing more than a sumptuously flea-ridden apartment house in which each boarder protected his or her privacy with cardboard partitions, scraps of moth-eaten curtains, or makeshift walls from old packing crates.

I was paralyzed with terror and shame. The flaked, scaly facade of the huge house, the odor that emanated from humans thrown together in such close proximity thoroughly repulsed me. I had grown up in the beautiful Delavigne residence. Gathering my courage, I clambered up the rickety steps of what was formerly a majestic staircase leading to the front porch. There, sprawled on a large straw armchair, Aunt Loulouze was holding court. Ah! If ever there was a character, she was it. I still get emotional when I recall how she greeted me in a way that was surly, comprehensive, and affectionate all at the same time. In what seemed like no time at all, she understood that Mélie had sent her a little bird who had fallen from the nest, a little bird whom she was to take under her protective wing and guide to safety.

"Ah! Ti Cocotte," she assured me, in her kind but booming voice. "Ti Cocotte, my dear child, life is complicated, yes, and full of surprises—always disagreeable ones for us poor folk—but, you'll see, when we take on a task together, it's very easy to get things done!"

Before noon, everything had been organized. I had my own corner all to myself in the room she shared with her daughters. She had given me something to eat, had comforted me, and we were already talking about what possibilities to investigate so I could begin earning my keep as soon as possible.

Aunt Loulouze was impressive. Her broad, proud face resembled that of a monarch. A disdainful pout (extremely Jeremiean, by the way) lowered the corners of her lips, as she tried stubbornly to mask the impulses of a heart quick to show sympathy. She had a baby's skin, smooth, black and shiny. First thing in the morning she rolled her hair into small, clever loops. Her large eyes exuded a profound knowledge of life and people. Because of her considerable dimensions, however, she didn't move around much. So, all the neighbors came to her, brought their problems, and asked for help and advice.

From her large straw throne, Aunt Loulouze controlled with implacable precision the smooth operation of the shop she had set up in what used to be the garage of the big house. You could hear her thundering voice from afar shouting orders, admonishing unruly clients, or hailing Marie-Lourdes, her oldest daughter, who served as her clerk, secretary, and scapegoat. Poor Marie-Lourdes was a silent, self-effacing creature, completely engulfed by her mother's powerful personality. She had a beautiful voice, as soft as her mother's was strident. In the evening it was pure joy to hear her sing those old provincial songs that are so quickly forgotten on the pavement of Port-au-Prince but that nonetheless lingered on in her mind.

Andréa, the youngest, was spectacular. She looked like a page right out of a catalog with her tight-fitting jeans ("Ay, you're going to suffocate in those things, my daughter!" snickered Aunt Loulouze) and Hollywood breasts that bulged out of her low-cut blouses. A pinup girl, yes sirree, exactly like those that papered the walls of her room. Each week, she tore them out of *Cinémonde* or other magazines such as *Star Magazine*. Ah, Andréa! It really did take someone with all her quiet arrogance to impress Aunt Loulouze. The little wasp-figured princess installed her "beauty studio" in one corner of the living room. On a pink sign decorated with small flowers, was written

STUDIO ANDRÉA

HAIRS IRONED AND ARRANGED AS WELL

From the way she wrote, it was obvious Andréa had never done very well in school. Besides, she had stopped school early in order to start her own business, to act sexy, and to devote all her time to her favorite occupation, which was driving all the boys from Bapedchoz crazy. She was, however, a "good girl." For a long time she put herself out trying to initiate me into Port-au-Prince slang, that street *Kreyòl*, a bastard language mixed with English and Spanish, and peppered with some of the most juicy linguistic finds imaginable. But all this was to no avail because I held fiercely to my Jeremiean accent, which used to make her laugh until she cried.

It is definitely far back in my memory, this time when, as a completely lost, provincial girl, I was welcomed by these three women:

Marie-Lourdes, who was too kind; Andréa, aggressive but generous; and especially Aunt Loulouze. Ah, that one—I'll never forget her!

The day after my arrival in Bapedchoz, Aunt Loulouze set out to discover more about Alexandre's fate. Tapping into her network of clientele, friendships, and other relationships, she quickly learned everything she needed to know. In all truth, Port-au-Prince is a strange city where sometimes the powerful, those "men-with-shoes" as they are called, are manipulated by the poor souls clumping around in sandals. Yes, there is an occult power that passes through the shanty towns and the hovels, but especially through the *ounfò*, a power whose tentacles reach all the way into the barracks and ministries in this city. But you have to know how to put it in motion. The golden rule is to use it only to get a friend or someone close to you out of trouble. It should never be used to demand what you think is coming to you or to threaten the livelihood of the powerful, that crab basket where they go to fatten themselves. It's only for emergencies, a personal safety valve.

The news concerning Alexandre wasn't very good. We had to act quickly. They had placed him in with the assassins and thieves, the anonymous and forgotten, in that section for common-law criminals where the conditions of incarceration were abominable. People died daily from hunger in that wing of the prison. Sometimes, they were killed outright by the other monster inmates locked away in there. That's just the way it was.

For us, the poor people, we have had no identity and as such the political prison hasn't been available. That particular option has only existed for handsome gentlemen, intellectuals, and career politicians, while we're tossed like dogs onto the public garbage dump. It's useless to try to claim our rights: they don't exist. But then there was also the fact I didn't know a soul in Port-au-Prince. The best thing to do was go ahead and use the friendships Aunt Loulouze had established with some of the guards in Gran Prizon, to appeal to the solidarity of humble people in hopes that Alexandre could be quietly transferred without fanfare to the section for political prisoners, where he would be treated better and where I would be able to visit him.

In fact, everything happened as Aunt Loulouze and her friends had plotted. I was finally able to visit Alexandre in his political prison. Ay, my friends, what a farce! It would make you split your sides with laughter, if it weren't a question of life, liberty, and death.

A corporal with roving hands and a small, protruding paunch was downright comical. A thoroughly ridiculous person, all puffed up, full of himself, he tried to push me into a dark corner. In the end, he accepted my bribe and at last I was able to speak with Alexandre, if you can call it that. They led me to a large metallic trellis separating the visitor's courtyard from that of the prisoners. From one side of the fence to the other, you had to scream to try to communicate even in the most minimal way. All these pitiful people were trying to pass on to each other their most intimate secrets through hints and innuendos, were trying to share a little love, trying to touch each other, under the mocking eye of the guards who patrolled up and down while chomping away on their chewing gum.

When Alexandre finally appeared as if from the dead, thin, pale, hairy, dirty, trembling with fever, his face swollen, tears came to my eyes.

"Ay! Alex, what have they done to you?"

"My Cocotte, if only you knew! Without a doubt you've torn me from the claws of the werewolf! But relatively speaking, this place is like the Palace Hôtel. At least now I know for sure I'm going to get out of here. I've found a lot of my old friends inside, too."

He continued to tell me about his life "in there," inside his prison, but I was no longer listening. I could only see this black hole, there, in the front of his mouth. My handsome Alexandre— they'd knocked out his two front teeth!

I was able to get some clean clothes to him, some medication, and then we all sent him a little food, as best we could.

. . .

I continue to spread out my cloth remnants, but I'm not really there. Around me, the activity in Bèl Antre is intense. Customers are arriving in droves. *Taptap* pour out loads of people that descend upon us. Everywhere horns are beeping and people are shouting.

Despite all that, I drift away, seeing myself as if in a bad dream. I'm somewhere all alone, being brushed up against by strange pres-

ences coming from every direction imaginable, the entire room resonates with the pounding of my heart. I've always heard there are
places overrun with witchcraft, saturated with evil spells. There,
you leave the world of appearances to enter into the very heart of
truth, openly, without being evasive or playing games. But at the
same time, you're doing nothing more than dreaming, because your
mind is making the journey, splitting in two, moving about in that
strange dimension reason shrouds from the eyes of our flesh. That
other mind watches your body seated on a small, shaky straw chair,
in a white-hot room at midday, in the very middle of Sanfil, the
toughest slum in all of Port-au-Prince. Overhead, the roof is made
of corrugated steel that is completely rusted and pocked with holes.
Sunlight pours through them, playing at your feet. Extreme poverty is all around you, but with its procession of cockroaches, its
stench of decay, its monotonous cries of children brutalized by
hunger, it all seems familiar. The floor is nothing more than packed
dirt. In front of you, a young man sits on a small chair just like you.
His hands are laden with rings and a chain that's too shiny and too
heavy to be real gold adorns his chest. He's speaking in a fluty
voice, affecting serpentine movements with his neck and hissing his
S's like a serpent.

What are you doing there, seated in that stark room filled with
burning incense, black candles, garishly colored pictures, a crucifix
hanging upside down, and dark bottles? And what about this human
skull bathing in a blackish oil right there ? And what are you saying
to this effeminate man who listens to you as he bats his eyelashes?

"Ay, my *fi*, be brave," Aunt Loulouze had said to me. "You
won't like this accursed child I'm sending you to for advice. He's as
vicious and evil as they come. He's a man-woman, a *masisi* of the
worst kind. But the spirits live in him, and he rules the roost in that
foul-smelling swamp of politics. He alone will be able to open the
door of the prison and no one else."

So, there you are, somewhat nauseated but thoroughly determined to explain your situation to the *bòkò-masisi*. It's unbelievable. He's barely twenty years old, yet they say seven devils can
dance in his body at the same time. He's listening to you, the bastard, smiling maliciously as he speaks.

"That will cost you a forrrr-tune, beautiful little lady. Because the devils tire me out an awww-ful lot when they come into my head. It's a tremendous amount of trouble, you know, to get an unknown youngster out of Gran Prizon!"

So what do you have to say about that?

"I beg you, I beg you. You can't do that to us. We're poor people, ourselves, and this boy is the apple of our eye, our hope and future. I don't have very much, not much at all. Here, take twenty dollars, it's all I have!" (Twenty dollars, a fortune, for sure!) A high-pitched laugh explodes in your face.

"But, my darling, I can't even buy a shirt with that! You must be absolutely crazy! Somebody gave you the wrong information. My clientele pay dearly for my services."

Something sinks in the pit of your stomach. But then right before your eyes, a strange phenomenon starts to take place. All of the beautiful young man's limbs begin to tremble. Ah! He's receiving a visitation from one of his evil Spirits because his body has suddenly become all bent and misshapen. His legs twist, his back stoops, and his arms shrivel. Meanwhile, his face is transformed into a hideous mask, its eyes rolling back into its head along with a deformed, swollen mouth, out of which oozes a whitish drool. A powerful rumbling echoes throughout the small room. Damn, this *is* a frightening devil! He approaches you, Cocotte, and then a wonderful woman's voice slips from his tightly contracted lips. You shudder because this harmonious, warm, sensual, feminine voice coming out of this monstrous body is more abominable that anything imaginable.

"You came along at the right moment today and are therefore quite fortunate! I was looking for someone like you. In fact, I need a young, untouched girl for one of my sons who has serious problems. There's a good chance he's going to lose all his magic. But to find a young virgin in this town is easier said than done. Ah yes, my girl, we're talking about a very rare merchandise indeed! If you'll submit to my son, I'll take care of your prisoner. Agreed?"

"If I can be sure you'll get him out of where he is, I'll do what you ask me," I answered, somewhat surprised at my own audacity.

"Very good. Agreed then that you'll welcome a man I'll be sending you. In return he will give you two magic cigarettes. The day your friend wants to get out of prison, he'll smoke one of them in the morning, the other right at the stroke of noon. At that point a white pigeon will come to get him in his cell. He'll have to follow the pigeon, and as he does, all doors will open before him. No one will see him. You will know my full power. This, I promise you!"

And then the evil Spirit goes away, leaving as abruptly as he came. The boy lies motionless on the ground. An ice-cold sweat covers his perfectly beautiful face.

And you, what are you going to do, huh? What is virginity after all? Nothing, a thousand times nothing, compared to Alexandre's life. No? You think I'm wrong? So now you're there waiting in the darkness.

The door opens, a tall, strong-looking man with a broad chest enters the room. He's very black and has an enormous head. You're able to smell the odor of his sweat mixed with Florida perfume. You don't want to look at his face because you're afraid. Without a word, the man knocks you down on the mat stretched out on the bare ground and lands on top of you.

He crushes you with his weight. You can hear him moan through his heavy breathing. A burning dagger opens you, penetrates you, tears you in two, as he continues to gasp for air. The taste of vomit fills your mouth.

At that moment you decide to let go, soaring high into the azure above. The empty cadaver lying down below doesn't belong to you anymore. You leave it for the brutish man to feed on as he wriggles around on top, noisily panting. You take refuge in the refreshing foliage of a tall mango tree, for you are a beautiful bird and not this pitiful thing that is bleeding, hurting, whose face is streaked with tears, spattered with mud, and who feels dirty, oh, so dirty.

So there, it's all over. Now you have to get the hell out of this pigsty. On the doorstep, the beautiful young man is there. He's crying, making faces like a punished child. He gives you the two cigarettes he promised. Then he reminds you in a rather mournful voice, sniffling as his whole body quakes, rippling with exaggerated waves: "Above all, he must follow the white pigeon! Don't forget to tell that to the prisoner."

You hurry off toward Bapedchoz, where you've been staying. And quickly!

Andréa is waiting for you. She takes you in her arms. You say nothing, but she understands, gently leading you into the bedroom. Still in the same place on the wall next to Andréa's bed, Marilyn, in her sequined satin sheath dress is smiling, her mouth in the shape of a heart. Next to her, Tyrone Power, with his velvety eyes, casts a glance full of promises. You throw yourself onto the pink nylon bedspread that smells of brilliantine.

Yes, Andréa understood, and without any hesitation takes charge and plunges you into a large basin, washing you from head to toe as if you were a baby. This is exactly what you needed. Her mouth stays shut, but violent tears burst from her eyes. Your face, however, remains perfectly dry. When you are completely clean and she has covered you with Johnson's talcum powder, she whispers in your ear while caressing your hair.

"My darling, never forget, this small treasure the good Lord placed between your legs is indestructible. It belongs to you, and to you alone. It's like a porcelain plate. Wash it, soap it down, and it becomes just like new!"

How did all these memories find a trail into my mind today? But you know, I've felt it from the beginning. Indeed, I'm sure, as I said only a short while ago, the day about to unfold is filled to overflowing. Great Master, please, just this once, send me a day with a full complement of joys, chase away the host of troubles you've continued to rain down upon my pitiful person for these past two years.

Sighing, I go back to my wares, my humble work. Ay, Alex! Saint Claire, please let some light penetrate Alexandre's damnable mule head! Every Sunday I've been going to see him at the prison, every Sunday throughout this whole insufferable period. He refuses to listen to me concerning the cigarettes. I weep with rage. But at least I know he hasn't thrown them away. He's stashed them under his straw mattress and, as long as they remain there, I'll continue to hope.

In the Wake

of "The Funeral Procession
for the King of France"

With the full intensity of its flames, noon blazes over Iron Market.
The racket is deafening. Not only are the tradeswomen and their
customers haggling and gossiping back and forth, but there is, also,
that piercing ring of the carbonated beverage bottles that the street
vendors like to clink together in a merengue rhythm in hopes of at-
tracting thirsty clients. Above all this can be heard the raspy voice
of Jo Carapate, the noisiest charlatan in the whole city, extolling his
miracle syrups, his lotions that he claims can cure "everything from
itch, intestinal worms, swelling, measles, blue balls, and kinky hair,
to sluggishness in bed." Thanks to prosperity he gives his sales
pitch through enormous loudspeakers that whistle and squeak.

This heat from the noontime furnace in the heart of Port-au-
Prince is fueled all the more by the intense accumulation of the
crowd itself. It's unbearable. You can see the air taking on a reddish
hue above the pointed minarets of Bèl Antre. Yes, I did in fact say
"minarets." Because this market, smelted in French factories at the
end of the last century by a man by the name of Baltard who was
crazy about the Orient, was originally destined for Turkey. It was
supposed to have displayed its cupolas and large steel archways in
Istanbul. A Haitian President, fond of metallic architecture, pur-
chased it through the intermediary of a swindler who was plying
his trade in the Caribbean area. In all truth, he got it for a steal. It's
one of those mysteries associated with business transactions. So,
minarets.

Cars of every variety from the provinces add the husky sound of their horns to the ambient cacophony. Passengers, dazed from their journey and deafened by the clamor of the marketplace, climb down, and are visibly unsteady as their feet struggle to rediscover the ground. A *taptap* from Petit-Goave plows its way through the crowd, honking people aside as it inches along. On the front of the vehicle is the solemn title "The Funeral Procession for the King of France." On its sides, an inspired artist has painted the King of France himself. His eyes are closed as he stretches out in his golden clothes along a straight line of precious gems bordered with crimson velvet and surrounded by paid mourners with generous backsides, all of which is very much in the style of the impoverished people of Port-au-Prince who admire nothing as much as the expression of abundance in all its forms. All in all it was a luxurious carriage, which was, in fact, transporting a load of chairs made of straw and mahogany, indeed those very kinds of chairs for which Petit-Goave is renowned. Down from the driver's seat climbs Clermézine Clermeil in all her finery, white scarf, flowered dress, and those huge gold earrings she always wears. And there is Violaine right next to her.

Who would ever recognize this strange creature obediently trotting along behind Clermézine, this crazy-looking girl with the wildly flowing hair, wearing a patched up dress, and one single earring, who could possibly identify her as Violaine Delavigne? Never under the harsh sun of Ayiti Toma had anyone seen a similar downfall! The Delavigne family—you have to understand what that means! Listen closely! They're rich people, so proud that their "hello" is a rare distinction doled out only in the most parsimonious way, such that you get the impression their feet barely touch the same ground the rest of us walk on. The Delavignes are people who only dress in silk imported from France and whose clear skin, so unblemished is it, seems to belong to another race altogether. Ay, Hector Delavigne, you're still the heir of your ancestors. You were supposed to make sure they weren't forgotten, your African ancestors. What game have you been playing? What duties have you failed to fulfill with respect to your guardian *lwa?* Why is your only daughter, born in the lap of luxury, stirring up the fetid dust with her bare feet in the marketplace at the lower part of town? Violaine follows Clermézine like a little obedient dog, yes, it's true, but her eyes are empty and motionless. She plods forward like a puppet without strings. And Clermézine's heart is not at peace leading this beautiful mulatto in distress in such a manner. What a disgrace! But it was written that Violaine would fall all the way to the bottom. It was also written she would bear our distress until the very end, that pain we all have in just existing, our vanilla suffering, our despair in all its colors along with the weight of that hatred that tears us apart without ever letting up for an instant. Yes, Violaine alone was to put that entire burden on her little, pointed shoulders. What will you give her in return, you in your kindness, o wise-hearted Papa Loko? What will you give her for suffering so much?

And Violaine and Clermézine continue walking in the boiling noon heat at Iron Market. They push through the crowd, which draws aside as they pass. Smiling with the smile of a child, Violaine accepts goodies and playthings the market gossips offer her. "Here, take this, my little crazy one, here's something for you, daughter of the gods, don't forget us." They caress her hair, take her hand. Violaine is still smiling, though not really reacting. Clermézine is heading for Bèl Antre.

Once in sight of its large portal, she turns toward Violaine and looks straight into her eyes. "You've arrived at the end of your journey, my darling. Who knows, perhaps some day you'll come back and see me when you have gotten your wits back and, maybe, at that point even tell me your real name! But in the meantime you're Loko's daughter. He's the one who has sent you here to Bèl Antre. Invoke him when need be, my little one, and may his good will be favorable to you!"

Deeply moved, Clermézine hugs Violaine very close to her heart. Then she pushes her off in the direction of Bèl Antre. Like a robot, Violaine lurches onward.

. . .

That morning, in his prison cell, Alexandre gives in to an irresistible desire to smoke one of Cocotte's cigarettes. Slowly, he savors it. It seems to him tobacco just like any other kind, perhaps soaked a little in something, no big deal.

The morning has unfolded strangely. It was endless, today. Wonder why, after all? Perhaps, he says to himself, this prison life has gone on about long enough. Right? my good friend, Alex! (Prisoners throughout the world are similar; and like all of them, Alexandre talks to himself all day long.)

At noon, unable to restrain himself, he smokes the second cigarette. Calmly at first. But when he blows out the last puff of smoke, his heart begins to beat like a clock suddenly out of control. "Oh! oh!" he wonders aloud, "what in the world could be happening to me? What in the hell is going on?"

At that moment, escaping from a large *mapou* in Carrefour-Feuilles, a white pigeon, no bigger than a turtledove, makes its way toward rue du Centre and ultimately Gran Prizon. Without any unnecessary turns, it traces its precise route in the sun-baked sky of Port-au-Prince. It flies over the red-light district. The little Dominican whores blow kisses to it. Next it crosses over Gran-Ri, then over the crowded and noisy commercial thoroughfares. It even flies over the large marketplace swarming with people.

"Hmmm, hmmm," mutters an *akasan* vendor, following the bird with her eyes while scratching her ear. "Who are you going after like that today, my little bird?"

Tiring somewhat, the fine little pigeon begins to lose altitude. But by now it isn't far from rue du Centre, as it gallantly glides above the neighborhood of those resourceful car mechanics at the lower edge of town, the ones who deal in all kinds of machines, vehicles, and motors. They can make anything you want, even parts for old machines for which the White Man who used to make them himself has long since lost the model.

One of the street kids, one of those starving little vagabonds with greedy eyes, hair red from malnutrition, dried-up limbs, and hunger wrenching his guts, is perched on the roof of a vehicle, and, while looking for opportunities, happens to see the bird approaching.

"*Kerte*," he exclaims in his street *Kreyòl*. "*Kerte!* Just look at that beautiful turtledove! That's a sugar-tit mama's sending for your little belly!"

Adjusting his slingshot and sticking out his tongue to get a better aim, he lets fly a superb, finely polished stone that scores a direct hit on the bird. The *lwa*'s pigeon turns slowly in the air, then crashes onto the macadam with a dull thud. The boy grabs it and slips it under his tattered shirt.

"Yes, damn right! I'm going to smoke you good, *ti papa!*" he murmurs as he bolts away.

Inside his prison cell, Alexandre suddenly becomes very dizzy.

· · ·

Violaine heads toward Bèl Antre surrounded by the squawking street kids who wander about the marketplace. Two tall vendors take the situation in hand, two good women who are very serious-minded and beyond reproach. Although they sell oranges, both are very active and are always working together on things—in short two large, strapping women who fear nothing, after all is said and done. With an air of authority, they escort the pitiful girl to where the *pakoti* vendors could be found. Their good friend Clermézine had asked them to do it.

When they arrive in front of the first counters at Bèl Antre, Violaine stops abruptly and stares at the display identified as belonging to Ti Fanm. Without any exaggeration whatsoever, it's the prettiest of all. Filled with wonder, she continues to look at the rows of glittering sequins, the pyramids of glass pearls, and the multicolored necklaces for some time. Her companions begin to grow impatient.

"So, this is it. This is Bèl Antre. Yes, this is what it's all about, my *fi*. But we have our own work to do; we've got to go. And now what are you going to do, hmmm?"

No sooner had they finished their sentence than a scream rang out behind them. It was Cocotte, who had come closer to see what was causing all the commotion.

Overcoming the emotions swelling within her, trying to suppress the trembling in her body, but especially not wanting to frighten Violaine, she slowly steps forward and gently takes her sister into her arms.

"My God, Jesus, Mary, have mercy! Papa Loko, have mercy! But where has she come from, my Lord Papa? My absolutely beautiful sister, my runaway, where has she come from like this? Has the Kingdom of the Dead given her back to me like this, my poor *marasa*, all disheveled, all out of sorts, completely lost, completely empty?" she murmured, closing her eyes as tightly as she could in order not to cry.

Violaine looks at her without saying a word. Then the first glimmer of a rational person begins to flicker in her eyes.

"Yes, my sister," responds Cocotte, whose agate-colored eyes search longingly within hers for some response. "Yes, you've made it, my dear. You've arrived. And, you'll see, you'll see how we're both going to stand tall, plant ourselves solidly on our Jeremiean feet once and for all. And we'll make our way along our own trail all by ourselves and in our own way, without *oungan*, without *manbò*, without anybody. We've paid our dues, and, yes, have finally finished paying the debt. Now, it all belongs to us!"

She sits Violaine down on her tiny vendor's stool and tenderly begins to untangle her cascade of hair that by now is filled with knots, blades of grass, and insect wings from the many trails she has traveled. Just then "The Funeral Procession for the King of France," obviously lightened of its load, passes by, squeaking noisily amidst thundering blasts from its horn, shouting, as well as groans from its rusty, old springs. Off it goes in the direction of Petit-Goave, and with it the last vestiges of Violaine's nightmare disappear. The children from the marketplace, clinging to the rickety frame of this old *taptap*, steal a short ride toward the southern gate of the city.

After returning to their domain of passementerie and lace, glass jewelry, fake gems, and penny perfumes, the tradeswomen have calmed the crowd and chased away the troublemakers. Already *te seʒi* is simmering on the portable stoves. A warm, inviting ambiance, so extraordinarily muted it seems lined with felt, has settled over Bèl Antre like a cocoon nestling around the two women. More than anything else, however, it is an ambiance created from all the common emotions and sense of solidarity.

"No! Cocotte, don't say that! No, you two are not all alone. We're all here for you, and don't forget it!"

So, Bèl Antre's generous heart, that collective heart of all those valiant, colorfully dressed, ever quarrelsome, tumultuous vendors of *pakoti* begins beating in unison around the living dead Violaine Delavigne and Cocotte, her long-lost *marasa* sister.

Roncégeac, January 1990

GLOSSARY

. . .

Kreyòl words, italicized in the text, are glossed below. Spelling follows the standardized system as used by Bentolila and Vilsaint (see Select Bibliography of Sources for Kreyòl Terms). There is no marker for the plural or gender in Kreyòl; for example, *zonbi* is singular or plural, masculine or feminine.

Ago bilolo *ago* means literally "I'm here" or "watch out!" Used for invoking Petwo spirits.

Agwe Woyo the *lwa* of the sea.

akasan a porridge made from manioc or cornflour.

ason a ritual rattle in Vodou made by filling a small gourd with pebbles or bones.

asowosi ritual herbs.

awona a whore.

ayibobo a Vodou invocation or expression equivalent to "amen."

Ayiti Toma the respectful term for Haiti; also, *toma* refers to the patriotic, skeptical Haitian.

bagi the inner sanctuary of a Vodou temple.

baka an evil spirit.

Banda a *lwa*; a Vodou dance.

Bapedchoz a neighborhood in the Turgeau section of Port-au-Prince.

Bawon Samdi the lord of death; also, Bawon Simityè (Baron Cemetery) and Bawon Lakwa (Divizyon).

Bèl Antre "beautiful entrance"; the name of the area close to the ornate, Byzantine entrance of Iron Market in Port-au-Prince.

bilolo see *Ago*.

Bizango a secret society akin to the *chanpwèl*; known for poisoning their victims.

bòkò a sorcerer.

bwa debèn ebony wood; slaves as cargo on slave ships.

chabin a mulatto with light-colored eyes and skin and reddish, kinky hair; also an adjective.

chanpwèl *kochon chanpwèl* (hairless pigs): a secret society practicing sorcery and violence.

chimen a road.

chwal a horse; a person possessed by a *lwa* in a Vodou ritual.

Dammari a port town at the tip of Haiti's southwestern peninsula.

Danbala a *lwa* represented with his wife as twin snakes; associated with Saint Patrick in Catholic rites.

degaye messy, disordered.

dlo kanpe a putrid liquid used to dispel evil spirits.

dodin a rocking chair.

dosou-dosa a child born following the birth of *marasa* (twins), possessing mystical powers.

Ezili the *lwa* of love, pleasure; associated with the Catholic Virgin Mary; various manifestations, such as Ezili Jewouj (red-eyed Ezili), who is also a Petwo Lwa full of jealously and vengeance.

fanm a woman.

fi a woman; *pitit fi* means daughter.

fi kanzo a female postulant in Vodou.

fistibal a slingshot.

foula *tafya* or other liquid sprayed from the *oungan*'s (or *manbò*'s) mouth onto a subject during certain Vodou rituals.

gangan a Vodou priest (*oungan*).

Gede Vodou spirits associated with death; *lwa* under the command of Bawon Samdi.

Gede Nouvavou   the triplet brother of Gede Oumson and Ti Wawè, sons of Bawon Samdi and Gran Brijit.

Gelefre Lwa   the spirits of Ginen.

Ginen   Guinea; a generic name for the lands (West Africa) from which slaves were transported, but also figuring a mythical land or paradise (under the ocean) to which they aspire to return.

govi   a sacred jar in which hair, fingernails, or other personal elements are preserved for ritualistic purposes; used as a receptacle for the *lwa*.

Gran Brijit   the wife of Bawon Samdi.

Grandans   the third largest river in Haiti (near Jérémie; also the administrative department where the river is located

Gran Prizon   a prison.

Gran Ri   "Broad Street," a main thoroughfare in Jérémie and downtown Port-au-Prince.

grimo   a light-complected Haitian with blond or reddish hair (female: *grimèl*).

gwo zouzoun   a "big cheese," important personage.

jennès   a whore.

kabwèt   a rough-hewn wooden cart.

kamoken   quinine; but also, a derogatory term of the Duvalier era for those who resisted the regime.

kanari   amphora in baked clay.

kanzo   see *ounsi*.

karabann   a wicker trap or cage for small birds and animals.

kasav   manioc cakes.

kasè   from the French *cassé* (broken: as in disjointed limbs); an erotic dance.

kay   a house.

kay chanmòt   a house rising two or more stories.

kayimit   a purple-colored fruit with a soft, fleshy pulp in the Sapotaceae family.

kay mistè   a synonym for *ounfò*.

kenèp   a tropical fruit, tree.

kerte!   an interjection of anger, disgust; an exclamation of extreme surprise.

kipe!   a noise made by sticking out one's lips as a sign of scorn or disgust.

kleren   unrefined rum.

kòb   a Haitian penny.

kokomakak   a club or walking stick made from a knotty branch.

komabo!   an exclamation of consternation or surprise.

konbit   communal agriculture work; also, a figurative expression denoting group unity, rallying to a cause.

Krik? Krak!   the question with which a Haitian storyteller elicits from his or her listeners the response that they are ready for the story to begin.

Laginode   a river near Jérémie.

lakou   a group of neighborhood dwellings, or a small village; family and neighbors who group together for work, worship, and self-protection.

lanbi   a conch shell; used as a horn to signal revolt among the slaves.

langaj   the mystical "language" of the *lwa*, sometimes incomprehensible to ordinary humans.

langlichat   a boneset plant.

Legba   the *lwa* who is the keeper of the crossroads or gateway and must be invoked at the outset of all Vodou ceremonies; associated with Saint Peter.

Loko Miwa   the *lwa* who protects healers and *marasa*.

lwa   a Vodou spirit (male or female); *lwa rasin*, the root spirits or manes.

mabi   a fermented drink similar to beer.

madan Sara   an itinerant woman vendor known for her sharp, sassy tongue; a small bird that sings continuously like the vendors.

madichon   a curse or bad luck.

madyawe   an apprentice to a Vodou priest.

makout   tonton makout: a member of the personal militia created by François Duvalier ("Volontaires de la Sécurité Nationale" or VSN); the *tonton* or *makout* has since been applied to various militia or pro-military groups under different regimes.

maldjòk   an article of clothing, such as a dress, made or quilted from multicolored or variegated pieces of cloth; a patchwork pattern; an evil spell (the "evil eye"); an accursed entity.

malfini   a hawk.

man   mama; often used as a title of respect for a *manbò*.

manba   peanut butter.

manbò   a Vodou priestess (has authority equal to that of the *oungan*); *manbò asire* is an authorized *manbò*.

manzè   Mademoiselle.

mapou   the ceiba tree, with a large trunk and palmate leaves. Akin to the kapok tree and a favorite dwelling place of the *lwa*.

marasa   twin or twins; the *marasa* are also *lwa*, with their own feast day. The *marasa* are especially revered in the realm of Vodou. They have mystical powers in rituals and are protected by Loko Miwa.

Marinèt Bwa Chèch   a Petwo Lwa known for her violence; patroness of werewolves.

masisi   a homosexual (pejorative).

mayi   a Vodou ritualistic dance step or rhythm.

mistè   a "mystery," *lwa* or Vodou spirit.

moun   a person: *ti-moun* is a child; *gran'moun* is an adult.

Ogoun   the *lwa* associated with Saint James the Greater in Catholic traditions; Ogoun Feray is the *lwa* of blacksmiths and metalworking similar to the Roman Vulcan.

Onnè!   "honor"; "Anybody home?" (a traditional greeting when calling on or meeting somebody). The response is *Respè!* ("Respect!").

ounfò   a Vodou sanctuary.

oungan   a Vodou priest (also, *gangan)*.

ounsi kanzo   female initiates; an *ounsi* who has undergone initiation by fire.

pakoti   knicknacks: cheap clothes, furniture, jewelry, etc.

papa   a term of respect for the *oungan* as well as a head of state or other dignitary; sometimes applied ironically, as with Papa Doc (François Duvalier).

pataswèl   a slap.

pè   a Vodou ceremonial alter.

pentele   having the varied colors of a guinea fowl: a pentele pheasant.

peristil   the public area of the Vodou sanctuary (often an open annex under the trees).

Petwo   a nation of *lwa*; the rites of Petwo Lwa are more associated with violence and sorcery than those of the Rada Lwa.

pipirit   a fragile raft, made of bamboo sheaves for temporary use.

pirouli   a sucker (candy).

piskèt   minnows or tiny river fish.

pitit   small, little; a term of endearment with respect to a child (a son or daughter), *pitit moun* or *ti moun*.

plàn   a pawnshop.

Plas Zam   the parade grounds from colonial times.

pwa kongo   a pigeon pea.

pwen   magical charms, extraordinary power.

rabòday   a Haitian dance with vigorous twists and turns of the hips.

Rada   a nation of *lwa* often associated with munificent acts; many of them have Petwo counterparts who tend to be more violent: Ezili is the Rada Lwa of love, associated with the Virgin Mary; Ezili Jewouj is her jealous Petwo counterpart.

ranchera   a "crying" Spanish "ranch" song.

rara   a Mardi Gras procession (rural in origin); also a proclaimed leader of this celebration.

restavèk   a child indentured to a family with means.

ri   a street; Gran Ri (Broad Street), Ri Gouvènman (Government Street), Ri Vyèj (Old Street).

sanpwèl   see *chanpwèl.*

saranpyon   a disruptive fever like measles or chicken pox.

saval   minnows, small river fish.

Simbi   a *Petwo lwa*, guardian of springs, ponds (associated with the Magi).

sor   "sister" (from Spanish); the term of respect for addressing a *manbò*.

tafya   *kleren*, raw rum.

taptap   a pickup truck, van or bus converted to use as a public transport; usually painted colorfully and customized with its own name, one of the *lwa*, a saint or some other fanciful name

te seʑi   herbal tea.

tèt gridap   wild, kinky hair; a *tèt gridap* lamp is made from an old tin can and burns oil; its wick resembles wild hair.

ti   "small"(*pitit*); a term of endearment; little, cute, or dear.

tiyon   a scarf tied on the head to make a peacock tail.

tranpe   a marinade mixed with *tafya*; rum flavored with herbs.

Trichopherous   a popular hair product, used particularly in Haiti during the 1950s and 1960s.

Venga, hombrecito! ¿Que quiere, mi amor?   Spanish for "Come here, young man! What do you want, my love?"

(la) vida, chica, buscando la vida   Spanish for "Life, girl, looking for life."

vlenbendeng   wandering spirits.

wanga   a charm or magic spell.

wont   "honte" (French: shame): a medicinal plant.

woy   a Haitian exclamation of distress.

yanvalou   a Vodou dance.

Zaka   the *lwa* of agriculture.

ʒobop   evil spirit; a sorcerer.

ʒoklo   a punch to the head.

ʒonbi   a person whose soul has been captured by a sorcerer; a "living dead" person.

ʒwaʑo   a little bird.

A BRIEF GUIDE TO KREYÒL

PRONUNCIATION

. . .

Most Kreyòl consonants are pronounced approximately as they are in English with the exception of *j* (/ ʒ / = zh) and *ch* / ʃ / (sh), pronounced as in French *(je* and *cher)*. The *g* is always hard (as in "get"). The *r* is velar (no Eng. equivalent) and is sometimes pronounced like a *w*. There are three nasal vowels, *an*, *en*, and *on*, pronounced like the French nasal *a, e,* and *o* (roughly like "p*aw*n", "p*a*nt", and "w*on*'t"). The only accented letters are the vowels, *à, è,* and *ò,* indicating that they have the open sound (like "palm", "get", and "s*aw*"). Stress is on the last syllable.

Kreyòl alphabet	*Kreyòl* word	English pronunciation
a	klas	f*a*ther
an	fran	d*aun*t
b	balon	ball
ch	chato	rash
d	deyò	daughter
e	chire	d*ay* (no diphthong as in Eng.)
è	kè	g*e*t
en	gen	r*an*t
f	frape	fair
g	gi	gone
(h) (often omitted)	(h)oungan	hair
i	glise	f*ee*t
j	jou	bei*g*e
k	ko	ro*ck*
l	lis	label

Kreyòl alphabet	*Kreyòl* word	English pronunciation
m	mèt	made
n	neve	near
ng	peng	a*ng*ry
o	onè?	c*oa*t
ò	mòd	b*aw*dy
on	konte	w*on*'t
ou	koud	rude
p	piti	put
r	Rada	route, *w*ood
s	glas	soar
t	tomat	tomatoe
v	vèvè	very
w	gwo	will
y	misyon; youn	p*ea*t; *y*ou
z	zanj	zero

SELECT BIBLIOGRAPHY OF SOURCES
FOR KREYÒL TERMS

. . .

Bentolila, Alain, et al., eds. *Ti Diksyonnè kreyòl-franse*. Port-au-Prince: Éditions Caraïbes, 1976.

Brès, Marjorie Villefranche, et al. *L'Expérience ti pye ʒoranj monte*. Montréal: Grafik Universel: Éditions, 1984.

Carbet, Marie-Magdaleine. *Comptines et chansons antillaises*. Montréal: Leméac, 1975.

Dauphin, Claude. *Brit kolobrit. Introduction méthodologique suivie de 30 chansons enfantines haïtiennes recueillies et classées progressivement en vue d'une pédagogie musicale aux Antilles*. Sherbrooke: Éditions Naaman, 1981.

Déita [Mme. Mercédes Foucard Guignard]. *La Légende des Loa. Vodou Haïtien*. Port-au-Prince: n.p., 1993.

Delbeau, Col. Jean-Claude. *Société, culture et médecine populaire traditionnelle. Etudes sur le terrain d'un cas: Haïti*. Port-au-Prince: Henri Deschamps, 1990.

Desmangles, Leslie. *The Faces of the Gods. Vodou and Roman Catholicism in Haiti*. Chapel Hill: Univ. of North Carolina Press, 1992.

Métraux, Alfred. *Voodoo in Haiti*. Translated by Hugo Charteris, introduction by Sidney Mintz. New York: Schocken, 1972. Originally published as *Le Vaudou haïtien*, preface by Michel Leiris. Paris: Gallimard, 1958.

Vilsaint, Fequiere. *Diksyonè Anglè Kreyòl*. Temple Terrace FL: Educa Vision, 1991.

———. *Diksyonè kreyòl/anglè*. Temple Terrace FL: Educa Vision, 1991.

Vilsaint, Fequiere ak Mod Etelou. *Diksyonè Kreyòl Vilsen*. Temple Terrace FL: Educa Vision, 1994.

CARAF Books
Caribbean and African Literature
Translated from French

A number of writers from very different cultures in Africa and the Caribbean continue to write in French although their daily communication may be in another language. While this use of French brings their creative vision to a more diverse international public, it inevitably enriches and often deforms the conventions of classical French, producing new regional idioms worthy of notice in their own right. The works of these francophone writers offer valuable insights into a highly varied group of complex and evolving cultures. The CARAF Books series was founded in an effort to make these works available to a public of English-speaking readers.

For students, scholars, and general readers, CARAF offers selected novels, short stories, plays, poetry, and essays that have attracted attention across national boundaries. In most cases the works are published in English for the first time. The specialists presenting the works have often interviewed the author in preparing background materials, and each title includes an original essay situating the work within its own literary and social context and offering a guide to thoughtful reading.

CARAF Books

Guillaume Oyônô-Mbia
and Seydou Badian
Faces of African Independence:
Three Plays
Translated by Clive Wake

Olympe Bhêly-Quénum
Snares without End
Translated by Dorothy S. Blair

Bertène Juminer
The Bastards
Translated by Keith Q. Warner

Tchicaya U Tam'Si
The Madman and the Medusa
Translated by Sonja Haussmann
Smith and William Jay Smith

Alioum Fantouré
Tropical Circle
Translated by Dorothy S. Blair

Edouard Glissant
Caribbean Discourse: Selected Essays
Translated by J. Michael Dash

Daniel Maximin
Lone Sun
Translated by Nidra Poller

Aimé Césaire
Lyric and Dramatic Poetry, 1946-82
Translated by Clayton Eshleman
and Annette Smith

René Depestre
The Festival of the Greasy Pole
Translated by Carrol F. Coates

Kateb Yacine
Nedjma
Translated by Richard Howard

Léopold Sédar Senghor
The Collected Poetry
Translated by Melvin Dixon

Maryse Condé
I, Tituba, Black Witch of Salem
Translated by Richard Philcox

Assia Djebar
*Women of Algiers in Their
Apartment*
Translated by Marjolijn de Jager

Dany Bébel-Gisler
*Leonora: The Buried Story
of Guadeloupe*
Translated by Andrea Leskes

Lilas Desquiron
Reflections of Loko Miwa
Translated by Robin Orr Bodkin